I0556032

Song of the Nightpiper

HANNAH MEREDITH

SpS

Singing Spring Press

SONG OF THE NIGHTPIPER

ISBN: 978-1-942470-04-5 (Print)
ISBN: 978-1-942470-05-2 (E-book)

Published by Singing Spring Press

To Absent Friends

Some gone from this earth;
Some lost through time, distance, and inattention.

Your laughter lingers.

❧ Perceived Truths ❧

Great Cheelum saw the goodness of those who dwelt below the Ice Shield and gifted the Lords of High Places with magic, so the lives of all those who lived under their care could be easy and peaceful. But a false prophet arose in the mountain fastness to the west. The people there rejected the Gift, saying they wanted no Lords over them. They believed the High Places belonged to all with legs to climb. The land welcoming Cheelum's Gift was called Fallucia and the land of the lost ones was called Rennic.

Over time, the Rennish, a dark and brutal people, came to envy the ease of life enjoyed by their neighbors and stole much of Fallucia's magic for themselves, warping it into something evil. And so the Lords of High Places called what magic remained unto themselves and shut the Rennish away behind strong, warded walls.

History of the Known World – by Aethem of Fallucia

Trust not Fallucians. They would steal our magic and our wives, for their lives are corrupt.

Rennish Folk Wisdom

1

Fallucia
Twelfth year of King Fremmor's reign

Lady Anlin of Giffard's Crest stood at the very front of the viewing box, her entire attention focused on the men assembling on the tournament field. Her absorption was such that she could ignore the pennants snapping in the wind, the milling crowds behind the barricades, and the loud cries of vendors hawking their wares. To her disgust, however, the increasingly strident conversation behind her was beginning to intrude on her concentration.

"You should *not* allow her to be here for the melee. It's unseemly. Look around. No other lady of noble blood is present. Viewing the jousting is one thing, but this..." Her brother Roland threw open his arms to encompass the achingly blue sky, the field of flattened grass, the lines of horses and assembled men in battle gear.

"Lower your voice," Phillip Giffard hissed at his son. "You're drawing attention."

"*I'm* drawing attention?" Roland managed to show his disdain even using less volume. "Impossible, with my sister standing there dressed in whore's red, eager to watch men bludgeon each other for her fair hand. Any melee is bound to produce bad injuries, regardless of the care we've taken to insure the weapons are blunted, regardless of how many referees we have on the field. This will be a bloody mess that no lady should see."

"Enough!" Lord Giffard raised his hand to signal the horns that would begin the mock battle.

"You act as if she's bewitched you," Roland said quietly. Too quietly for their father to hear him, but Anlin understood every word.

She could have told Roland that their father was motivated by guilt rather than by any magical compunction. She obviously had no magic. Had she been one of the Talented Giffards, she would not have been abandoned to ten years of horror in Rennic. But if guilt were the only weapon she had to get what she wanted, then that's what she'd use.

Either Roland hadn't heard a thing she'd said in these past few months or he'd purposely chosen to ignore her admittedly brief descriptions of her captivity. Was it willful misunderstanding that he could think she'd be affected by the sight of blood? Blood? She knew all about blood—knew that it felt surprisingly hot on her hands compared to the cold steel of the knife.

The horn sounded. Men and horses dashed forward with a cacophony of shouts, rattling harnesses, and clashing weapons. The formerly peaceful field was transformed into a disturbed anthill. Anlin was unable to follow the progress of any individual participant. All was chaos.

Only the yellow robed referees and their bobbing yellow banners were obvious markers in the confusion. They scuttled to and fro, tagging those who were deemed to be captured and leading them to holding pens where they awaited those who had vanquished them to eventually claim either their horses and equipage or accept a reasonable ransom. The men who were judged to have been killed simply quit the field to the jeers of the spectators.

Somewhere an injured horse thrashed, its piteous cry rising above the din and cutting through Anlin like a blade until someone mercifully silenced it. She remained rigidly upright, her face carefully schooled to utter blankness. She knew those who didn't watch the fighting watched her—and whispered about Giffard's ruined daughter. How damaged was she? What had really happened to her in Rennic?

They could look and gossip all they wanted. She'd worn the scarlet so none could miss her. But Roland was wrong about its being a whore's dress. There wasn't a whore in all the kingdom who could afford to buy such silk. Others would stare at her and see only the outside. What lived within belonged only to her.

The field was becoming less crowded, giving the fighters more room for broader, more punishing strokes and thrusts. Few knights retained their lances and were still astride, making them conspicuous. One of the mounted men wore a moss green surcoat, the muted color distinctive among the reds, blacks, and blues favored by most.

Anlin vaguely recalled seeing the man in the lists. She remembered him because he seemed at odds with himself. He rode a big, gray gelding, the altered nature of the horse proclaiming him a man-at-arms. But a green surcoat with some emblem on it draped his hauberk, attesting to his having been knighted.

Without moving her head, Anlin tried to make out the knight's badge. It looked like a fat bird. Before she had time to study it, the man's lance broke. He swung from the saddle and pulled the sword that rode in a scabbard on his back. She lost sight of him in the milling confusion.

She allowed the scene again to go slightly out of focus. All the combatants were helmed and indistinctive. She really had no preference. One man would do as well as the next, as long as he was a competent, brutal fighter. The purpose of the tournament was to present her with just such a man.

She was not so foolish as to think that any of them fought for the honor of marrying her. That idea was ludicrous. All these men had come to fight at Giffard's Crest because her father had offered a substantial fief as well as her hand in marriage. It was the hunger for land that drove each of the contestants. She let her eyes drift over the field as the yellow-garbed referees led more and more men away.

And then there were only four. The man in moss green remained. He dispatched his opponent at nearly the same time as a knight in black and silver. The two men turned to face one another.

"Yes!" her brother exclaimed beside her. His boyish enthusiasm reminded her of how truly young he still was, just two years less than her own twenty-two. Anlin, however, had felt very old for a very long time.

"The man in the black and silver," Roland said. "That's Sir Charl. He's presently one of Lord Tarn's retainers, but he's here with Tarn's blessing. I've heard the man is unbeatable."

"Tarn's man you say? I'm not sure that's much of a recommendation." Her father's voice suggested he was not so excited about this particular finalist. "Who's the smaller man?"

"I've no idea. I don't think I know him—or his emblem. Obviously, a nobody. But I doubt it will make much difference if he's going up against Sir Charl. And Sir Charl will be a good addition to our fighting men.

Perhaps Anlin's crazy scheme will work out after all."

Whatever her father replied was lost in the loud cheering as the last two men approached and circled each other. Sir Charl had the greater height and reach, but the green clad knight seemed fresher. His moves were a little crisper than his opponent's.

The two men met with a tremendous clashing of metal. Anlin knew how heavy the great swords were, yet both knights swung theirs repeatedly with a speed that made the weapons nothing but blurs. The surrounding crowd had quieted. It breathed in and out like a great beast in time with the laboring combatants.

Sir Charl logically kept pressing the advantage of his greater reach, making the smaller man move back. Then the green clothed knight appeared to stumble, and Sir Charl lunged. Anlin, like most of the spectators, gave a quick intake of breath. This must be the end.

But the smaller man deftly sidestepped the blow and returned with his own stoke, low and across the legs. Even with the swords padded, the stroke must have been punishing. Sir Charl's knees buckled and he crumpled to the ground. The green knight moved to a dominant position over his opponent, and the referee called an end to the match.

The spectators broke into a frenzy of cheering. Anlin remained frozen in place. This, then, was the man who would have command of her body until the day she died. Cold uncertainty leached into her bones. Then she reminded herself this could only happen if this warrior agreed to bend to her will. She felt her shoulders relax as the man approached. She yet had control of the pieces in play.

"That last stoke was unsporting," her bother complained. But their father ignored him and stood to receive the victor.

The man strode forward, stopping directly in front of the dais. He didn't take a knee or even bow his head. He stood with his feet slightly apart, his stance proclaiming confidence more than arrogance. He knew he was the last man on the field. He brought with him the smell of combat—leather, oiled metal, and the sharp tang of sweat.

With a surprisingly graceful movement, he reached up and removed his helm. Tucking it under one arm, he pushed back the mail coif with the other hand. Fear— the despised fear she'd thought safely bound by her iron will—shot through Anlin. In that first instance, the man's features had a decidedly Rennish cast, with sharp cheekbones, dark skin, and black hair.

Then she blinked and remembered to breathe and the similarity was gone. His features were chiseled, but definitely Fallucian. His skin was tanned from hours in the sun, slightly lighter lines radiating from the corners of his eyes attested to the fact. His hair, wet and matted from his exertions, could have been any color.

He looked directly at her father with a proud lift of

his chin. "My Lord Giffard, I am Faulk of Jarburgh, and I am the last man standing." His voice was deep. His diction that of an educated man.

"Welcome Faulk of Jarburgh," her father replied. "You are the day's champion and the promised rewards will be yours. We will await you in the castle to confirm your possession of the offered prizes."

Her father's hand might have made some motion in her direction, or perhaps the man just wished to ascertain for himself if one of the prizes was worth the winning. He looked directly at Anlin and she saw his eyes. No, this man was not Rennish. No one in that Cheelum forsaken country had such eyes—green with yellow flecks, surrounded by a solid ring the color of moss on a wet rock. He looked at her without compromise.

He was a hard man. The one she needed. For the first time that day, she felt her face relax. Her lips quirked up into a slight smile. The final piece was on the board. The next move was hers.

෯•෯

Faulk nodded to the calls of congratulations. He suspected men would be pounding him on the back had he not been leading Fiddian. Only a fool made a quick move toward a knight when his warhorse was near, particularly when the animal was still keyed up from what for him had been a totally realistic battle. This was not the first time the big gray had protected him, even if these approaches wouldn't be lethal.

With effort, Faulk kept his stride measured and dignified. No one could know his heart was bouncing around in his chest like a cricket in a box. His lips wanted to curl into an idiot's grin. It had taken him a few moments to realize that what he felt was happiness, the emotion was so foreign. Not since before Lord Lealand's arrest and execution had he felt this uncommon flush. But, Sweet Cheelum, the fief was now his! The fortified manor house was substantial, well situated on a bluff above a river ford. It wasn't a keep, of course, but when he'd inspected the property, Faulk had seen where the addition of a few walls could make the place adequately defensible.

The land that went with the manor was lush and well-watered. The attendant village, while not large, was prosperous looking and even boasted its own temple. It was a place to put down roots, a place that would be his heirs for generations. In the space of one day he'd been raised to the ranks of the landed. Oh, he'd never be one of the Lords of High Places, but he was now so much higher than he had been, it was unsurprising the air he breathed at this elevation seemed dizzying.

His return to his encampment after his victory brought him back to reality. There was no pavilion with fluttering pennants here at the place he'd staked for himself. He'd made a lean-to out of canvas that was supported on one side by the curtain wall of the castle. A fire pit for cooking stood to one side. Other than a fine horse and good mail, this had long been the extent of his wealth.

He was surprised when two men unfolded themselves from where they squatted next to the cold fire. Then he recognized them as Kevin and Waylon, two men-at-arms he'd supped with the previous night. By rights, he should have eaten with other knights, but he'd been a man-at-arms himself for more years than he cared to remember. He was comfortable with these men who made up the backbone of all armies and lived on hope.

Kevin and Waylon both sported the idiot's grin he'd been trying to hide. "Sweet Cheelum, Faulk, you did it," Kevin said, coming forward to grasp Faulk by the forearm. When Fiddian's ears slicked back and his great, square teeth appeared, however, the man had sense enough to step back.

"We thought you might, you know, need some help now that you're to be a land holder," Waylon said with a shy smile. He wisely kept his distance.

"Oh, you've come to apply for the position of squire?" Both men's faces exhibited such horror that Faulk broke into a laugh. Men-at-arms generally belittled squires, who were thought to be trying to jump up in rank by being ass-kissers. The two men got the joke and laughed. Faulk suspected they were looking for jobs at his new holding. While neither had seemed particularly brilliant, both men were solid and steady. Not the worst people to have at your back in a fight. It was something Faulk would consider.

Like a wash of cold water came the realization that his tenancy of the fief was not certain. Lady Anlin had the right to approve the final choice. And he had no idea what the lady was particularly looking for. He felt some of his joy drain away.

"I'd appreciate your help," he said. "I'll take care of the horse. He can be a bit twitchy when he doesn't know you. But I'll not show my teeth or stamp my feet if you get me out of this damned mail."

"That we can do," Kevin said. "I'll even sand it some so no rust develops. Especially if you happen to have some ransom money you can afford to spread around."

Faulk thought of his very full purse. He'd purposely chosen to fight the Lords' younger sons early in the melee. They were a parade of peacocks with limited fighting skills and so were easy targets. And wealthy ones. Even if he hadn't won the day, this tournament would have left him with more coin than he'd seen at one time in his entire life. "Yeah, I've got a bit I can spread around."

Both men leaped forward and in record time divested Faulk of his mail. He'd worn mail for much of his adult life, was accustomed to its pressure on his shoulders and waist, but he still felt as if he could float away when the pressure was gone. He flexed his shoulders and rotated his neck. Ah, that was better.

He stripped off Fiddian's tack and smiled when the big horse seemed to sign with a relief that was similar to his own. Then he began to brush out the saddle marks.

Kevin diligently went to work sanding Faulk's mail. The scrape of grit on metal seemed to provide a counterpoint to his own brush strokes across the gray's back. They were the comforting sounds of day's end.

Not to be left out, Waylon appeared from inside the lean-to, shaking out Faulk's only good tunic. "I figured you'd want to look your best to go up to the castle. Is this what you'll wear to meet your intended bride?" When Faulk nodded, he continued, "Too bad the woman is so old, gray haired and all. It'd be nice to get some heirs to pass your land on to."

Faulk stopped brushing Fiddian and looked at the man-at-arms. "She's not old. She's just got a white blaze in her hair. Probably from an injury. There's a little star-shaped scar on her forehead below the blaze."

"How do you know that?"

Faulk stepped back and tossed the currycomb in the direction of where his saddle sat on its tree. "I was standing right in front of her, you dolt, and I looked."

How could any man not look at her? Even during the worst of the fighting, some part of his brain had been conscious of her. She shone like a pillar of flame.

The sheen of her dress varied from scarlet to apricot in the shifting light. It gave a false appearance of motion. The woman herself was immobile, as if she were some stone saint in a temple. No expression crossed her face; her eyes were shuttered windows. She was of middle height, slender, and had a finely drawn face. The small scar and the white streak in her dark hair made her unique. Other than these physical attributes, however, she remained a cipher.

"Then let's hope she's not as mad as some say," Kevin said from his position on the ground.

"Who says?" Faulk lowered his voice. It was not a good thing to talk about the madness that stalked the High Places. Lord Lealand might be alive today had anger not pushed him to question King Fremmor's sanity.

"Oh, you know, just gossip." Kevin looked around, evidently realizing his error. In a quieter voice he said, "I've heard everything from her being howling mad to just a bit peculiar. But I guess strange is strange. I mean, her father couldn't get one of the local Baron's to marry her, nor one of the local Baron's heirs, and he had to be willing to lay out plenty of inducement in the dowry. Look what he offered to anyone who could win her, regardless of family or background. I figure the lady is plenty strange."

"I suspect any sane person who was enslaved in Rennic for years would end up a bit peculiar." Faulk hoped to end the discussion right there. "But unless the lady suffers from a lack of smell, I need to wash before I go up to the castle. I smell worse than my horse." Actually, he smelled much worse. He'd stripped off his sodden gambeson when he'd removed his hauberk and the breeze had dried the sweat on his naked chest, but he still exuded an odor reminiscent of a civet cat.

He scooped up an odd scrap of linen and some soap and headed toward the river. Ironically, now that he had funds to pay for a bath in a bathhouse, he lacked the time. He'd definitely indulge himself with a long soak in hot water before the actual marriage—assuming there would be one. If not, he'd collect the five gold els that were offered as a consolation and buy his own damned land. It might not be as nice as the prize fief, but it would be something. The essential part was that it would be his.

The river water was cold, no help for aching muscles, but it drained away the heat of combat. Faulk ran the sliver of soap over his whole body, not having to be careful with its use. The odd feeling he'd identified as happiness rose up within him again and, being alone, he smiled. All the soap he could ever want, a big, square bar. Another set of small clothes so he didn't have to wash them on himself and wander around wet-assed until they dried. Hell, maybe two sets. He laughed at himself. His dreams were modest for a man with such a heavy purse, but most important was the land.

He'd just stepped onto the river path on his way back to his bivouac when he felt a hand on his arm. "Faulk? Excuse me, Sir Faulk?"

Faulk turned to look into a face he hadn't expected to see. Hadn't wanted to see. Edmund Tarn stood looking down at him. Tarn, the damned, tall bastard. Tarn loved the way everyone had to look up at him.

"Sir Edmund," Faulk said, pasting a patently false smile on his face. "Excuse me, Lord Tarn now, right?" Two could play this game of being uncertain of the other's elevation in rank. "Sorry to hear about your brother's death." Insincerity oozed into his words. The only thing that Faulk was sorry about was that he hadn't killed Edmund Tarn's brother himself. The man had been an asshole. It was unfortunate that Edmund, the younger brother, wasn't an improvement.

"Thank you for your condolences," Edmund said. His face reflected the same artificial camaraderie Faulk's own expression signaled. "I stopped you to say congratulations. You'll be a worthy addition to those sworn to Lord Giffard. Of course, I'm still distressed that things worked out the way they did for Philip Lealand. Damned fine man. But he should have known not to question the king about that disputed holding." Tarn shrugged. "The vagaries of power. One never knows how some of these things will work out."

It took all of Faulk's considerable self-control not to push his fist through Tarn's falsely concerned face. Tarn had the ear of King Fremmor, and Faulk suspected the man had been the one urging the king to reject Lealand's suit. Faulk gritted his teeth. "It's kind of you to express your concern."

Edmund raised one eyebrow, the only indication that he'd not missed Faulk's sarcastic tone. "I came with one of my men, Sir Charl of Shorely. He took part in the tournament. The holding that was offered was superior to anything I'm able to give him, and I wanted him to know that I supported his desire to improve his lot in life. A good man, Sir Charl." He gave another false smile. "You know Sir Charl. He was your opponent there at the end and probably would have carried the day if you hadn't used that stumble trick."

Faulk kept his face carefully neutral. "It wasn't a trick. It was a win." He thought Tarn's coming with his retainer showed more than just the normal support of ambition. If Sir Charl had won and taken a Giffard holding, to which man would Sir Charl really be sworn? Was there any reason Tarn wanted to insinuate "his" man, even once removed, into the middle of Giffard's vast domain?

This was a time of shifting loyalties, and it was often difficult to tell where fealty resided. Philip Lealand, the most loyal of men, had been betrayed by his own liege lord, the increasingly unstable king. Madness stalked magic in all the High Places. Faulk felt the familiar impotent rage and with difficulty retained his bland expression.

"It was kind of your new lord to release you for this pursuit." Edmund gave him an unctuous smile, a smile that said he knew there was no new lord but that he just wanted Faulk to have to say so.

"In this I was fortunate." Faulk's shoulders were tight, but his smile was in place. "I've recently been a garrison knight on the Rennish border. The tower is on Hannon land, but I've not sworn to him, so needed no one's leave to be here." Unsaid was the fact that many felt that Faulk was tainted by his former Lord's fall.

"Oh, a hired garrison knight." Tarn feigned surprise, but he said the words with the same inflection that one would say *rag picker*. "Well, if Giffard's daughter decides you're not what she wants and you're looking for a position, please feel confident that I'd be glad to take your oath. You had Lealand's high estimation and that's enough for me."

"That's kind of you, milord," Faulk said, thinking that he would swear to the likes of Tarn only when birds flew north for the winter, "but I suspect that I'll be swearing to be Philip Giffard's man. That's a requirement to hold the prize fief."

Edmund laughed. "Well, if all doesn't go as you've imagined, I'm in the striped pavilion to the west of the walls. I was serious about the offer."

"Again, you are too kind." Faulk's face ached from holding his tight smile, and he was glad to turn away and continue down the path. A miasma of corruption always seemed to follow Edmund Tarn. Lealand had hated the man. He'd felt the Tarns were part of the cabal that guided the king into some of his more bizarre decisions. Lealand had thought that all the Tarns held more magic than they'd admit to, and that what was hidden was twisted. Faulk hadn't the ability to see any of this, but he did still get a strange feeling around the man.

One thing Faulk was sure of—he'd never swear to Tarn. But it suddenly dawned on him that he'd hopefully soon be swearing to another Philip—in this case Philip Giffard would replace Philip Lealand as his liege lord

The symmetry felt like inevitability.

2

"*Well, at least it should be easy* to convince the winner to take the money instead of the holding." Roland sat on the edge of their father's desk, idly swinging his foot. "Sweet Cheelum. How did we end up with such a champion? A garrison knight. Not a drop of noble blood in him. Supposedly knighted from the ranks of the men-at-arms. The second man standing would have been a better choice. Perhaps we can defer to him when the first is out of the way. Unless you're done proving that you control the situation and will accept the obvious choice of Sir Kenteth." This last was a statement addressed to Anlin where she sat by the solar's window.

Anlin stared stonily at her brother. Could he tell from her expression that she thought him a fool? "I've told you repeatedly that in my mind, Kenteth will always be my brother-in-law, Sybil's husband. Her death makes no difference. Neither he nor I have any desire to change this relationship. I was the one to press for this tournament—and I'm the one who will live with the results."

She'd held on to Sir Kenteth's image through the first months of her ordeal in Rennic, tried to wrap her mind in his former kindness to cushion the brutality around her. But over time, she'd made a shocking discovery. Sir Kenteth was not the man she needed. He was kind. He was considerate. And he was soft.

She now knew she needed someone who was ruthless, someone who would do what was expedient to get what he wanted. That had been the entire purpose of this tournament. The winner should have been the hardest, meanest fighter who was present. She hoped she'd gotten him. She personally didn't care if he'd ever been knighted. His only disqualifying feature would be an affinity for magic. But this was something the two of them would discuss privately.

"Well, the 'results,' as you name him, is certainly taking his own sweet time about coming to claim you," Roland said.

Her father reached over and put a hand on her brother's knee. "Enough, Roland. We're already well acquainted with your opinion. I promised Anlin that we'd abide by the rules she set down. As for Sir Faulk's tardiness—he sent a referee's assistant asking me to give him time to arrange ransom for those he'd captured, and I agreed."

"I noticed he captured only those who could pay well to get their mounts and equipage back," Roland continued in the same vein. "I doubt that was happenstance. Sir Faulk is a man looking to increase his income, not marry and swear fealty to you. I'm sure he'll take the money and you'll not have to give your daughter, as well as one of your best fiefs, to some unknown man-at-arms."

The two men continued the discussion, dismissing Anlin as though she'd left the room. She didn't mind. Regardless of what was said, she was the only one who could reject this man, this Sir Faulk.

What did she know about him? Her brother had been bludgeoning her with his humble origins, "raised in a monastery, obviously someone's bastard, supposedly knighted and pledged to a lord in the north who got himself killed fighting the king." Yes, she'd heard all the damning evidence. But she'd also seen him fight.

And fighting was something that Sir Faulk did very well.

A knock came from the door, the sound stopping Anlin's reverie and ending her brother and father's conversation. "Come," her father called.

As the door opened, both men rose to their feet as if expecting trouble rather than an anticipated visitor. With difficulty, Anlin remained seated in the window alcove. She schooled her features to reflect none of the tumult she felt.

The man who entered was subtly different from the one that she'd seen on the field. He was taller than she expected, nearly of a height with her father and brother, but he walked with the same powerful, self-contained movement she remembered. He was a man comfortable in his own skin and confident that he could control most situations. He wore a tunic of the same moss green as his surcoat. His dark hair, poorly cut and showing a tendency to curl at his neck, glinted a deep, dark red in the light from the setting sun that slanted through the solar window.

"Sir Faulk of Jarburgh?" her father said, more a statement than a question.

"Lord Giffard, Sir Roland." Faulk acknowledged the standing men. Then no one seemed to know how to proceed.

Anlin stood from her position by the window and inserted herself into the awkward silence. "I am Lady Anlin Giffard," she said moving toward them. Three pair of eyes swiveled toward her.

Faulk was the first to acknowledge her. "My lady." He bowed with graceful courtesy, something she hadn't expected from the man she thought he was.

Her brother wasn't about to be similarly courteous. "Go back and sit down," Roland said. "I reluctantly agreed to father's decision to let you remain, but this is a discussion for men. You should stay out of it."

"I'm the one most involved," she said, giving her brother a cold stare. Anger simmered—anger that she'd carefully suppressed all these months. Anger at abandonment. Anger at men, any men, determining her future with no regard to her own feelings. She sometimes felt there was little difference in her position here from that of a slave in Rennic.

"She *is* the one most involved," her father said, slanting Roland a quelling look. "Any decisions made are hers, not yours, not mine, and ultimately, not even Sir Faulk's. Normally the men work out the property distribution, and the lady is presented with the decisions after the fact. This situation is hardly normal, however, so I think it would make most sense if we all sat down, had some wine, and came to our conclusions jointly." He gestured to the table and benches that sat before a cold fireplace. "Sir Faulk, if you'd please be seated."

Faulk walked to one of the benches, the rest of them filling in the open spaces. Anlin and her father ended up on one side of the table. After her brother had poured the wine, all the while frowning at Anlin because she'd not done so, Roland rather hesitantly took the place beside Faulk. Anlin noted the fragile Tremellian glasses had been placed on the table. She doubted Faulk understood the honor that was being accorded him.

"We understand that you're not sworn elsewhere. Is our information correct, Sir Faulk?" Lord Giffard asked.

"Yes, sir." Faulk looked down at his hands gently holding the stem of the expensive glass. "I was sworn to Lord Philip Lealand, was part of his household for the past eighteen years, but I was released by his death over a year ago."

"And in that time, you've sworn fealty to no one

else?" Roland asked.

"No, Sir Roland. Due to the nature of Lord Lealand's death, and to the knowledge that I'd been his man for so long, I've received no offers that I would consider." Faulk gave Roland a look that Anlin couldn't quite interpret. She tried to remember what she'd heard about the death of Lord Lealand. She'd never met him, but knew that his estate lay in the North, knew he'd rebelled against the king in some way. As with much of what had transpired in Fallucia during her captivity, however, she really didn't care what had happened.

"If you were with Lealand for eighteen years, you must have come there when you were a boy," Lord Giffard said.

"Yes, sir. I was eleven. Previously I'd been at the monastery at Jarburgh, but by eleven it had become apparent that Cheelum had other plans for my life." Faulk gave a deprecating smile. The smile changed his face and made his remarkable eyes glow. "That's a nice way of saying that I didn't fit at Jarburgh, that it had become obvious that I'd never make a monk, and that I was more trouble than I was worth. Lord Lealand was the brother of one of the monks there, and after one of his visits, Lord Lealand took me to live at his castle.

"I started out working in the stables. I've always liked horses. But, like all the young boys in residence, I was given arms instruction and was good at it. I eventually became a man-at-arms. Four years ago, I was knighted for valor in the field. I believe you know the rest."

"All those years and your previous lord never felt you were competent enough to have your own holding?" Roland asked. Anlin didn't need to notice the way Faulk's fist tightened on the glass's stem to realize her brother's question contained an insult.

"Lord Lealand had limited land," Faulk said with studied evenness. "There was a disputed holding that he thought to give into my care, but the dispute was settled against him." He stared hard at her brother. Roland flushed and looked away.

"You understand you'll have to swear to me if you take up the tenancy of the holding I offered the winner of the tournament," Lord Giffard said. "I'm indisputably the king's man. Can you, in good conscious, do so?"

Faulk looked directly at her father. "I thought about this carefully before entering the lists, my lord. I've heard only good things about you and feel you'd not misuse my loyalty. If you believed a cause was just, either in the king's behalf or simply in your own, I feel I could honorably follow you. I would give you the full extent of my loyalty and fighting skill."

Anlin could see only sincerity in Sir Faulk's face, but she felt he'd somehow skirted the issue. He'd indicated his loyalty would be to her father, which was right, but he'd also seemed to suggest that this loyalty didn't extend to the king. Sir Faulk appeared to indicate he'd be willing to fight for Giffard either for or against the chief magnate in the land.

Her father leaned back, however, as if satisfied with the answer. Her brother started to speak, but Lord Giffard held up his hand for silence. "Then I think there'd be no impediment to your taking the holding. It's named White Ford. At some future time, you might want to style yourself Faulk of White Ford, unless you have a strong continuing connection to Jarburgh."

"I would gladly accept the honor you offer me," Faulk said. "But I was led to believe the Lady Anlin had the final say in the matter. We two should discuss her concerns."

He looked at her with such concentration that Anlin realized Faulk had been acutely conscious of her presence throughout. To the others she'd disappeared, noticed but not noted, like a tapestry on the wall. Faulk, however, had had part of his mind constantly attuned to her.

He was correct, though. The decision was ultimately hers. He was not a bad looking man. His face would have been just average had it not been for the striking green eyes. Remarkable for one who had fought for so many years, she saw no scars on his face except for a recently won bruise darkening along his lower jaw.

His shoulders were wide. The fabric of his tunic stretched tight across them. The same rather poorly-designed, fat-looking falcon that had been displayed on his surcoat now decorated the upper left shoulder of his tunic. For all its slightly misshapen appearance, a talented hand had carefully embroidered the bird. The work of a mother, or sister, or lover?

If it was the latter, it made no difference. Anlin hadn't planned to demand any sort of fidelity. Faulk's faithfulness and loyalty could be reserved for her father. If the man would accomplish her goal, that would be enough. To get what she wanted, she would pay with her body, she'd done so often enough before, but she hoped he would find that sort of activity elsewhere. She suspected what he really wanted was the land, and if he would follow her instruction in just one thing, it would be his for as long as he lived.

"Yes," she said, "I believe it would be best if Sir Faulk and I came to an agreement before we proceeded." When neither her brother nor father made a move to leave she added, "Alone."

Her brother's face darkened, and he looked as if he'd disagree. What? Did he think he needed to stay here to protect her? She had nothing left that needed protecting. As if her father understood better than her sibling, he abruptly stood, bringing the other two men to their feet.

"Yes, I think it is time for Anlin and Sir Faulk to see if they can find common cause. Roland, it's best we leave."

Although her brother frowned, he followed their father out the door, the sound of its closing making her think of a lid being placed on a coffin. Not a happy thought to begin a discussion of lifelong commitments. Despite the misgivings she suddenly felt, she forced a smile onto her face. It was time to cast the dice and see if the game were winnable.

❧ 3 ❧

Faulk stood next to the table, consciously relaxing his shoulders, willing to wait in silence under the woman's scrutiny. She smiled at him, a quirking of the lips, but the expression didn't extend to her eyes. He couldn't read Lady Anlin's emotions. He wondered if there were any to be noticed or what it would take to engage them.

"What is the bird?" she asked. "A falcon?"

It was hardly the first question he'd imagined she might ask. His right hand unconsciously came up to stroke the embroidery that sat just above his heart. "It's a nightpiper."

The smile now seemed to reach her eyes, but he feared it was the humor of derision. "A nightpiper? Your insignia is a nightpiper? A little bug-eater instead of a soaring raptor? You're an unusual man, Sir Faulk."

"Not so unusual." He felt the fine stitches beneath his fingers and remembered all they had once promised. "I happen to be an admirer of the nightpiper. They're clever birds. They can hide in plain sight. Their flight is as soundless as an owl. Their cries are not beautiful, but they punctuate the night. Heard but unseen, like a ghost in the darkness. Something mysterious. I developed an affection for the nightpiper as a boy, when I hoped that as an adult I'd be mysterious." His own mouth curved into a smile at the memory.

"So, are you?"

"Am I what?"

"Mysterious."

"No, I'm a quite average man. My behavior is easily readable to those who bother to notice. As a child I tried to imagine some attribute that would set me apart from others, and I chose mysterious." He didn't go on to explain how that same child had lain awake many nights, listening to the chirring of the pipers and envying the freedom the birds enjoyed.

"Does this discussion of the emblem I've chosen have something to do with determining my suitability?" he asked. "I'm obviously fond of it, but if you find it particularly offensive—"

"No, no, it was just a curiosity. I thought the bird was a poorly done falcon or hawk." Silence fell between them. Faulk waited for her next area of discussion, but she just tilted her head and looked at him. "I can see why a hawk or a falcon wouldn't work for you. Both of those can be tamed, and I don't see you sitting on anyone's wrist."

"I don't think you would easily be tamed either, my lady." Faulk thought it was a courtly thing to say. This woman could still reject him, and he would lose the holding. He wanted to make a good impression. He was surprised when a look of anger flashed across Anlin's face.

"I promise you that I will not be tamed at all. If you expected me to be some meek maiden, you're mistaken. I haven't been a maiden for these past ten years, through no fault of my own. I've endured more abuse than I want to remember, and I'll not now suddenly become meek and endure dominion from you. If you think to tame me, I warn you, I killed the last man who thought to do so. And I would do it again. I *will* do it again, if I need to."

She'd come to her feet and was leaning forward with her hands on the table. Her breath was audible as if she'd just run a distance. Faulk had wondered what could call forth emotion from her stoic demeanor. He'd never imagined his innocent remark could do so. The whispers about her possible mental instability came back to him. Had he just seen an example of potential madness?

"My comment was meant as a compliment, not as a threat. And I promise you—if I ever do threaten you, you will know the difference."

Faulk realized he was also leaning across the table. His voice had lowered to a growl. What was he doing? What was he saying? He'd never threatened a woman in his life. He was looming over her. He straightened and abruptly sat down.

"My apology, Lady Anlin. I don't know what came over me. I can only make the excuse that, for me, more is riding on this than what is usual. I thought I'd relinquished the possibility of ever marrying. A man without land cannot support a wife, at least not in the way I'd want to support one. I thought the opportunity to ever have my own holding had disappeared with the death of my former lord. In your anger, I saw a dream slipping away."

Faulk looked directly into Anlin's flushed face. Mixed with the anger he saw a fear he'd probably never fully understand. He'd been beaten as a young boy, but he'd always had faith that somehow, he could make things different, better. He'd been confident that eventually he would simply grow larger than his tormenter. A woman had no such guarantee. He could understand her fear of larger, more muscular men.

"Please sit down," he said, trying to keep his voice even, as if he were speaking to a spooked horse. "Let us talk honestly together. If we're unable to come to an accord, I'll not press you to honor the agreement to marry and bestow the fief of White Ford on your husband. I will simply take the money and disappear from your life. It isn't what I want. I'd hoped for the land. It's your choice, however. If it would ease your mind, I'd be willing to add a codicil to the agreement that should I ever physically mistreat you, the land would be forfeit."

He continued to sit calmly and watch her, willing

her to comply, seeking the sign of sanity that was necessary if they were to proceed at all. Her breathing slowed. With a sigh, she eased back onto the bench, her face resuming its emotionally frozen appearance.

"I'm sorry for my outburst. It was uncalled for. I too have been under a great deal of stress. I too have much riding on this outcome. Can we perhaps go back and resume a normal conversation?"

"Of course, my lady." Relief flooded Faulk. He felt the strange giddiness that sometimes comes after battle.

"Do you think me mad?" she asked after a moment of silence. "There are some who say I returned from Rennic in that state. I can only assure you that, while I have moments of extreme anger, I think I'm quite sane."

"I don't really know you well enough to form an opinion," he said. "I'm sure captivity by the Rennish had an effect on you. It would be strange if it did not."

Silence again filled the chamber. Somewhere outside a man whistled a tune. Faulk unconsciously strained to catch the melody.

"I was just a girl when I was taken by the Rennish," she said, the intensity of her voice pulling Faulk's attention away from the whistler, "a headstrong, heedless girl. We, my sister and I, were on the way to Giffard's Crest from our fosterage. My sister was coming home to celebrate her betrothal to Sir Kenteth of Clee. And I was angry." She made a short, chopping sound that might have been a laugh. "Ridiculously angry because Sybil had been given Sir Kenteth and I wanted him."

She shrugged. "I was twelve. What did I know? Sir Kenteth was nice to me, and he seemed all that was wonderful. Everyone else seemed to favor my sister Sybil. And why not? Sybil was pretty and tractable and polite and magically Talented. And I was—well, I was not. So, when the Rennish swarmed out of nowhere and attacked our cavalcade, I was dressed in a drab work kirtle. At the time, I thought dressing poorly would show my parents that I didn't care if they loved Sybil best." She brought her eyes up to look him directly in the face. "Adolescence is a confusing time. Now, I can't understand the thought process of the girl I was."

"You were captured? Your guard let this happen?" Faulk found the idea repellent. Unless Lord Giffard was incompetent, and he had never heard such, then a large contingent of fighting men should have been sent to accompany his daughters. All would have to be either dead or unable to hold a sword before their charges could be taken. Or at least that would have been the case if he'd been in charge.

"All the men in our escort were either killed or incapacitated. In retrospect, we didn't have enough armed men with us. Our foster father made the arrangements. Our own father might have been more prudent. But then, it was ten years ago. There had been few problems with the Rennish, and we were a distance from the border." She shrugged. "At this point, it makes no difference. It happened long ago."

While it had, indeed, happened long ago, Faulk could still envision how the fight had ensued. The Rennish would have boiled from their hills in vast numbers, so crazed they would continue to slash at their opponents after they'd sustained fatal wounds and should have been writhing on the ground. Having served at a border garrison, he was well acquainted with Rennish tactics, which were fearsome. A small group would easily have been overwhelmed.

"But the Rennish usually want only horses and weapons," he said. "Prisoners of value are almost always ransomed back. Why were you retained?"

She gave another short chuff of laughter. "Oh, they ransomed my sister Sybil back to our parents. But because I was poorly dressed and hadn't the least bit of magic, they wouldn't believe I was also a Giffard daughter. And since I had no ransom value, I was sold as a slave in the market in Hightor."

All animation left her face and she became a graven effigy. "A frightening thing, being sold. To somehow suddenly become less than human. To be stripped naked and groped and prodded like an animal by men with dirty hands. It's odd, but through all the horror, I remember the hands. The hands and the stench, a feral smell of unwashed bodies and leather tanned with piss."

Her voice had taken on the cadence of a storyteller, as if she were relating a tale that had been heard and remembered, not something she'd actually experienced. But then, she'd only been twelve, so perhaps the memory did seem to belong to someone else.

"There are some here in Fallucia who think the Rennish are not really human," she said. "But I can assure you that they are normal men, with men's desire to dominate anyone weaker than themselves. And a girl child is easy to dominate, to force to your will, to train to do all sorts of abominable things. Of course, I didn't remain a girl, but I was always Fallucian, always unique. I was passed from one man to the next to be dominated, to be used."

She paused. The distant whistling could still be heard, sounding, to Faulk, like the soft melody used by a harper to accompany his tale.

"I had a son. It was for him that I chose to live instead of die, since this most basic of choices, whether to live or die by my own hand, was all that was left to me. When he was three, my then-owner found him an inconvenience, and my son was taken from me. At night, I still imagine I can feel him, curled up next to my heart. After he was gone, I chose to live to find him again and get him back.

"The land you covet will be yours if you come with me into Rennic, find my son, and bring him back. That is the agreement you will be asked to sign. There is no need for a codicil. There is nothing you can do to me that hasn't already been done."

Her recitation ended. She just ran down as if she'd spoken all the words she knew. Faulk fought the urge to reach for her, to offer the human comfort of touch.

Something in her attitude rejected sympathy, however, rejected pity, and that was how she'd have viewed his action.

On more than one occasion, Faulk had fought across ground that was slick with blood and entrails. He knew what men could do to one another. Anlin's story sickened him, nonetheless. He hated brutality practiced on the helpless.

Her tale called forth more questions than answers, however. Why had she been left there without rescue? And why, on her return, had her powerful father not mounted a campaign to regain her son? He longed to ask her these questions but feared that he would again tread into the prickly area of her anger.

Anlin seemed to read rejection into his silence. "You said that we should deal honestly with one another. If this is more honesty than you bargained for, I'm sorry."

"No," he said, "I appreciate your telling me this. It can't be easy for you to remember such things. I was just trying to absorb your experience, to understand all that has happened. How old is your son?"

"He's seven."

"You realize it's very possible that he no longer lives." It was a hard thought, but one Faulk could not pretend did not exist.

"He lives!" She touched her heart. "I'm sure I'd know in here if he did not."

"Then why didn't your father take a host of knights and look for him right after you returned? This action would seem to have the greater opportunity for success than just the two of us riding over the border."

"Do you have magic?"

The question seemed to come from nowhere. Did she hope for someone who had a powerful Talent? If so, he was going to be a grave disappointment. His grasp on the holding, on White Ford, again became tenuous. "I've exhibited no special abilities," he said slowly. "I'm generally good with horses, but I think that this is a skill more than a Talent."

"Good," she said to his relief. "Fallucian magic is abhorrent to the Rennish. They can feel it. One person with ability is, to them, a tickle. But massed power, such as a group of Fallucians, has a strange effect. They swarm like hornets from a disturbed nest. They're almost mindless in their fury. This is the reason Fallucia has made no incursion into Rennic. It is not just their mountains that Fallucians find daunting."

"Is this the reason no rescue was sent when you were taken?"

"No. My family was convinced I was dead. My sister Sybil's Talent was scrying—in her case, the ability to see distant happenings in water—and she could find no evidence of me. There is something in Rennic that deadens Fallucian Talent." She shrugged. "It is of no matter now, except my father's guilt at leaving me there is the bludgeon I use to get my way for what I plan to do."

What she planned to do was to rescue a half-

Rennish son. Not an easy task, but one she thought Faulk could help her accomplish. "Am I correct in assuming that you too have no magic?"

She laughed without humor. "Yes. I'm particularly well-suited for the task I've set myself. I have no magic. My family has found me a great disappointment. It's an embarrassment for any woman in a Baron's family to be without a shred of Talent, but I've managed to achieve that distinction."

Faulk could understand her attitude. The man he believed to be his father had magic—and exhibited all its negative aspects. The man imagined that he heard the voice of Cheelum. Faulk thought of this as god-madness and most fervently hoped it wasn't inheritable in any way.

"The two of us should then be able to enter Rennic without complication," Anlin continued. "Even if we are seen, we will not be perceived as a threat and allowed to go on our way. An amazing number of Fallucian traders travel in and out of Rennic, regardless of what the law says. We'll travel as traders, except that we'll take only silver to trade for my son."

"And no one would think to relieve us of a pack horse loaded with silver?"

She gave him a tight smile. "That's why I needed a warrior to go with me."

Faulk now saw Anlin's plan—and understood how he fit into it. She needed a warrior to protect her and a large quantity of silver, a warrior with a strong arm and a lack of magic, a warrior willing to take direction from a woman and venture into Rennic.

"What if we don't find your boy?"

"We give it one year. If we've not found him in that time, I'll return with you to Fallucia and never mention him again."

Faulk rather doubted the latter, but felt that in much less than a year, they would either find the child or determine he was dead. "I'll undertake this journey with you. Are there any other stipulations that could hinder our going forward with our marriage and my tenure of White Ford?"

"No. That's all I require."

Faulk smiled at what he assumed was understatement. All? As if a potentially perilous journey was something easily granted. But it was, wasn't it? He envisioned the comfortable manor house, the fertile acres, the small but prosperous village. Yes, almost any price for White Ford would easily be granted.

"I agree then," he said. "But you need to know I have some requirements of my own. Ours must be a real marriage, not just a transfer of property. I want heirs of my body who can inherit my land. Without this continuation, the ownership of property has little appeal. You also need to know that under no circumstances will your Rennish son inherit my holding. Don't think to deny me children in the hope that your son will follow me at White Ford."

"I won't expect that to happen," she said.

"The only other requirement I have has to do with our vows. I want a vow of binding fidelity. For as long as we live, there will be no other for either of us."

"But I thought that most men—"

"I'm not most men. I've been careful not to sow bastards in my wake up until now, and I do not intend to start." As an unacknowledged son, Faulk had no desire to father any unacknowledged children himself.

"Fidelity will not be a problem for me. I will enter your bed and no other's. But you will have access to only my body. My mind, my heart, will always belong only to myself."

The latter was not what Faulk wanted to hear. In his imaginings he'd hoped for a true marriage, such as he'd observed between Lord Lealand and his lady. But he'd overcome this objection. Over time, he'd make this a true meeting of souls. "Then we'll be married tomorrow at the small temple I saw in White Ford's village. I want the people on the estate to know that as their overlord, I have full legitimacy. I'll need some time to get the estate organized, but we should be able to leave for Rennic once the planting has been done. Is that acceptable?"

She hesitated and Faulk felt a tightening in his gut with the knowledge that even at this late point, failure might loom.

"Yes."

With that word, all possibilities lay before him. He would be landed, something he thought had forever moved beyond his reach.

"You should go get my father. He has the documents already drawn." It was dismissal and acquiescence together.

Faulk went down the winding steps to the hall below feeling lighthearted. A holding of his own. And he thought that Lord Giffard would be a worthy overlord.

Lord Giffard and Sir Roland stood by the dais, obviously waiting for him. "The Lady Anlin and I have come to an agreement," Faulk said.

Lord Giffard's face immediately reflected relief. Sir Roland's gaze was more cautious. Faulk could only hope he and Sir Roland had reached an accommodation by the time Sir Roland succeeded to the title. With luck, this occurrence would be many years away. Hopefully, when Roland became Lord Giffard, Faulk would be firmly planted at White Ford with a brood of sons ready to follow.

He suddenly felt his face flush. Lady Anlin would be the mother of those children. He'd found her anger and hoped he could soon find her passion. Then the begetting of those sons would be even more delightful than walking his own land.

4

As had long been her habit, Anlin was up before the sun. In Rennic, long before the men arrived at first light, she would have stirred the kitchen fire to life and made porridge. If the steading was fortunate enough to have a few dairy cows, she would have milked the animals and seen to their needs. She had learned to embrace those pre-dawn moments that belonged to her alone. They gave her the illusion of freedom.

The chores themselves hadn't been that onerous. The biting air of winter had been refreshing after the stench of smoke and unwashed bodies that permeated the house. She liked making new tracks in the snow as she made her way to the barn. She found comfort with the animals themselves, with their easy acceptance and warm, mournful eyes. In summer, watching the dew catch the sun's new rays and turn a meadow into a sparkling landscape filled her with peace.

This morning she wished she were out walking through that wet grass instead of watching the sliver of sky visible through the arrow slit change from black into a pearly gray. She never thought she would find anything to miss from her captivity, but she missed those stolen moments when she belonged to no one but herself.

If she now decided to walk outside in the pre-dawn hours, men-at-arms would appear to shadow her progress, and later, her father and brother would attempt to *reason* with her, explaining that any erratic behavior could only fuel more rumors of her mental instability. Ladies of her standing did not scamper about barefoot in the dew. So, she could only pace her chamber and fret as the sky began to lighten.

Today she'd sell herself to a man, as surely as she'd been sold at the slave market in Hightor. But this time she would willingly do so, in the hope that her son, Telm, would be reunited with her. He's been Cheelum's gift in her darkest time. His return would mend the hole in her heart, and she could move forward.

Of course, Faulk would also be constantly at her side. That was the price she would pay.

Faulk was the unknown in her plan, a tumbling die that could change all the other equations. She was sure he'd entered the tournament solely to possess the fief. Marrying her would simply validate the transaction. She was not the prize.

She now owned a mirror. The woman reflected there was fey looking, still too thin for any consideration of beauty, the puckered scar on her forehead and the white streak in her hair marking her as different, odd.

For this reason, she didn't understand his insistence that vows of fidelity be included in their wedding ceremony. She'd neither expected nor wanted that to be the case. She little cared where the man sowed his seed. She would remain faithful to him simply because she wanted no man, but she would put up with Faulk's invasion of her body to hold Telm in her arms again.

She stopped pacing and leaned her head against the cool stones of the wall. Her heart fluttered, and her breathing was shallow. She would not think of that bestial act. She would not remember the pain and the fear. She would put it out of her mind as she'd learned to do. When the time came, as it surely would, she would escape to a place where dew sparkled on the grass and leave her body to be handled as it would.

She took a deep breath and centered herself. She had nothing to fear. Regardless of what happened, she'd mentally be gone. Later, it was a simple matter to wash away the smell and stickiness left from a man's rutting. She would then find herself again and go on, as she had always done.

She heard the light tap on the door. Straightening, she called, "Come."

Gilda, one of the serving women, entered, her face wreathed in smiles. "Oh, my lady, you're already up." The woman chuckled. "But that's to be expected on such a happy day. Exciting, isn't it. The wedding and all. I'll go down and tell the kitchen staff to hurry up your breakfast. You'll want to eat before you bathe and that will give us time to get the big tub in here and filled. And have you chosen yet what you want to wear? The yellow, perhaps? It has those pretty, little flowers sewn around the neck. I bet we could find some flowers to put in your hair. You'll look so lovely. And then..."

"Breakfast first, if you please." Anlin felt washed away by the torrent of words. She'd never known Gilda to be so loquacious. The woman was like a child's toy wound too tight. Excited. Yes, that was it. Gilda was excited about Anlin's wedding. How could the woman think being married was a cause for rejoicing? But most women in Fallucia seemed to think a wedding was a woman's crowning achievement. She wondered if it held true in Rennic, but she had no basis of comparison. The whole time she'd been there, she'd not met any wives, or even those destined to be one.

Gilda was taking a breath, obviously readying herself for another deluge of words. "Breakfast," Anlin said again, this time with the arrogant authority she'd often heard in her father's voice. It worked. Gilda scuttled out the door.

ᔯ•ᔰ

Poked, prodded, curried, exclaimed over—Anlin felt like a prize ox being readied for a fair. Gilda and several other women finally decided Anlin was resplendent enough to descend to the hall and leave for the ceremony in White Ford. She wore the yellow tunic but had drawn the line at a circle of flowers that one of the women offered. Seeing the servant's disappointment, Anlin felt a moment of hesitation, but enough was enough. The farce had gone on for as long as she could stand it. It was time to be off.

She thought the final ridiculousness had come when Gilda pulled her aside as she was about to exit the room. "Is there anything that you'd like to ask me about... eh... this evening, my lady? I mean about the... eh... marriage bed. Since your mother isn't here, may she rest in Cheelum's arms, I thought you might have some questions of an older, more experienced woman. I mean, there's nothing to be nervous about. It's all quite natural. Once you get the rhythm, it's like a dance, a happy dance. Just let your husband do the leading."

"Enough!" Anlin shouted. Startled faces looked at her. "I'm sorry," she said in a softer tone. "I just need to leave if I'm not to be late."

What were these women thinking? Did they have no idea what had happened to her in Rennic, or did they just choose not to know? Certainly, all her ordeals had not been made public, and there had never been any mention of a child, her father believing either Telm would never be found or he was dead. But to tell any bride what she faced was a happy dance... Anlin could barely control her fury.

Seething with anger, she marched down the narrow, winding stairs into the hall. Her father looked at her with a smile that quickly vanished. "Is something wrong?" he asked.

Anlin wanted to tell him that he was ten years too late with his solicitous enquiry. Instead, she gritted her teeth and said, "I think it is best that we're off."

Totally misunderstanding, her father said, "I know it would have been easier to have the ceremony here, but I can see why Sir Faulk wanted it to take place at his own fief. I think it was wise of him."

Anlin made no response. She just strode through the hall and out into the courtyard. Grooms held eight horses at the ready. A small wedding party to be sure, but decidedly a wedding party. And then the final indignity—her horse had green ribbons and bells braided though its mane. Bells! Sweet Cheelum, bells! Was this to be the music used as a prelude to the happy dance?

Rounding on her father and those who had hurried to keep pace with her, she asked, "Who did this?"

"What?" Her father stopped abruptly, eyes darting to see what was amiss.

"The horse. The ridiculously decorated horse."

Her father looked confused, so she transferred her suspicions to her brother, but he too appeared perplexed.

"Sir Faulk," said one of the grooms, his voice nervous. "Sir Faulk gave me money to buy the ribbon and bells and paid me to braid them in. He said it was something that he'd seen as a boy in Jarburgh."

Faulk? Faulk had spent good money for this

mummery? Anlin had a sinking feeling that she'd totally misjudged the man that she was bargaining herself away to get. She needed a strong man, a knight who would kill without compunction. She needed someone who could overcome any threat they might find in Rennic. She needed to *belong* to such a man, for her own safety and the safety of her son. But instead of a warrior, she seemed to be tying herself to a man who decorated horses. Sweet Cheelum!

She fought the urge to yell that this was all a mistake, to run back into the keep and hide. And then what would happen? Her father would marry her off to someone else, probably Sir Kenteth. Her father still wanted a blood tie with Sir Kenteth's family. He'd lost that when Sybil died birthing remarkably unattractive twin daughters. For all his mixed blood, Anlin had safely borne a son, something her nearly perfect sister had failed to accomplish.

Schooling her features to reflect a bland good humor, Anlin walked to the horse and ran her hand gently over the bells. "How interesting," she said, unable to think of any other word. But she felt those around her relax. Lord Giffard's crazy daughter wasn't going to make a scene on her wedding day.

She allowed a servant to lift her into the saddle, and she followed her father out of the courtyard and through the streets of Giffard's Crest. People gathered at intersections and hung out of windows to see the procession pass, calling out good wishes and the blessings of Cheelum upon the bride. The damned bells tinkled and Anlin smiled—smiled as others expected her to.

Once they'd cleared the town, the group picked up speed, but that only made the bells ring more frantically. Villeins waved and called from the fields. Never had the ride to White Ford taken longer.

They arrived to find what appeared to be the entire population of the fief crowded around the squatty little temple. There was a festive feel about the crowd, and everyone wore their market-day best. Faulk—tall, broad-shouldered, and smiling—stood next to the temple door. He wore the same moss green tunic he'd worn the previous day. Anlin suspected it was the only good tunic he owned. She also realized that the ribbons woven through her horse's mane were nearly the same color green. She had an uncomfortable feeling that he had chosen the ribbons to show his ownership even before the ceremony.

With this in mind, her frozen smile slipped from her face. She noticed that his smile also slipped some, but he came forward and lifted her from her horse. "My lady, are you ready to begin?"

No, she was not ready to begin, but she would go forward. Just as long as the end included Telm being back with her. "Yes," she said, placing her hand lightly on his arm so he could lead her into the temple. The wedding party from Giffard's Crest and the crowd from in front of the building filed in behind them. She could hear everyone rustling and shuffling behind them.

The priest's face held the same beatific smile as had been carved on the statue of Cheelum that sat on the altar. The similarity of expression and the mob of people in attendance lent a feeling of unreality to the proceedings. If, as a girl, she'd ever dreamed of her wedding, she couldn't remember it, but she was sure this wasn't what she would have imagined. She wondered if Faulk felt the same, but standing next to her, he appeared relaxed and sure of himself.

Faulk repeated his vows in the same low, serious voice that he'd used when he'd sworn fealty to her father the day before. Anlin must have followed the proscribed wording since there was no confusion in the ceremony, but when it was swiftly concluded, she really had no memory of what she'd said. The only thing that surprised her was the ring that Faulk slid on the middle finger of her right hand. She wondered when he'd had time to get one. It hung loosely on her finger and she had to fist her hand to make sure that it didn't fall off.

They had to wait until the crowded temple cleared, then Faulk led her out and lifted her onto her horse. He walked, holding her horse's bridle, back to White Ford manor house. The entire throng followed then.

"Why are all the people following?" Anlin quietly asked as Faulk lifted her down. She was curious, that was true, but she also needed to distract herself from the alarming feeling of her body sliding against his.

"For the wedding feast, of course." He flashed her a

quick smile. His teeth were white and straight. He looked different from yesterday, younger. Then Anlin realized he'd shaved. No stubble glinted red in the sun. "When I arrived yesterday evening and told the people here we'd be wed today, they dashed into a flurry of cooking and baking. They wanted to welcome us and wish us well."

Of course, the people of White Ford wanted to make Faulk welcome. He was their new lord and held their lives and livelihoods in his hands. But for herself, she suspected the people were simply curious to get a good look at Lord Giffard's odd daughter. She didn't look forward to another stoic performance.

But what was done was done. She felt her face slide into its impassive mask. She took little notice of the manor's hall and let the throng that filled it drift into an unfocused kaleidoscope of colors. Faulk spoke to her throughout the interminable meal, but his voice seemed to come from a distance, and she wasn't sure exactly what he said.

Anlin was surprised when her father came to her and kissed her on the cheek. "I wish you happiness, daughter," he said. Her brother followed, but simply took her hand and mumbled something about hoping this was for the best. And then they were gone.

Faulk took her chin in his hand and turned her face toward him. "You may retire to the solar now if you wish. I know this has been a tiring day."

Unease threaded through Anlin's numbness. Retire?

Now? Sunlight still slanted through the hall's windows. It was only late afternoon. Did Faulk think to assert his rights while there was yet light in the sky and the hall still filled with people? Could he not wait until the decent cover of darkness? Her breath quickened and she felt her heart pound in her chest.

"I don't know where the solar is," she said.

Faulk beckoned a woman forward. "This is Hilmar. She'll act as your maid for now. If you'd prefer to have one of your old retainers come from Giffard's Crest, I'll make some sort of accommodation with your father. Until then, Hilmar is yours to command. She will see you to our chamber. I need to stay and get acquainted with the villeins and freemen of the fief. But I'll be up later." He said the last with a smile and squeezed her hand.

Anlin felt dismissed and couldn't decide if she were relieved or angry. Faulk rose from his seat when she stood. Anlin gave him a slight nod and followed Hilmar. Anlin walked with her back straight and head high. She was sure that no one could tell how franticly her heart beat.

Hilmar led her to a wooden stairway at the back of the hall. Of course, the solar would be up the stairs. At the top, she gazed back over the length of the hall. Faulk's green tunic stood out among the more common browns. He'd left the dais and was standing by the lower tables.

Hilmar pushed open the door. "Here, my lady," she said.

The solar was pleasant. Two carved chairs stood on either side of a now empty fireplace. Other small benches were scattered around the room, and there was a large expanse of windows on one side, their openings covered with real glass. White Ford must be a prosperous holding indeed. Faulk had to be pleased with his bargain.

"You can see the ford from here," Hilmar said, leaning over the window seat and pointing. Anlin looked where she was directed and saw the shallow rapids that allowed easy travel across the Milk River.

"And here's the Lord's chamber," the woman said, scurrying to open a door on the same wall as the fireplace.

This chamber was as spacious as the solar and had a matching, large, glass-covered window, this one overlooking the courtyard below. It was a much more comfortable room than any available at her father's keep since the manor house had not been built with defense in mind. Besides the abundance of light, the room boasted its own fireplace for winter comfort. Chests dotted the walls and a large bed with the hangings pulled back held pride of place on the longest wall. It was a room that Anlin would have liked very much had she not had to share it. The problem was... she did.

"Your belongings were brought over from the Crest while you were at the temple." Hilmar said, "and I put them in here, next to Sir Faulk's." She opened one of the larger chests.

Faulk's chest was significantly smaller, but his mail had been installed on a T-shaped support in the corner. It brooded there like an unfriendly ghost, as if to remind her this was the Lord's room and not really hers.

Anlin suddenly wanted to be gone from this room with its big bed and man-shaped mail. "I'll think I'll wait for Sir Faulk in the solar." She turned and quickly exited, Hilmar at her heels.

"Do you want me to brush out your hair? I couldn't find a night robe when I put your clothing in the chest, but if you have one elsewhere, I'll retrieve it." Hilmar was obviously trying to think of any way she could be helpful, perhaps fearing that her position would be taken by someone from Giffard's Crest. Anlin looked carefully at the maid. She was young with a wide peasant face that might coarsen with age but was now appealing in its youth and freshness. Anlin felt old and used by comparison.

"I want for nothing," she said. Then a grumble from her stomach gave the lie to her statement. She hadn't been able to force down a morsel at the wedding banquet. "Actually, I'd like to have some bread and cheese and a flagon of ale."

"I'll get it immediately," the girl said, giving Anlin a wide grin that showed a slight gap between her front teeth. "Shall I bring enough for Sir Faulk as well?" Hilmar's face suddenly flushed. "You are most fortunate, milady. Sir Faulk is such a handsome man."

She whirled and was gone before Anlin could tell her to bring food and drink for only one. Oh, well, it made little difference. At the worst, there would be some food left over—and additional ale might be welcome. In Rennic, Anlin had never had access to any type of liquor. She wondered if she could drink enough to make her numb.

She settled into one of the carved chairs, thinking it would be more comfortable if it had a pad on the seat. The solar would be her room, where she met with her ladies to do needlework and to make things like attractive pads for chairs. She wondered if Faulk cared her needlework was limited to the strictly functional. Did he imagine that she would create lovely wall hangings to soften the walls? Did he picture her as being something other than she was?

Hilmar thought Faulk handsome. Strangely, Anlin couldn't remember what Faulk looked like as a whole. She thought of him in pieces—the odd green of his eyes, the breadth of his shoulders, the whiteness of his teeth when he flashed an unexpected smile. But as a complete person, his appearance eluded her. Perhaps because his looks made little difference to her. But they had obviously intrigued Hilmar.

Anlin wondered if Hilmar's mother had told her the lies about what transpired between men and women, if Hilmar too had been told the myth of the happy dance. People told such lies to make the bitter draughts of life taste more palatable.

Anlin laid her head against the back of the chair and watched the sky through the window. Eventually, the sun would set. Was that when Faulk would come to claim his marital rights, to prove he was master of her? It made no difference. He would come, and all she could do was wait.

5

Faulk laughed at a story told by Hettle, the reeve. It had something to do with a plow team and the miller's wife, but Hettle laughed so much during the telling that the tale had been difficult to follow. The others at the table, being familiar with the occurrence, had also joined in the hilarity, and the laughter had pulled Faulk along. Straightening from a somewhat awkward position where he had been leaning on the table, Faulk bid the men there a good night. He looked around the hall. Most of the families had finally left, and only some single men remained, gathered into congenial groups and getting down to serious drinking at their lord's expense. Faulk couldn't blame them. He'd done it often enough himself.

But now, he was the lord. This was *his* hall and these were *his* people. Such a miracle was worth the expense of a few casks of ale.

He'd visited every table and spoken to most of the people in attendance. While some of the names and faces melted into one another, he felt he remembered a lot of them. Enough to stop and talk intelligently to many of the fief's inhabitants. Lealand had always told him that, while all the people on a fief would give their liege lord enough service to avoid being disciplined, a wise lord made each person feel he had a stake in the success of the holding and by doing his job well, he was working for his own betterment. The way to do this was to show a personal interest in each and every one.

Today Faulk had started doing this. He knew loyalty was earned and not coerced. He was very willing to earn it.

He leaned back, stretching muscles still tight from yesterday's tournament, and checked to see how close it was to twilight. The sky through the high windows had taken on a reddish glow. It would not be long until he could comfortably leave the hall and approach the next task of the day.

Task? Faulk smiled at his own choice of words. He hoped that consummating his marriage would be more a pleasurable than an onerous job. Unfortunately, he was unsure of exactly how the next few hours would play out.

He couldn't figure out what Anlin was thinking. During the meal, she had reverted to the expressionless and silent person he'd seen in her father's hall. Perhaps she was just terribly shy and hated to sit on the dais, although he would have guessed her to be more argumentative than retiring. There was no way to tell. But Faulk greatly preferred the prickly woman he had spoken to at their post-tournament meeting to the frozen one who had sat next to him at the wedding meal. He wondered which would meet him when he went up to the lord's chamber.

Faulk smiled at his own uncertainty. He'd never had trouble with women. To put it simply, women liked him—and he liked them back. Although women had never entered the picture while he resided at the monastery at Jarburgh, once he arrived at Maylea, Lord Lealand's fief, there was no missing them—or what they had to offer. Privacy was something difficult to attain at a busy keep, and he heard and saw a lot of what went on between men and women long before he was ready to participate.

He'd just moved to the men-at-arms' barracks prior to his sixteenth birthday when Dort, one of the laundresses, sought him out. Dort, nearly double his age, was broad of face and broad of hips, but possessed an earthiness a young man would find enticing. She smiled at him. She accidentally brushed against his body. She kissed him in ways he'd never imagined. And finally, she showed him the delight that lay between her powerful thighs.

For nearly two months, Faulk had walked around in a state of perpetual arousal. Days were long and tedious, but nights were filled with wonderful adventures in the barn. To this day, Faulk found something compelling about the scent of laundry soap mixed with fresh hay.

His mistake had been in trying to expand his

horizons. Sir Landis had come to Maylea with his family from an outlying holding, and one of these family members was his daughter, Clare. Blond, blue-eyed Clare had also smiled at Faulk. It had seemed like a good idea to see where a few kisses might lead, and Clare appeared interested in experimenting.

Lord Lealand had caught them in the stillroom, Faulk's mouth pressed to Clare's, his hand groping for hidden treasures. A powerful hand had snatched him away from his prize, and then a granite fist connected with his jaw, bringing him to his knees. It was the only time Lealand ever struck him in anger.

The girl, perhaps grasping the situation more rapidly than Faulk, ran.

Lealand shimmered with anger that seemed inappropriate for what had been taking place. "Sir Landis is my guest," he said, his voice hoarse. "His daughter is my guest. I'm disgusted that you would seek to dishonor her."

"I meant no dishonor," Faulk said, torn between an answering anger and despair at disappointing Lealand.

"A noble's daughter is not someone to trifled with. She is not some kitchen wench who is happy to share her charms with you."

"I didn't see her resisting," Faulk said, wiping the blood from his lip.

The anger flowed out of Lealand with a sigh. "Faulk, as you age, I fear women of every class will have trouble resisting you. So, you must be the one who knows when to stop—or, as in this case, knows when not to start. What if you'd succeeded in the direction you were going? What if you'd lain with Sir Landis's daughter? You would have stolen her virginity—the virginity she's expected to bring as a gift to her husband if she's to make a good marriage. Would a few minutes of carnal pleasure be worth destroying a young woman's life?

"No," Faulk said, suddenly feeling childish. "But I could have married her."

"Now that's an impossibility." Lealand stared at him with a knowing, almost sad, look.

"Why, because I'm a bastard? I'm not good enough for the likes of Sir Landis's daughter?" Hurt and anger mixed when Faulk thought Lealand would so judge him.

"No, because you have no way of supporting someone like Landis's daughter. Do you think she'd want to move into the barracks with you?"

"Of course not." The idea was ridiculous. There were eight men in the barracks, and they slept practically on top of one another.

"Then you have nothing to offer her."

It was the truth, but it hurt. Faulk could do nothing but nod.

"It's my hope that someday you'll marry a noble's daughter, Faulk, and you'll then be glad no one took advantage of her in a stillroom or the stable or the barn. You will be the only man to ever lie with her, and I hope you'll then forsake other women in honor of her. The two of you will form an indivisible unit. It is one of the greatest gifts that Cheelum bestows.

"Until that time comes, you must be very careful whom you bed." Lealand arched his brow and gave Faulk a slight smile. "You notice that I didn't say I expected you to avoid rutting with women. I too remember what it was to be young and unmarried. I do not expect the impossible. But I do urge caution. Do you understand me?"

"Yes, sir."

"Good." Lealand turned to go and then swung back to face him. "Has Dort at least taught you to withdraw so you don't sow bastards from one end of the country to the other?"

Faulk flushed with embarrassment. "How do you know about Dort?"

Lealand laughed. "Oh, Faulk, you are so very young. When a young man gets a decent breadth to his shoulders, when his face sports a fuzz that might someday be a beard, it is always Dort."

Faulk smiled at the bittersweet memory. Lealand was, as always, right. As Faulk got older, he watched Dort become broader, but other young men still followed her nightly into the barn.

Faulk's eyes again went to the window. The red in the sky had leached away, leaving a smear of dark blue-gray. It would soon be dark. His attention focused on the stairs to the solar. He hoped that Lealand was also right about what would happen when he married a lord's daughter. Oh, he knew that Anlin was not in the position to gift him with her virginity, but he hoped the rest was true. He hoped he and Anlin could form the indivisible unit that Lealand and Lady Patrice had managed to form. It was to this end that he'd asked to include the oaths of fidelity in the marriage ceremony. It was his pledge to Anlin and a promise to himself that a true union was possible. To end his perpetual aloneness was very appealing.

He walked to the stairs, ignoring some good-natured comments from the dedicated drinkers. He felt the tightness in his gut that usually preceded a battle. He realized he was nervous, as nervous as an untried boy. It wasn't just a woman who waited for him in the upper chamber; it was his wife. Wife. An unknown quantity. The eventual mother of his children.

He mounted the stairs, wondering if perhaps Anlin felt the same nervousness. Was she as worried about how this evening would play out as he was? Well, as with the people in the hall, he'd go slowly, making her feel he held her as important. He would start as he meant to continue.

He pushed open the door. Candles gave the room a soft glow. His bride awaited him in this room instead of the bedchamber. She was obviously not nervous. She was asleep.

Anlin sat in one of the carved chairs, her head resting against the back. A soft snore came from her open mouth. She looked totally relaxed; her body slumped with the bonelessness of a sleeping child. Faulk smiled at the innocence of the scene. Anlin looked pretty, younger, the fine lines on her face smoothed away. The white blaze in her hair flashed in the weak light.

Her right arm had slipped from the arm of the chair, her hand hanging down limply. His betrothal ring glittered where it lay on the floor. It was too big. He'd known it when he'd placed it on her finger. The ring had been made for another's hand, back when Lealand was alive and all things had seemed possible. Faulk bent and retrieved the ring, absently stroking the nightpiper carved on the flat surface of the gold. He'd have the ring sized to Anlin's finger. Giffard's Crest was a decent sized town. There was bound to be a goldsmith there.

Then he noticed the empty flagon and glass on the table next to her. Ah, Anlin too was nervous about this night. He'd never before seen her do more than take a sip of wine and couldn't imagine her emptying an entire flagon.

Now what was he to do with a drunken wife? Carry her to bed as he would the sleeping child that she resembled, he supposed. He squatted down, sliding one arm under her bent knees. With the other, he gathered her to his chest and stood.

She stiffened and jerked back from him so suddenly he nearly lost his hold on her. "What are you doing?"

"I thought you too soundly asleep to wake, so I'm carrying you to bed."

"I can walk," she said, squirming against him. She

was a slim woman, but the breasts that rubbed his chest so enticingly felt firm and round. He gently lowered her to her feet.

"As you wish," Faulk said.

She shook off his arm that still encircled her shoulder and marched, straight-backed, to the chamber door. There was no wavering to her steps. Anlin was evidently not the worse for drink. And she was most definitely awake. Awake and walking to their bed. Faulk smiled.

There were no candles alight in the chamber. Faulk started to go back and retrieve one, but the moon, riding amid low clouds, filled the large window with a pale, gray glow. When he'd first seen the windows in the solar and the chamber, Faulk thought they'd have to be considerably reduced in size, such openings impossible to defend. But with moonlight limning the room, he decided he might want to reconsider.

Anlin stood in the middle of the room. She seemed frozen, as if unsure of what to do. It was somehow comforting that she was as unsure as he was. When he walked up to her and touched her shoulder, she jumped.

"Why don't you take down your hair? It can't be comfortable to sleep with it pulled back so tightly." Faulk knew the suggestion was more for his benefit than hers. He wanted to see her with hair falling to her waist and perhaps beyond. He wondered if the white streak flowed to the ends.

"Yes," she said in a crisp voice as if she were

obeying a command. Her hands reached up and removed the combs that held her hair tight against her crown. But when she reached behind to loosen the snood that covered the gathered locks at her neck, she removed the whole thing. Her hair fell to just short of her shoulders.

"What…" he began, reaching for her shorn hair, finding it soft and springy.

"It was kept short in Rennic," she said. "This is as much as it's grown."

"Why short?" he asked, twisting the strands around his fingers, glad that she didn't pull away.

"It marked my servitude," she said, voice flat. "But an unintended consequence was that it made it easier to control lice." A brief, ironic smile ghosted across her lips.

Faulk couldn't imagine what her life had been like. He knew of no way to make up for whatever had happened to her. He fisted his hand in her hair and pulled her toward him, angling his head down until he claimed her mouth.

Her lips were firm but unmoving. Faulk lightened the pressure and nibbled slightly at her bottom lip. No reaction. No anything. Had the woman never been kissed? He held her face immobile and brushed kisses across her cheeks and eyes. She stood as though frozen. He dropped his kisses to the hollow between her neck and shoulder. There he could feel the erratic beat of her heart. While she showed no reaction, she wasn't immune to his kisses.

She suddenly pushed back, away from him and walked to the bed. "There is no need for all this," she said. "There's no need to sugarcoat mating. It is what it is." As she spoke, she pulled her tunic and under-tunic up over her head, leaving her nude.

Now it was his turn to stand unmoving in the middle of the floor. With her hair stopping at her shoulders, she looked somehow more naked than any women he'd seen. Her body seemed to glow in the moonlight. Breasts high and firm and surprisingly large. Her waist tapered in abruptly, her stomach nearly concave. Her legs were long and lanky, the curls at the junction of her thighs dark against the paleness of her skin. Faulk realized that he was fully aroused, his erection pressing against his braies.

"I wasn't trying to sugarcoat anything," he said, his voice rough.

"Of course you were," she said. "The whole day has been nothing but icing designed to disguise a bestial act. Sweet Cheelum, I was wrapped up like a holiday package and displayed through the countryside on a mummer's horse decorated with ribbons and bells. All so I could stand with you before an unctuous priest and have us mysteriously bound for life. After all that, there is no need for slobbering and rubbing. The purpose of all this falderal was so that you could bed me. Well, I'm here and you're here, so just get on with it."

"I..." Faulk was at a loss for words. He had done the

things she denigrated because he thought they would please her. Or had he done them for himself? He'd seen a merry wedding procession when he was a young boy and thought to reproduce it. The household staff here at White Ford had suggested, no insisted on, the wedding meal, but, again, it fed some fantasy that Faulk had been unknowingly harboring.

She'd warned him, had said that she was no maiden, but still... he'd thought there would be, or could be, something precious and good between them.

"If you're unable, perhaps it would help if I got on my hands and knees. Some men seem to have found that stimulating." Her tone was one of detached disinterest, as if she were discussing the weather. Faulk felt some emotion spiral through his body. Anger? Hurt? He didn't want to analyze it. He only knew that at that moment he hated her and desired her in equal measure.

"I'm quite capable of mounting you," he said in a stranger's voice. "But I'm choosing not to do so."

He turned abruptly and strode out of the bedchamber, slamming the door behind him. He was trembling like a spooked horse. He'd know he would not be the first. But then, he'd never been *any* woman's first, so he couldn't imagine it would make any difference. But this... this aberration, this distortion of something good, was beyond his imagining.

Unconsciously, his hand came up to stroke the nightpiper embroidered on his tunic's shoulder. Lady Patrice had sewn it for him. Lady Patrice, beloved of

Lealand. She'd stood with Lealand until the end as if the two of them formed a multitude. The precise stitches reminded Faulk that such a connection between people was possible in this world.

It seemed, though, that it would not be possible for him. He and Anlin would not be forming an indivisible unit. The barrenness of it all stretched out before him. He went to where the ale flagon sat on the table but found it indeed empty. The gold ring winked at him in the wavering candlelight. He knew now it would never fit.

Then the newly named Sir Faulk of White Ford, the holder of a fine fief, a man who knew the feeling of a sword sliding through muscle and sinew, a knight who had watched the light fade from the eyes of friends and foes alike, a warrior who had seen the man he honored above all others traitorously hanged, this man who had never showed his distress—this Faulk—buried his face in his hands and wept.

6

The manor folk were beginning to gather to celebrate the completion of spring planting. Laughter and loud greetings echoed around the meadow next to the house. Anlin realized Faulk was wise to give the people such a festive occasion. Of course, to her surprised discomfort, she was discovering Faulk was wise about many things.

Anlin leaned against the trunk of a sprawling oak, resting and enjoying the scent of fresh-turned earth that floated on the soft breeze. She'd overseen the preparation of the food and the moving of the trestle tables to the meadow. At least, she'd gone through the motions so it would appear to most that she'd been in charge. She knew it would have been a woeful celebration had everything been left to her. Fortunately, the household staff at the manor knew how such things should be organized and covered for her lack of knowledge.

The last month had been a bizarre mix of boredom and panic. Anlin had had only minimal training in what the lady of the manor was supposed to do. Her fostering at Hannon's Heights had given her some grounding, but she'd been a captive in Rennic during the period when the bulk of her education should have taken place. The skills she'd developed as a slave were not needed here. At White Ford there was staff to care for the animals. At White Ford there was staff to prepare food. At White Ford there was staff to sweep floors and clean fireplaces and skin animals.

The Lady of White Ford wasn't really supposed to *do* any of these things, but she was expected to be able to oversee others doing it. Even in her areas of limited competence, however, the scale was so different she might as well have known nothing. She knew what to do with the milk of one or two cows, but what did one do with the milk of ten?

"Make cheese," the housekeeper quickly declared with confidence. It sounded good, but how did one go about doing this? Anlin had had to ask how to accomplish basic tasks at every turn. The chatelaine keys she wore on her belt seemed to laugh at her when they tinkled. She may control the locked cupboards at White Ford, but she had no idea if people were stealing massive amounts whenever she opened them.

Since there was nothing she was competent to do, time hung heavy on her hands. The stables and the barn called to her. The quiet acceptance of the animals had always been a balm to her soul. Her first foray into that territory, however, led to a direct order from Faulk.

"Do not go out there again," he said. "It makes the stablemen nervous. They don't know what to do with you there."

"Then what am I supposed to do with my time?" she asked.

"Sew. Make something. That's what the ladies I've known do. The hall could use some nice hangings. A tapestry or something similar." He looked at her with infinite patience. She was coming to hate that look. "Can you do that?"

No, she couldn't. She had neither the talent nor the inclination. But she hated to say this, so she just nodded in what might be construed as a positive response. She did not want to admit she was a failure at every task associated with running a manor. So, when she didn't have something else to occupy her time, she hid in the solar. Perhaps Faulk thought she was happily making a wall hanging. He never asked, though. He never mentioned the lack of a tapestry frame. He seemed to notice very little about her.

They slept in the same bed, but that was all they did, sleep. After the first night, Faulk had announced he would not again sit in a Cheelum damned chair and that since he was the lord, he would use the bed in the lord's chamber. He cared not where Anlin laid her head.

For the first week, she'd stayed in a chair, on the floor, anywhere but the bed. One night, exhaustion made her collapse in the bed long before Faulk arrived from the hall. When she awoke, he lay beside her. But he made no move to touch her that night or any night since. They lay in isolation like effigies on a tomb. One night she came awake to find the bed pulsing in time with his hand as he found his own release, but he did not then, or since, turn toward her.

She didn't want anything to do with him. She knew this. But a loneliness closed around her that was different from any she'd known.

Anlin's morose thoughts scattered when a noise arose from the corner of the village and the plow team came into view, joyously followed by those who were just quitting the fields. The two big oxen moved at their customary slow pace, massive heads and broad horns swinging from side to side with every step. The horns had been decorated with green ribbons and, as the team drew closer, Anlin could hear the jingle of bells.

The realization these were the ribbons and bells from her wedding procession made her feel a flash of sadness. It was a ridiculous emotion. When her maid Hilmar had brought the bells and ribbons to her as a keepsake, Anlin had said that they were of no importance. But seeing these items now put to a different use caused an ache in her chest.

She'd thought the trappings of their wedding had held some significance for Faulk. Not that he'd said so directly. Faulk never talked to her about anything of importance. Oh, when they sat on the dais at meals, with many eyes watching them, he talked expansively about his plans for the fief, and he talked about the weather and the crops, but that was the extent of their conversations. Whenever he inadvertently met her in the courtyard or the hall, he was always polite. Distant and polite. As if taking their cue from Faulk, everyone else on the fief treated her the same way.

Sweet Cheelum, she was lonely. Since Faulk had forbidden her the solace of working with the animals, she tried to find contentment in riding, traveling to the furthest boundaries of the fief. Whenever she did so, she was always followed by either Kevin or Waylon, the two new men-at-arms that Faulk had brought to the fief. Followed. Respectfully and politely followed, not ridden with, not talked to, but never out of their vigilant sight.

The only time she and Faulk had made any sort of connection was the morning after their wedding feast. Looking back, this had probably been what led to all the following politeness.

She'd awakened in the pre-dawn hours, surprisingly alone. The faint streaks of light creeping across the dark sky called to her. She'd slipped on a tunic and, barefoot, had stealthily opened the bedchamber door and crossed into the solar. A hand shot out and grasped her wrist. She jerked with surprise.

"Where are you going, milady?" Faulk was a darker lump in the darkness, insubstantial and unreal, but his hand felt like an iron shackle.

"I was, I was..." What? Escaping? In need of the garderobe? No, the truth. "I was going outside to watch the sunrise."

He sifted his weight and released her wrist. "Is this your normal behavior or are you in distress?"

"I usually waken before the sun."

"Oh." Then there was only a lengthy silence. Anlin wasn't sure what she should do.

"Last night was..." His voice trailed away. "I've never forced a woman. I promise I will not force you. I won't rut with you like a wild boar. And I don't want you to act the whore for me." Faulk sounded as if he spoke from a distance, even though she knew he hadn't moved.

She felt confused, disoriented, there in the dark without a visible anchor. "But you made it plain you wanted heirs to follow you. And I agreed to it from the first. I'm well able to endure it."

"Endure it?" His voice was a growl. Faulk stalked toward the window, stopped part way across the room, and turned back toward her. He was a broad, dark shadow against the hint of gray in the sky. "All you anticipate is endurance?"

What did he want her to say? What did he expect? There was obviously something in the act that men liked, or else why would they do it even when procreation wasn't the desired result? She had a vague remembrance of men taking her before she learned to escape into the peaceful place in her mind, and even they had seemed to be in pain, stiffening and moaning. She often wondered if it were some sort of penance placed on humans to ensure that their offspring would be born without sin.

"It is a penance I'll gladly endure, if it means the return of my son," she said without thinking. Faulk just stood there, taking deep breaths. She wished she could see his face. Into the silence, she ventured, "When do you think we will be able to leave for Rennic?"

He turned from her then and went into the bedchamber. In silhouette, she saw him pull on braies and hose and drop a tunic over his head. He didn't speak, but she could hear his breathing, harsh and deep. He approached her, standing close.

"I'm sorry you think of being married to me as a penance." He sounded angry. No, beyond angry, furious. "I'll try to bother you as little as possible."

Anlin suddenly feared that Faulk would go back on their agreement. That he wouldn't take her into Rennic to look for Telm. "We will soon go to Rennic, though," she said, hating the quiver in her voice.

His open palm slapped the wall behind her with such speed, the noise so loud in the morning silence, that she cried out. The brutal warrior she originally thought she'd married suddenly loomed over her. The man with the shy smile and bells and ribbons had vanished.

"Have I not sworn it?" He seemed to force the words from is throat. "I keep my bargains, as I expect you to keep yours. At some point you will come to me and we will make my heirs together." He strode from the room.

When she reached the hall, she heard a loud chopping sound. She followed it to the area outside the gate and saw Faulk methodically attacking a tree with his sword. His movements looked like a deadly dance, controlled and powerful. The pale morning light showed that the tree was deeply girdled.

If Faulk knew she was there, he ignored her. He just kept pounding the tree with great sweeping strokes, sweat running down his face and darkening his hair.

He left that afternoon, saying nothing to her. She wondered if he were gone for good, perceiving his anger but not understanding it. He returned two days later with Kevin and Waylon, saying only that the fief could support two fighting men and that her father was pleased. From that time onward, the early morning rang with the clang of metal on metal, the two men-at-arms taking turns sparring with Faulk. The girdled tree, however, put forth few leaves and seemed destined to die.

From his return until now, Faulk had been distantly polite.

Anlin felt she knew no more about her husband than she had on the day they'd met. He remained a mystery, his behavior unknown and unknowable. The one thing that was abundantly clear was that he was a good steward of the land he held. Most of the people on the fief liked him, villein and freeman alike responding to his keen interest and ready smile. But those who shirked their work or who sullenly performed their tasks saw a stern-faced Faulk, and they rapidly did their work out of fear.

With Anlin, he neither smiled nor frowned. He remained blandly courteous.

"Lady Anlin." Waylon's lanky form had appeared by her side while she was woolgathering. "Sir Faulk asks if you'd join him and the priest for the libations to Cheelum."

"Of course," she said, carefully resting her hand on the man-at-arms' sleeve and allowing him to guide her to where a cask of ale had just been tapped. She stood next to Faulk, the priest on his other side. Faulk gave her a quick smile, genuine and heartfelt. She felt her own heart lift.

The fief's inhabitants milled around, ready to begin the celebration. The priest held a shiny copper cup beneath the froth of ale and then stood, raising the cup over his head. The crowd quieted.

"Cheelum admonishes us to plant our fields with joy so that we may harvest the same," the priest intoned. "Today our toil is done and we pray for the arrival of green shoots of joy."

He then spilled some of the ale onto the earth and the assembled people called out, "Green shoots and joy."

Then there was a general movement toward the ale casks and Faulk pulled her back from the surge. "It's good to celebrate a task accomplished," he said. "Now we can only pray for the right amount of sun and the right amount of rain. If all that we've planted flourishes, we'll have plenty of fodder to winter over some sheep, and we'll be able to get them cheap in the fall." Anlin had heard a great deal of talk about sheep and how well they'd do on the higher pastures. Faulk was already planning where to put shearing sheds and carding houses. All he lacked were the actual sheep.

She felt the enthusiasm radiating from him as they walked back across the meadow, as he smiled and nodded to people who called greetings. She relished this moment when Faulk seemed to have forgotten to be polite to her, when his reactions were genuine. He was genuinely happy. He walked her back to the tree where she'd earlier been standing, however. Anlin suspected he was soon to leave her in splendid isolation while he returned to the throng.

"How soon do you want to leave for Rennic?" he asked.

Anlin was caught off guard, had not expected him to speak of this now, in the middle of the celebration, but the joy that the priest had prayed for surged through her. Without thought, she swung about, grabbing Faulk around the waist and hugging him. "Two days," she said, looking up at his starkly sculpted face, gazing into his amazing green-flecked eyes. "I can be ready to leave in two days."

He seemed surprised to find her pressed up against him, but his arms slowly came around her shoulders, holding her lightly. "Is this what it took to thaw you?" he asked. "You knew I'd sworn to go when the planting was done."

His eyes never left hers as his hand slid along her shoulder and gently cupped the back of her neck. Then he leaned down and lightly brushed her lips with his. The touch of a feather, the weight of a sigh, but Anlin felt that touch to her toes. It was an odd, fluttery feeling, nice in a way, but then he pulled her tighter to him and she felt the beginning of panic. She unconsciously jerked back from him—and he let her go.

He left her by the tree and made his way back into the crowd. Different people came up to talk to her, and she tried to be gracious. Her eyes followed Faulk's progress, however. Saw him talking and smiling to those around him. Saw that hers were not the only eyes that stayed on Faulk. Hilmar, her maid, also watched with the look of a hungry child barred from a feast. Anlin could not name the reason this bothered her.

That night she waited for him in the solar. She wanted to make sure he knew she had almost everything ready for their journey. She felt she needed to remind him they had to retrieve the silver her father had promised as ransom for her son. While she waited, she paced between a table and the fireplace. She would not go to sleep. She couldn't take the chance that he would avoid her as he usually did. She didn't want there to be any question of his going back on his word.

She was finally rewarded by his tread on the stairs. When he pushed open the door, he seemed surprised to see her there. "Still up?"

"Yes, I wanted to show you some of the maps I've drawn of parts of Rennic and to discuss the supplies you think we should take. Of course, if we're gone a year, we'll have to get supplies as we go…" She had moved toward the table, conscious of Faulk following in her wake.

"We won't be gone a year," he said. "I'd hoped to be back by harvest, or before the snows close the passes at the latest."

"You agreed to a year!" Anlin felt a crashing disappointment. He was trying to go back on their agreement.

"It's not going to take a year." Faulk had come up beside her and was leaning over the desk, looking at the maps. "These are good," he said. "Are they accurate?"

"Of course, they're accurate. What good would they be if they weren't?" Anlin had been planning her return to Rennic since she'd escaped and had spent weeks carefully recreating the features and trails she remembered. She might not be able to weave a tapestry, but she could draw a map. "And what makes you think that our search will take less than a year?"

"Your maps show it," Faulk said, smoothing out a crimped corner on the largest map. "Rennic is a small country. Yes, it's very mountainous and there could be many hidden valleys in which to search. But why would they hide the boy if they could exchange him for more money than they could possible steal in a year. If he's there, the Rennish themselves will find him."

"You don't know the Rennish."

"You're right. I only know the few who trade near the pass that borders on Hannon land. And those would have gladly given us their grandmother if the price were right. The biggest problem we had in the border keep where I was stationed was pilferage."

"As I said, you don't know the Rennish. The men we'll meet are of a different order than those who haunt the border and pick up Fallucian leavings." Anger simmered. She knew the Rennish very well.

"Anlin, you must consider that the boy may be dead." As she opened her mouth to refute him, Faulk continued, "I know you don't want to consider this, but you must be realistic. I don't want to make you unnecessarily unhappy." His voice had lowered and he brought a hand up to lightly stroke the side of her face.

She didn't know whether to lean into his stroking hand or to pull away from it. Her impulse was to pull away. But she wanted to make sure that Faulk would be totally committed to finding Telm, however long it took. To guarantee this she owed him acquiescence. She leaned into his hand. She would keep her bargain so he would keep his.

Faulk's reaction was immediate. He gathered her to him, enveloping her, lowering his head to nuzzle the side of her neck. "We'll find him if he's there to be found. I promise you."

It was what she wanted to hear. But the power of his arms surrounding her and her feeling of vulnerability frightened her. She felt tremors shake her body.

"It's alright," he said, running his hand down her back, pulling her against him. "We can make this work." Then he kissed her. He nibbled at her lower lip rather than pressing tight. His tongue traced the edges of her mouth. Excitement and fear fought each other. She could feel his erection pressing into her stomach and knew, then, what he wanted. What all men wanted.

His hand grazed her breast—and the panic won out. She slipped into the peaceful place of green grass and dew. From a great distance, she heard someone say, "Shit!"

7

It had been difficult to leave White Ford, more difficult than Faulk had ever imagined it would be. After the fief had been given to him, he'd thought he would feel pride of ownership and nothing more. Instead, he felt as if he'd been given *to* the fief, as if he were owned by the land in a way more binding than that placed on the lowest villein. He feared White Ford wouldn't prosper unless he was there—guiding it, protecting it. It was a ridiculous fear. Hettle, the reeve, was competent and well respected. Hettle could easily oversee the day-to-day business of running the fief. He'd ably done so before Faulk had arrived. And Faulk had hired Kevin and Waylon to insure the protection of the land and its people.

Of course, there was an additional bonus to having the two men-at-arms at White Ford. Faulk had offered them positions on the fief because they were the type of men with whom he was comfortable. They were the whetstones on which he could hone his own fighting skills. And, perhaps most importantly, they were men who reminded Faulk of who he was. He was a man who had won land and wife through his own ability. And what he had won, he would hold.

Faulk had thought he would meet resistance from Lord Giffard when he asked permission to hire the men-at-arms. Lord Giffard's enthusiasm for adding to the overall fighting force available in his demesne gave Faulk pause.

"They're solid men?" Lord Giffard had asked when Faulk rode to Giffard's Crest to talk with him.

"Yes, sir. I met them here, at the tournament, and was impressed by them. I could also tell that they weren't happy in their present positions. They're with Lord Hemple's garrison and, while they like their lord personally, he has a large group of men-at-arms. Kevin and Waylon are way down on the seniority list and, consequently, assigned all the tedious, menial work. I think they'll come because I can offer them greater responsibility. And I think they'll come cheaply."

Lord Giffard had laughed at how quickly Faulk had realized that the stewardship of land often required cheese-paring economy instead of providing unlimited wealth. Faulk found that he liked Lord Giffard very much and was pleased that he'd sworn to him.

"I'd be delighted for you to take on these two men, then," Lord Giffard said. "Extra swords may not be amiss in the future. You know I'm a King's man. Always have been. But even I can see that King Fremmor's behavior has become erratic. The king is, unfortunately, easily led, and I think he's getting very poor advice from people he trusts."

"Such as Lord Tarn?" Faulk asked.

Lord Giffard looked surprised and then said, "That's right. Your former lord ran afoul of Edmund Tarn, didn't he?"

"Lord Lealand's dispute was actually with Montcliff, but it was Lord Tarn who brought the king in on Montcliff's side. And Montcliff's claim was totally without merit. The disputed fief had been under Lealand's purview for years. An elderly knight who wasn't active held it until his death. He didn't fight, but he was sworn to Lealand. Always had been."

The old guilt washed over Faulk. Lealand had pressed his claim to the fief because he intended Faulk to have it. Would Lealand have been so adamant if Faulk had not just met Shay, Sir Clemmet's daughter, and hoped to marry? It was a question that forever chased itself in Faulk's head and for which there was no answer. If he'd not aided Montcliff in getting the disputed fief, wouldn't Tarn have found another way to discredit Lealand?

Faulk needed to remember he had a fief now—and a wife. If it was not the original dream, it was one he could live with. Something tightened in his gut at the thought that Tarn and an increasingly mad king could again threaten him.

One more reason that he'd not wanted to leave White Ford. But he had, because it was part of his bargain. He truly believed Anlin's son was dead and selfishly hoped this could be established quickly. But until either the boy's death or his whereabouts could be ascertained, he would dutifully follow Anlin into Rennic.

And so, Faulk found himself riding down a trail though heavy woods in the borderlands of Fallucia and leading a packhorse loaded with a fortune in silver coin.

Faulk watched Anlin carefully maneuver around a deadfall tree that blocked the narrow trail and marveled at the changes in her. In just a few days, her anger and incompetence had become calm assertiveness. He'd thought it would take her weeks to prepare for a long trip, remembering the baggage carts that had always followed in Lady Patrice's wake. But Anlin had been ready in the two days she had estimated—and much of that time had been spent in collecting supplies that were normally not a woman's purview.

He'd sent Kevin to Giffard's Crest to get the silver to use as ransom for Anlin's son, although she said no ransom would be involved. They would simply buy him. To the Rennish, her son would be a slave, not someone of value. Kevin returned with many more bags of coin than Faulk had anticipated. Lord Giffard was being more than generous. One entire packhorse was needed to carry the money.

"We can only manage one more packhorse," he'd said, "or else we'll be so strung out that we will definitely invite attack. And that one additional horse will have to carry everything else we need, so plan accordingly."

Anlin gave him a look that suggested she thought he was auditioning for the position of court fool. "I know that. Everything I need is already laid out on the window seat in the solar."

From a quick inspection, he could tell what she'd placed on the seat would make a small pack indeed. There was a neat pile of nondescript clothing that he'd never seen her wear, the colors mostly browns and grays. Next to this were two pairs of boots, newly made of soft leather. The real surprise lay in the assembled weapons—two sheathed knives and a recurved Rennish bow with a quiver of well-fletched arrows. Faulk slid one of the knives from its sheath, finding inside a slender blade, wickedly sharp.

"That's the knife I used to kill Martic when I escaped."

Faulk turned quickly to see that Anlin had silently come up beside him. She took the knife from his hands and touched it lovingly. "The slenderness of the blade allowed it to slip easily between the ribs," she said. The smile on her face was chilling.

"And am I to assume that you can also competently use this odd bow?" he asked, confused as ever by this woman he had married.

"I can bring down enough small game to feed a number of men," she said, now stroking the bow with the same loving look. "In Rennic, they never gave me arrows worthy of killing anything very big. It was the first thing I asked for when I got to Giffard's Crest." She now looked up at him. "These arrows should be heavy enough to bring down a man."

No, this was not the woman he thought he'd known. Her behavior was different from anything he could have imagined, or, perhaps, would have wanted to imagine. But this was the woman who now led them unerringly toward the border with Rennic.

The first night out, she'd helped set up camp with the quiet efficiency of a well-trained man-at-arms. She had even made a surprisingly tasty meal, frying thin corn cakes on a flat rock in the fire and rolling the cakes around a mixture of dried meat and some spicy herb. She spoke very little, but Faulk hadn't press her if silence was her choice. She continued to be quietly competent every time they stopped.

There was something comfortable about looking across the fire at her, her dark clothes blending into the shadows behind her, the white blaze in her hair standing out. Anlin's face was composed, as if she were in deep thought. She was pleasing to watch. Faulk hoped that this trip might put some of her ghosts to rest, that she might later function more normally. He knew her years in Rennic had left her scarred, but since he couldn't see those scars, there was no way to know how they could be healed.

"We should cross the Tarsell River tomorrow," Anlin said, suddenly breaking the silence. "The Rennish consider that the border, even if we do not. There's a suspension bridge, and that's where our presence will be challenged. When that happens, all you have to say is 'This is my woman and she will speak for us' as I've taught you to say in Rennish."

Faulk disliked the fact that the Rennish he'd learned while serving at a border keep was limited to simple greetings and curse words. He realized that he'd have to rely on Anlin to do the talking, but he worried that his inability to understand wouldn't allow him to react as he perhaps should. He wasn't sure that he could understand a verbal threat if he heard one. "And you're confident we won't be attacked at the bridge?"

"Not there. At least I don't think so. As I said, Fallucian traders come into Rennic more than is thought. The closer we get to Hightor, however, the more dangerous our way will become."

"But we may not need to go as far as Hightor."

"That's what I'm hoping," she said. "But we'll tell everyone we meet that we're delivering previously ordered goods to Headman Creel in Hightor. That will assure that no one wonders why we're not trying to sell them anything. An order meant for the Headman will be off-limits to anyone else."

Faulk stretched his legs out in front of him, a comfortable position after a long day in the saddle. "Yeah, we definitely don't want to open the silver packs—although I bet we'd have quite a few buyers." He chuckled at the thought.

Anlin gave him a ghost of a smile. "That's where you

come in. You're supposed to look threatening, and we'll hope that it's enough to keep the peace."

Faulk hoped that was the case as well, but he didn't have much confidence in this assumption. He wondered if looking threatening would encourage an arrow in the back. He decided he would start wearing his mail hauberk tomorrow.

Acting on his intentions, the next day found Faulk sweating slightly under the familiar weight of his mail as they left the woods and came upon a deep chasm filled with frothing water.

"The Tarsell River," Anlin said. Obviously in full spate from spring rains, the Tarsell was very different from the placid Milk River that ran by the manor house at White Ford. There would be no ford over such a wild flow.

They followed a trail along the edge of the gorge, the air filled with mist from the turbulent water below. When they rounded a bend, Faulk saw the bridge. Made of rope and planks, it floated above the river like a dream and seemed about as insubstantial. "We're supposed to cross that on horses?" Faulk asked, doubt filling his voice.

"It's the only way across," Anlin said. "We'll have to lead the animals."

"Have you crossed it before?"

"No, but I've met many people who have. It's the main trade route into the country."

If this was a trade route, Faulk thought, Rennic was

obviously a country that didn't get much trade. Faulk was also loath to admit that the very sight of the narrow bridge made him feel nauseous. Heights had always been a problem, but he'd overcome the feeling of vertigo by sheer will.

He was all right as long as he had something very solid under his feet—preferably a mountainside or a stone keep. The bridge was most definitely not solid. Even from a distance, he could see it swaying slightly in the wind. He shut his mind to the imagined motion that two people and four horses would cause.

By the time they reached the entrance, the bridge seemed to have grown even narrower. The supporting ropes, staked into the ground and tied to tree-sized posts, looked thin and worn. The planking was too thin to support a horse the weight of his gray, he was sure. And the water was way, way down. Choosing to look across rather than down, Faulk saw guards on the other side—just a handful, but it wouldn't take many to defend such a bottleneck.

"There are men on the other side," he said, swinging down from his horse, trying to sound assertive. "I'll lead in case there's trouble."

"No, I'll lead," Anlin said. "You can't talk to them and would most likely end up in a fight we could avoid."

It irked him that she was probably right. Talking their way into Rennic was preferable to fighting their way in. The bridge made an effective barrier. Anyone approaching would have to arrive single-file, leading a horse rather than mounted. Although Fallucia might dispute that the river was the border, defensively, the Rennish were smart to claim it as such. Faulk certainly saw no Fallucian host attempting to change Rennish geography.

Anlin dismounted and grasped her sturdy mare by the cheek strap of the bridle. "Let's go then," she said, her face very serious.

Faulk appreciated her resolve. It had to be very hard to go back to a place where one had been held in bondage, but her steps were confident as she started across. The packhorse she'd been leading dutifully followed.

Faulk gave Anlin's packhorse some room and then started over. There was room for him to walk next to his horse's head—just barely. The support ropes along the side of the bridge seemed no barrier at all. There was only mist-filled nothingness beyond. Faulk concentrated on placing his feet firmly on the planking. He refused to think of how quickly a man in mail would sink into the turbulent water below. Then he realized that he needn't worry about staying afloat. The fall itself would kill him.

Fiddian, his big gray gelding, was, as always, solid and steady. He'd ridden Fid into too many battles to have any doubts. A horse that didn't shy at pikes and swords flashing near its face was not going to bulk at crossing a bridge.

The packhorse was another story, however. The moment its hooves touched the planking, the packhorse was pulling back on the lead line, its eyes rolling white. It thrashed its head and planted its legs against the pull of the line.

There was no room for Faulk to get around Fiddian to calm the packhorse. Meanwhile, Anlin, with her two horses in tow, was nearly at the middle of the bridge. She wouldn't want to stop, even if Faulk could make himself heard over the roar of the water. Seeing no other option, Faulk pulled back on Fid's bridle and touched him on the chest, getting him to slowly back off the bridge.

Once on solid ground, Faulk walked back to the packhorse, speaking calmly and softly, but the horse still pulled back violently against the halter. The packhorse was having absolutely nothing to do with the bridge. Faulk looked over his shoulder and saw that Anlin had made it to the far side. She was now surrounded by the guards. A fine protector he made, stuck on the wrong side of the bridge. But there was no leaving the packhorse since it was the one carrying the silver.

He walked the horse around, trying to get it to settle. Any approach toward the bridge was met with instant resistance, however. Finally, Faulk got one of his hose from the pack on Fiddian and tied it around the packhorse's eyes. Blindfolded, the horse was still skittish, but controllable. Faulk had no option but to lead the packhorse with a hand on its halter and let Fiddian trail behind.

With the two horses in this position, Faulk again tried the bridge. The packhorse snorted and jerked its head back, but Faulk managed to cajole it onto the planking. Slowly, oh so slowly, they inched their way across. Faulk talked constantly to the recalcitrant horse, the words as much for his own benefit as for the horses.

"See, we can do it," he said. "This bridge is sturdy. Anlin has crossed it. There is no problem." He repeated this over and over like a chanted prayer.

All went well until they'd arrived at the mid-point of the bridge. Maybe it was the increased sway in that location; maybe the packhorse had simply had enough of walking blind into the unknown. Whatever the reason, it suddenly reared up, front legs trashing.

Faulk hung on, trying to avoid the flailing hooves and wrestle the horse down onto all fours. The bridge shuttered. Faulk was flung against the side ropes and felt them give. He again briefly wondered if the fall would kill him or if the weight of his hauberk would simply drag him under to drown.

Pushing the thought aside, he fought to get his other hand on the far side of the halter, hoping his weight would pull the horse's head down. Panic lent the packhorse strength. Holding tightly to both sides of the horse's head, Faulk was jerked away from the rope railing. The planking underfoot danced about.

Fiddian, perceiving his rider was in danger, did as he was trained to do. With a loud trumpet, he tried to force his way past the packhorse, biting the smaller horse hard on the flanks. Blind, frightened, and now under attack, the packhorse went down, legs thrashing. Faulk could do nothing but hang on and hope he wasn't caught by a slashing hoof. The bridge flooring seemed to move in four different directions at once.

The packhorse miraculously didn't tumble off the bridge. It found its legs, staggered up, and blindly bolted. Fiddian thundered after him. Holding the headstall, Faulk was pushed before both horses like a leaf before a strong wind. His only conscious thought was to throw his weight from side to side in an effort to keep the horse pointed down the length of the bridge. Just as the packhorse's hooves struck solid ground and disaster seemed averted, Faulk was driven into one of the huge support poles. The packhorse pounded into him and then slipped to one side.

The world took on black edges. Faulk was unable to get his breath. Sound receded. His legs refused to support him, and he slid down the support pole to the ground. The sky seemed an unrealistic blue. Suddenly, Anlin's face inserted itself in his vision. Anlin's face and four Rennish faces, dark and tattooed and scarred.

Anlin knelt beside him. "Are you all right?" she asked.

It took a moment for Faulk to be able to reply. "I think so," he said, trying to get up. But he finally had to be hauled to his feet with a Rennish man on either side. He swayed like a three-flagon drunk but finally found his balance. He seemed to be in one piece, although his shoulder throbbed. The Rennish men released Faulk, patted him on the back, and shifted away. One said something incomprehensible, and Faulk looked to Anlin for a translation.

She had an odd, frozen look on her face, but said, "The guard captain said that since you are uninjured and the horses seem to be fine, everything has turned out well. But he also said your entrance into Rennic was the funniest thing he's seen in years." Then Anlin's control slipped and she started laughing. The guards joined the hilarity until all five of them were gasping for breath and had tears in their eyes.

His pride as bruised as parts of his body, Faulk found no humor in the situation. He did, however, make use of his collection of Rennish curse words. This made the guards slap each other on the back and laugh harder.

"We can leave when you're ready," Anlin said, wiping her eyes, her breath still coming in hiccups. "I think they see no danger in us."

Of course, the guards wouldn't think of Faulk as dangerous. Instead, he was a buffoon. The entertainment. His crossing the border into Rennic was about to become a tavern tale that eventually no one would believe.

But cross they had, and it was probably a good idea to move on before someone decided to look in their packs. The frightened packhorse stood with his head down but seemed to be no worse for his experience.

Faulk stiffly mounted Fiddian, cataloging pain in his left leg to match that in his shoulder, and gestured for Anlin to lead the way.

He would look at her maps tonight to see if there was another route home.

$\approx 8 \approx$

A faint rustle of mail, which could have been wind in the brush, was the only indication that Faulk had returned. He slid through the trees and back into the clearing where Anlin waited with the horses. It was the fourth time he'd doubled back since leaving the bridge.

"No one's following," he said, sitting down on a large rock. He leaned forward to put his head beneath his knees and breathed deeply. The day was unusually hot for early spring and mist hugged the ground like a pale blanket for miles around the Tarsell River, making it damp as well as hot. They'd also been traveling uphill as they climbed out of the river gorge. The ground looked almost level, but the laboring of the horses told otherwise.

"That's good news," Anlin said, "but I rather expected it. The man with the three ritual scars on each cheek was a shaman. He scanned us for magic and was satisfied that we were both without Talent. Had it been otherwise, we probably would have been attacked when we entered. And, then, we did look pretty non-threatening when we crossed the bridge."

She smiled when she said this to take some of the sting out of her last words. But she still enjoyed the flush of embarrassment that darkened Faulk's face. A laugh suddenly bubbled up, making Faulk frown. "I'm sorry, but once I was sure you hadn't been hurt, it *was* funny."

Anlin didn't explain that laughter was a release of tension for her. Standing at the end of that bridge, alone, surrounded by Rennish men, she had been acutely uncomfortable. She had held her betrothal ring out, repeating over and over, "I belong to him." And then, when her "owner," her protector, looked like he was getting himself killed, the old, hated fear had seized her in its uncompromising grip.

She thought she would die of fright as Faulk finally came shooting off the bridge and into their midst like a doll thrown around in a fair day puppet show. That had been terrifying, but when she knew that he was uninjured, her tension had dissolved into laughter.

"Yeah, funny." Faulk rotated his shoulders as if working muscles that had been banged around on their crossing.

"There should be a stream off somewhere to the right," Anlin said. "Why don't we go on and make camp for the night. There's no way that we can make it to Chirlon by nightfall anyway, so we might as well stop here."

"How do you know about the terrain in this area? Was this near where you were held?"

"No, the closest I lived to here was on a steading near Chirlon, where we're headed. I wasn't allowed to wander more than an hour's walk away from my master's holding. My last owner, Martic, had some good maps of the border area, however, and I memorized as much as possible once I determined to escape."

As much as she'd hated the man, Anlin was thankful that Martic had been an area commander and had maps of Rennic's border with Fallucia. She'd poured over those maps every time Martic left the steading—planning, always planning, her escape.

Martic had been careless with his maps. He'd assumed no mere female slave could read them. Of course, he'd also thought no mere female slave would kill him. Unbidden, Anlin's mouth turned up in a smile that had nothing to do with her previous humor.

"This might be a good time to stop, if you know of a likely spot," Faulk said. When he'd mounted after crossing the river, he'd given a soft grunt. Anlin suspected his abused muscles were now stiffening, and he was carrying around a great deal of extra weight by wearing his mail.

She led the way off the trail and was gratified that within a few minutes she came to a rapidly flowing stream. She followed it until they came to a place where the trees drew back from the water, forming a small meadow. It was a good location, and they quickly made camp, accustomed to doing specific tasks in a coordinated manner.

When the horses were cared for and hobbled and a fire cheerfully burned to heat the rocks to use in making flatbread, Anlin retrieved her bow from where they'd stacked the supplies. "I'm going to walk the meadow and see if I can scare up some hares," she said. "Fresh meat would be nice."

Faulk looked up from where he'd dropped a load of wood. "I'll go with you."

"No, I'll stay in the meadow where you can see me. There's no one else around, so I should be fine. If you're out tromping around too, rabbits will be popping up everywhere, and I won't know where to shoot. It's better if I go alone."

He smiled deprecatingly. "I've done such a superb job of taking care of you up to now, haven't I? But don't leave the meadow." He shrugged his shoulders. "I'd appreciate it if you could help me get this mail off before you go. If nothing else, it would be cooler."

Anlin walked to where he stood and tugged on the mail shirt when he leaned over. As it began to slip free, the weight amazed her. She was glad she could quickly drape it over a rock. "How can you wear this all day?"

Faulk laughed. "All day is easy. It's sleeping in the thing that is sometimes difficult, but I've done it plenty of times. I guess the ability to sleep in discomfort depends on the level of exhaustion." The gambeson under the mail was sweat-sodden, and he removed that as well with a contented sigh. He looked at his left shoulder and flexed it back and forth. "Yeah, a nasty bruise as I expected from that damned horse whacking me into the support pole."

Anlin glanced at his shoulder, but her gaze focused on his back. Sculpted muscles flowed with his every movement, but the skin, Sweet Cheelum, the skin. His back and upper shoulders were a mass of welted scars, crisscrossing each other in odd angles, a map of destruction wrought on his flesh. She must have made a sound, a quick intake of breath, for he swung back to face her, gambeson still in his hands.

"I'm sorry. I forgot you'd never seen my back. Fortunately, it's a bit of ugliness that I never have to look at." He held his arms wide and glanced down at his chest. "But see, no scars on the front. I learned to defend myself and have done a good job of it, tussles with a recalcitrant horse notwithstanding."

"What? How?" She couldn't make a coherent sentence. Even on other Rennish slaves, she'd never seen such scars. It seemed impossible that anyone could have sustained such damage and lived.

"A scourge. The patterns on my back were made by a metal-tipped scourge. It's an outward sign of my failure to hear the voice of Cheelum. The abbot at Jarburgh was convinced that the marks of blackness on my soul were much worse. I think he tried to erase those marks with ones of his own from flogging." His voice was clam, dispassionate.

"But how could you let him…"

Faulk's head came up and his eyes bored into hers. "Let him? I didn't *let* him. I was a boy, a child; there was no 'letting' involved. I thought being beaten was the normal way of the world. I didn't know what happened to me was unique. And the scourging itself wasn't nearly as painful as when the brine was poured over the cuts to aid in healing. That's when I screamed. I tried to scream the walls of Jarburgh down. There was no sweetness in the Cheelum that I called upon."

He turned his back to her. "You can look at these scars all you want. I'm not ashamed of them. While the scars are on my body, I'm not the madman who put them there. You can touch them if you want. They don't hurt. If anything, there's a lack of sensation. Some women I've been with wanted to touch them, something I never really understood." His voice took on a softer tone. "But I'm beginning to see the attraction. If I could see your scars, if I could touch them, maybe I could make them better."

Anlin turned and fled, angry that the tears in her eyes blurred the meadow grass. She wanted to shout, "I have no scars!" But she knew this wasn't the truth. Her own injuries were there, just hidden. So much of Faulk's story had sounded similar to her own… *I was a boy, a child; there was no "letting" involved.*

She had been a child and knew not how to stop it when a man had violently spread her thighs and plunged into her, invading her body, injuring her soul.

But unlike Faulk, she had scabs instead of insensate scars, and she feared their removal, knowing that the pain hidden beneath them would then come flooding out.

Wiping her eyes, she stopped to string the bow and continued into the meadow, ignoring the man who stood behind her.

⤝•⤞

"The rabbit was good," Anlin said.

"You were the one who killed it, for which you have my thanks. I just made sure it didn't burn over the fire," Faulk said.

Yes, she'd provided the hare, but when she'd brought it back to camp, Faulk had surprised her by taking over the cleaning and cooking duties. No Rennish man would have done that. She was confident even her father and brother would have expected her to cook if there were no servants around to do so. Faulk's behavior was just another piece of the puzzle that was the man she'd married. None of the pieces seemed to be making a decent whole, however.

She'd intended to tie herself to a callous man, to a fighter who would give no quarter. This is what she imagined she'd need on this trip into Rennic—the type of man who could make her feel safe. But Faulk didn't seem to be brutal enough. She knew he was a marvelous fighter. That much was true. But he personally seemed to be nice instead of ruthless. The people of White Ford didn't fear him; they liked him. Sweet Cheelum, *she* liked him, and that wasn't something she'd thought could ever happen.

Faulk lay on his back, some distance from the fire, his head supported on his saddle. He seemed to be studying the stars. Anlin wondered what he thought about in the long moments of silence between them. Did he think of the beatings that left such horrendous marks on his back? She hoped not. She hoped he'd found a way to block the pain and ugliness as she had done. She thought of his scarred back now. Thought of all the times she'd lain just inches from him in the dark and had never known.

"If there are Rennish around, it wouldn't do for you take over any chores that might rightly be mine. They wouldn't understand why you treat your slave with such leniency and would probably judge you to be soft. It's better they think you a hard man. They can understand this type of man."

Faulk turned his head to look at her. His eyes seemed to be without color; they just reflected the firelight. "But you're not my slave; you're my wife. I'm sure the Rennish understand the concept of having a wife."

"I'm sure they understand the concept, but, in all the time I lived here, I never saw anyone's wife. Any women you see in public will be slaves, and that's what the Rennish will be expecting me to be. Wives and marriageable girls over the age of eight are sequestered."

"And never seen?" Faulk rolled to a sitting position.

"Never. The guards at the bridge assumed I belonged to you, as your slave. I used the betrothal ring as a sign of ownership. In Rennic I would have been collared, but the ring worked as well."

"Anlin, you can use it to show ownership to fool the Rennish, but I hope you know it was never meant to signify that. I just... well... I thought when we married, a ring would be appropriate. I'm sorry I didn't get around to having the ring sized to your finger before we left," Faulk said. "I'd meant to, but it kept slipping my mind."

Anlin thought he probably would have remembered it more readily had she actually worn the ring while they were at White Ford, but she'd put it in a small cask along with a necklace that had been her mother's. It occurred to her to use it as a sign of ownership just before they'd left. She'd wrapped the back with thread so that it wouldn't slip off. She unconsciously fiddled with the ring now as she said, "It wasn't important. I've made it fit. I noticed that it has a nightpiper on it. You had it made for someone, didn't you?"

He didn't answer and Anlin wondered if she'd wandered into a personal area where she wasn't supposed to go.

"Yes," he finally said. "I had it made for Shay Landis when I thought we would marry. But when Lord Lealand fell, and I was left without a lord and without a fief of my own, her father wisely married her elsewhere."

"You knew her, then. She wasn't someone who was chosen for you. She was someone you wanted." For some reason, the thought that there was a woman Faulk had wanted to marry bothered her.

"Of course, I knew her. Even when I was sworn to Lealand, I wasn't in a position where fathers approached me to make a politically advantageous match. Shay and I met, we liked one another, and we thought we could make a life together."

He suddenly got up and added more wood to their small fire. "But that's not what happened. You're my wife now. I'll get you your own ring when we get back to White Ford. One that fits you from the beginning." He paced to the edge of the light. "I'll go make sure the horses are set for the night."

Then he faded into the darkness before she could say that she didn't want another ring, that this one was just fine, that a ring made no difference to her.

But she did wonder about this woman who had attracted him. What had she been like? Obviously larger than Anlin was, judging from the size of the ring. In her mind, Anlin imagined that Shay looked like her maid Hilmar. Hilmar who watched Faulk with such concentration. They would have made an attractive couple.

Why did she care? Faulk could be attracted to anyone he wanted. It made no difference to her.

But it did.

ॐ • ॐ

It rained in the night and continued into the next day. Everything dripped and squished. While it luckily wasn't cold, it was still uncomfortable. They broke camp with the minimal of talk, each eating some of the flat bread from the night before—damp flatbread with the consistency of congealed mush.

Anlin had not slept well even before the rain, awakening once from a dream in which someone who looked like Hilmar tenderly stroked the scars on Faulk's back. She felt irritated and jerked the lead line of the packhorse harder than was necessary when she started off.

She could have used the miserable weather as an excuse for her foul mood, but she suspected her attitude was more likely caused by nerves. When they arrived in Chilton, she would again come face-to-face with her second owner, Nerth. By sunset, she would have demanded answers as to what had become of her son Telm. Or, more correctly, Faulk would have demanded those answers. She would simply stand back and look subservient. But regardless of who asked the questions, she would know what had happened to her son after he'd been pulled from her arms.

She'd gone over every possible scenario with Faulk so he'd be prepared to get the needed information, regardless of the reception awaiting them at Nerth's steading.

"I don't understand these people," Faulk said after their discussion. "They hide some of their women and then misuse other women. I can't grasp such inconsistency. And for a man to sell his own son is incomprehensible."

"Telm wasn't Nerth's son," she said. "When he bought me, I was already pregnant. Think of it as buying a cow already with calf. You get two for the price of one."

"Sweet Cheelum. You sound as if you think this is normal."

She paused for a moment. "I probably did come to think of some of my life here as normal. I hated Nerth for selling my son, but I understood his position. Telm was eating food and providing little labor. The child was worth money, however, and only a fool would spend coin on food when he could have been making more coin from a sale. So Nerth sold him."

She could now calmly recite the bald facts. She'd come to accept what happened. But her tone gave no indication of the anguish that she had felt at the time. She had cried for weeks until Nerth, normally mild-mannered, had cuffed her frequently.

It was probably her constant distress that had led Nerth to sell her to Martic less than a year later. Martic was a very different kind of man than Nerth had been, however. He was more than happy if she cried. It made him feel powerful.

"Do you want me to kill this man, this Nerth? After

we've gotten the information, of course." Faulk showed no emotion. The stark lines of his face seemed more prominent. Anlin realized he would kill Nerth for what had happened to her in the past without any compunction. She'd been concerned that Faulk might not be as hard a man as she'd anticipated, as she felt she needed. But only a merciless man could ask so calmly about murdering someone who had done him no personal harm.

"No, there's no need to kill him. It won't change the past. Did you kill the man who marked your back?" Anlin considered it a real possibility.

"No," he said. "When it happened, I hadn't the power to do so. And when I was older, I understood that the abbot was mad, that he truly thought he was doing Cheelum's bidding."

"It was fortunate that you were sent to Lord Lealand's when you were."

Faulk laughed. "I wasn't *sent*. Lealand basically stole me from Jarburgh. He had come to visit his brother who was in orders there, and Lealand heard my screams. He simply wrapped my battered body up in a sheet and carried me to his keep. There his wife, Lady Patrice, tended me until I was healed. Had I stayed at Jarburgh," he shrugged, "I would have been dead. Lealand being the good man that he was, his being at Jarburgh at just the right time—these are the workings of fate."

Anlin hoped that fate was at work now, that Faulk would be the man who could save her son. She kept this hope before her like a bright flame and rode through the sodden day toward a steading near Chilton.

Faulk was frustrated by the slowness of their travel. When he'd imagined the journey, he'd thought they would be traveling on roads. Instead, the best they could do was to slog down meandering trails that the local inhabitants—and Anlin—*thought* were roads. They avoided the steadings and mean villages they passed and slept rough in whatever shelter they could find.

And so, it had been nearly a turn of the moon since they had left White Ford when they finally arrived at their destination.

Faulk and Anlin rode into Chirlon in the late afternoon. Faulk had hoped the village would contain an inn of some sort. They'd ridden in a steady downpour for most of the day and the idea of sleeping some place dry was compelling. It was obvious from a cursory inspection, however, that Chirlon didn't have an inn. It didn't have much of anything.

The village was a collection of huddled huts and odorous pigsties situated along a trail that the rain had turned into a quagmire. Faulk wondered if Chirlon would seem more appealing on a sunny day but decided it would take more than sunshine to make the place look prosperous. Furtive faces peered at them from dark doorways, but no one came out to either greet or challenge them. Except for the pigs and one bony, sway-backed milk cow, the place was lifeless.

"We turn here to get to Nerth's steading," Anlin said. Her hood was sodden, lying flat against her head. Water made rivulets down her face. She had to be as uncomfortable as he was. But underneath her subdued manner, Faulk recognized that she quivered like a hunting hound that had gotten the scent of prey. He hoped this Nerth would have the answers she sought. If the man was forthcoming, Faulk would not kill him, although images of Anlin, little more than a child heavy with a child of her own, skulking around this mean village as a slave, made his hand itch for the feel of his sword.

Anlin led them down a narrow trail that wound between gloomy, dripping pines and finally opened onto a small clearing. The long, low crofter's cottage that sat there was in better repair than most of the dwellings in the village. The thatch on the roof looked fairly new and watertight. The wattled walls had at some time been limed and still held a hint of white. Candlelight leaked around the edges of the closed shutters.

Anlin hurriedly dismounted and moved toward the door. "I'll knock," Faulk said, swinging off his own horse.

"You stand near me to translate."

She shot him a look that was far from the subservient one she was supposed to keep on her face, but she gave way to him. He pounded on the door with more force than perhaps was needed. The door opened a crack. A dark Rennish woman peered at him, her eyes wide with fright at seeing a Fallucian armed for battle standing at the door.

"I wish to see Nerth," Faulk said. Before Anlin could begin translating, the woman tried to close the door. Faulk stuck his foot inside the frame and pushed; the door flew open and the woman stumbled back.

A Rennish man jumped up from a bench on the far side of the room. He dropped a harness he'd evidently been mending and held an awl in the position of a knife. Faulk's hand went for his sword. Anlin, pushing through quickly behind him, put her hand over his and began speaking rapidly and insistently in Rennish.

The man slowly lowered the awl. "Anny?" he asked. More Rennish flowed around him, Faulk at a loss as to what was being said.

"I speak Fallace," the man said, his accent heavy but understandable. "I make talk with you." He indicated that Faulk should sit on the bench, but Faulk merely nodded his head, thinking that being seated would not be a good defensive position.

"Please sit," the man said again, slowly placing the awl on the table and sitting down himself. Faulk moved to the bench and sat down. He sensed Anlin standing behind him. The man said something in Rennish and then changed to Fallucian. "I am called Nerth. The women will get us drink and then put your animals in barn. Then they be dry. It is best that men discuss without women."

Faulk started to protest but felt Anlin's hand on his shoulder. "It's proper," she said and drifted away. The man said nothing, and Faulk did likewise until wooden mugs were set in front of them, and Anlin and the Rennish woman had gone out the door.

"Take, drink." Nerth said, raising his mug. "I make. Is good."

Faulk didn't think Anlin would have left him to be poisoned, so he took a tentative sip. The liquid seemed to be a dark, frothy ale, very bitter, and judging from the fumes, very potent. Nerth took a gulp, obviously liking his own brew. The man was probably about ten years older than Faulk, typically Rennish in appearance, short and stocky with dark, nearly black hair and inscrutable black eyes. His face was tattooed so it looked like a blue spider rested on his right cheek.

Faulk raised his mug as if a salute and then lowered it to the table. "Very good."

Nerth grinned. "Anny say she now belong to you and that you want to own her son too. She say that you will pay." His grin widened and he took another drink.

"Yes, I want to return Anlin's son to his mother. I vowed to do so when we married."

Nerth gave an explosive cough into his mug,

blowing froth in all directions. He set his mug on the table with a thump and wiped his face. "Married? Anny wife? No. No. I have wife." He pointed to the tattoo on his cheek. "Anny for work. Anny for night comfort, to keep seed strong. Anny not wife."

It took all of Faulk's self-control to not reach across the table and throttle the little bastard. Regardless of what Anlin had been here, she was now his wife, and he would not see her disparaged. Nerth's saying that Anlin was for night comfort was particularly aggravating. Unless her behavior was very different when she lived here from what it was now, Faulk could see little comfort in nights with her unless the Rennish ideal was screwing a corpse. "Anlin *is* my wife," Faulk said through gritted teeth. "And we want her son."

He evidently communicated his anger to Nerth. The man held out his hands in a pacifying gesture and vigorously nodded his head. "Yes. Fine. Anny wife. Fallace strange. But good."

Faulk wondered why Nerth would think it would please him to be called strange. It was possible that something was being lost in Nerth's broken Fallucian. "And the boy?" he asked, trying to appear calm. "Where is Anlin's son?"

"Had to sell. Made Anny cry. But boy was *traked*. So had to sell. No choice."

"What do you mean, *traked*?" Faulk feared Telm had been diseased or handicapped in some way. It was possible that Nerth had sold the boy before his condition became apparent and Nerth couldn't get as much for him. If this were the case, it was highly likely that the boy was dead.

"*Traked.*" Nerth said the word with force, as if saying it louder would suddenly make Faulk understand. "Shaman say boy *traked.* Any *traked* boy go to Ridgemere. To be safe. Little money for *traked* boy. But, no choice." The Rennish man shrugged in resignation.

"So, Anlin's son was sold to Ridgemere?"

"Yes," Nerth said with something like relief. "Telm boy go to Ridgemere. You pay now?"

Anlin had evidently offered a reward, but Faulk's first impulse was to offer Nerth his life in return for this information and nothing else. He wished Anlin were here to give him some guidance. "I'll pay," he said. "But you must tell us how to get to Ridgemere. Is it far?"

A strange look, almost like fear, crossed Nerth's face. "Go Ridgemere only when called. For wife. When wife call. I have wife." He again pointed to his tattoo.

"Good for you," Faulk said with exasperation. "But how do we get there?"

"Secret way. Only when called."

"Listen, you idiot. I'm not going to be called. And the way can't be secret if you know how to get there. So, how do we go?"

"Secret."

"Shit." Faulk stood up. The little man also bounced to his feet, grabbed the awl again and held it in front of him as if expecting attack. Faulk made no move toward him. Instead, he crossed to the door on the far wall that his nose suggested led to the attached barn. He threw open the door and saw Anlin and the Rennish woman seated on upturned stumps. "Anlin, I need you, whether your presence is proper or not."

The Rennish woman leaped back from him, but Anlin immediately came forward. "Did you find out where Telm is?" Her face was incandescent with hope.

"Yes, I know where he was sent from here, but Nerth doesn't want to tell me where that is. He keeps saying the way to Ridgemere is secret."

"Ridgemere?" Anlin's face paled.

"Yes. Do you know where it is? Nerth said Telm was sent there because he was *traked*, whatever that means."

Anlin reached blindly for his arm and grasped it as if she were drowning. "*Traked* means tainted, specifically by distorted magic. It's the term the Rennish use in referring to Fallucians, since many of us have this type of magic. It is anathema to them. So, this means that Nerth thought Telm had magical abilities."

"Nerth said the shaman told him that Telm was *traked*. But what has that to do with Ridgemere?"

"That's what doesn't make sense. Ridgemere is the place where the wives and potential wives are sequestered. I can't figure out what that has to do with a tainted slave boy."

"Whatever the reason, he's supposed to be there. Do

you know where it is? Is it shown on any of those maps that you've pored over?"

"No, the way is kept secret. I'm not sure that Nerth would tell you even if you threatened to kill him. He's very proud that he has a wife, that he has the face tattoo that proclaims him a husband. If he told us the way or guided us, he'd lose his wife at the least. And having a wife is the only hope a Rennish man has for what they think of as 'continuation.'"

Anlin tightly gripped his arm and worried her lower lip with her teeth. Faulk was about to suggest that he threaten to remove the portion of Nerth's anatomy that would make having a wife useless and without which there would definitely be no "continuation."

Then Anlin suddenly smiled. "Nerth's pride in being chosen to be a husband is second only to his love of money. Can you get my maps and one of the bags of silver from the packhorse? I think he might be persuaded to accidentally point to a place on the map if coins kept hitting his tabletop."

"You know him." Faulk said. "I've been having a difficult time just trying to figure out what he's saying."

Faulk made his way to the back of the barn where their horses were tethered. He removed the map case and some of the silver from the hipshot packhorse and returned to the cottage. Anlin was carrying on a quiet conversation with Nerth, who smiled shyly at her.

Faulk wished he knew what they were saying. The look on Nerth's face suggested that he had some tender feelings for Anlin. Anlin hadn't wanted Nerth killed, so Faulk wondered if there was some sort of emotional connection between the two of them, regardless of how foreign the possibility seemed to him. The idea curdled his gut.

"Here's the map," he said, throwing it on the table and startling them both.

Anlin spread the map out and continued her soft conversation. "Count out twenty coins onto the table," she said, switching to Fallucian. "And then pick one up and return it to the bag every time I tell you to."

Faulk carefully counted the coins, watching Nerth's face. He looked lovingly at the money. Anlin evidently knew her man, or, at least, she knew what motivated him. As Faulk placed the money on the table, Anlin kept up her monologue, gently stroking the map in front of her. When the money was neatly arranged in two tall stacks, Anlin picked up Nerth's hand and drew it over the map. Then she took her hand away.

Nerth sat there a minute, unmoving. "Take away one of the coins," she said. Faulk did so, purposely knocking over one of the stacks and having to arrange the coins again. Nerth didn't take his hand from the map. He sat looking at Anlin. "Take away another," she said.

"No," Nerth said in Fallucian. His hand moved and his right index figure tapped on the map three times. He smiled. "The money is mine, yes?"

Anlin leaned forward to make sure that she knew

exactly where his finger pointed. She nodded.

"It is yours," Faulk said, pushing the coins across the table to Nerth. The Rennish man smiled broadly and raked in the coins.

"You stay in barn for the night?" Nerth asked. "You already pay for it." He clicked the coins against each other and smiled.

Faulk realized that Nerth was pretending to sell them a place to stay for the night instead of admitting that they'd paid for directions. As much as he hated to think of camping in the rain, the idea of staying in Nerth's barn was even more uncomfortable. It was too easy to imagine the man suddenly having an attack of conscience and trying to kill him and Anlin so they couldn't travel to the secret location of Ridgemere.

"Thank you, but no," Faulk said. "There is still daylight left and we should be on our way." He switched his attention to Anlin. "Anny, go ready the horses and bring them around." The last was definitely an order. If Anlin wanted to play at servitude, he'd give her the opportunity. He was rewarded with a veiled and decidedly angry look from her, but she gathered up the map and immediately left to do his will.

❧•❧

As the last of the light faded from the gray sky, they were fortunate to find an abandoned barn just a short way off the track they were following. It was derelict, the sides gaping open, but a portion of the roof was still intact and provided shelter from the worst of the rain.

They made camp with their usual efficiency, but without conversation. Anlin had said nothing to him except to give some terse directions. As he was putting his tinderbox away, after coaxing a smoky fire into life, she finally deigned to talk to him.

"Don't call me Anny," she said, her voice tight.

Faulk straightened and turned toward her. "Why not? You seemed to be having a nice little conversation with Nerth and that's what he called you." The apparent ease with which Anlin and Nerth had dealt with one another ate at Faulk. He was not proud of his evident need to strike back at her.

"It's a slave name, a diminutive that is intended to diminish. And I wasn't having a 'nice little conversation' with Nerth." Her eyes slid away from his and she busied herself getting something out of her pack.

"It certainly looked that way to me. It made me wonder exactly what there was between you two. Nerth told me that part of your job when you belonged to him was to be a night comfort. How comfortable were you two?"

Her eyes came slamming back to his, anger shimmering in their depths. "Comfortable? You think that I found any comfort there? I can tell you what too many of the nights were like. Nerth would order me to strip naked, then, watching me, he would handle himself to arousal and mount me. That was it. If he found comfort in it, I certainly didn't."

"And yet you don't hate him?"

"Why should I? Nerth was kinder in many ways than my other owners. His behavior was typical of all the other Rennish men I knew. And I can't see how it is appreciably different from the way Fallucian men treat women."

Anger now flashed through Faulk. He was confident that he was the only Fallucian man she'd been with. Hell, he was her husband and had the *right* to do anything he wanted to her. And he had treated her only with consideration.

Yet, she felt she could prose on about the way Fallucian men treated women... Well, he would not, most *definitely* would not, be classed with the behavior she'd described. He fought the desire to strike her. Such behavior would only prove her point. He consciously relaxed his clenched fists.

"I object to being included in your confused idea of the behavior of all men." His voice was amazingly steady. "I have never treated you thus. I have avoided physical contact with you, since it was obvious you disliked it. I have done so even though I would have been within my rights to lie with you every night. I'd hoped you would come to know me as a human being. I'd hoped you would stop fearing me and my sex."

"You have never treated me thus? I think that is hardly true."

Faulk thought with discomfort of their aborted wedding night. "How would you know?" he asked. "All I have to do is touch you and you're gone. Oh, your body stays near me, but that is just a husk. Whatever makes you yourself has fled. If you'd mentally stayed on any occasion when I touched you, you might have discovered there is a great difference between what happens between slave and master and between husband and wife."

Anlin looked at him without comprehension. "What great difference would this be?"

Faulk realized she really didn't know. "Men and women who care for one another can find great joy in physical love," he said. "Even without emotional attachment, the act itself is pleasurable, or at least, it should be if done properly. Was there no obvious caring between your parents? Have you never wondered why even the villeins will disappear into the darkness holding hands and smiling?"

Conflicting thoughts obviously crossed her face. The effect was startling since her expression was usually so tightly controlled. "My parents may have liked one another. I was a child when I lived with them. How was I to know and how can I, at this point, judge? I never saw my sister Sybil together with Sir Kenteth. By the time I returned, my mother was dead from a fever and Sybil had not survive the birth of her twins."

She gave an odd, sad smile. "It's pathetic to admit that I felt superior to Sybil for the first time in my life when I learned she had died in childbirth, and I had survived. Perhaps there is something so lacking in me that I could not have recognized affection between these married couples in my family even if it had been plain. As for strangers—I've come across couples rutting in the barn or the field or even the hall late at night. But I saw none of the joy that you speak of. They seemed to only be answering a need to procreate, similar to that of the castle dogs."

Hopeless, Faulk thought. Trying to change Anlin's attitude was hopeless. She had never known pleasure in coupling. She had never seen the soft caring that could surround a couple as it had Lealand and his Lady Patrice. Anlin would always flee to some place in her mind at his touch. He was bound for all time to a sterile relationship.

The sadness of this fact was sharper since he'd seen a side of Anlin on this trip that had been hidden at White Ford. She'd emerged as a competent woman with a quirky sense of humor, someone he would have found attractive had he just met her. He felt an acute sense of loss and wondered how you could lose what you never had.

"It makes no difference," he said. "We're wet. We're tired. This is not the time for this discussion. We need to get dry and have something to eat." He turned from her and leaned forward, beginning to loosen his hauberk so that it would slide off.

"I can help with that," she said from close behind him.

"No need." He had handled the removal of his

hauberk by himself many times. He really didn't want her near him right now.

"There's some bread and cheese," she said.

"Good." It came out as a grunt as he got the mail moving off his body and onto the ground. His wet quilted gambeson followed. He wiped his head, chest, and back with a piece of linen from his pack. It would have been nice to completely strip and dry, but that didn't seem like a good option at the moment. He smiled wryly at himself. As if he could frighten Anlin away more than he already did by just existing. He reached for a dry tunic, thankful that the heavily waxed packs were doing their job. He froze his motion when he felt the tentative touch on his back.

✤ 10 ✤

Anlin reached out and touched Faulk's back. She had no idea where the impulse came from; it was just something she had to do. She wanted to reassure him that she was there, as she had done when Telm awoke crying from a dream. It was a ridiculous impulse. If there was ever a man who did not need reassurance, it was Faulk. Yet, when her hand grazed the mass of scars on his back, he immediately stilled.

She slowly moved her fingers over the ridges and welts, amazed that they felt polished, as if large drips of candle wax had flowed over each other. She'd expected the ruined skin to be harsh and coarse. She had also not anticipated the heat. Warmth spread into her hand and seemed to creep up her arm, as if she held her fingers to a fire.

She trailed her fingers up over his shoulder, the skin there smooth and soft, the muscles beneath firm and hard. She walked around him, concentrating on her stroking hand, not looking up at his face. His chest too was ridged, but only from the shape of the muscles lying close beneath his warm skin, skin that was pale, lighter than that on his face and arms. A cross of hair, soft and springy to the touch, ran from one flat nipple to the other and then arrowed down across his taut abdomen to disappear behind the tunic he held in his relaxed hands.

She rubbed her fingers from side to side across his chest She was fascinated by the tightening of muscles wherever her questing hand touched. Different. Faulk felt so different. He was nothing like herself. And he was also not much like the Rennish men she'd known, whose chests were narrower and hairless. She would never have been allowed to touch them in this manner, however. Such stroking was not the province of a slave.

Her fingers circled around one of the darker, flat nipples. To her surprise, when she brushed the tip, the nipple puckered until it sat like a small pebble on Faulk's chest. There was a strange, answering response in her own breast, a tingling, a tightening. She transferred her attentions to the nipple on the other side and watched it change, fascinated by the transformation. She stroked her hand down the long, vertical line of hair until she touched the tunic that Faulk clutched below his waist. Although he hadn't moved, Faulk's earlier relaxed posture had disappeared. He held himself stiffly and his knuckles showed white as he clasped the tunic as if it would be torn from his grasp.

"Don't," he said, his voice scratchy.

Anlin stopped contemplating the progress of her hand and looked up at Faulk's face. His expression was blank, but the look seemed to be one that was willed rather than natural. The firelight accented the plains and hollows of his face. His green eyes appeared dark. "Don't touch you anymore?" she asked.

"No. I've told you that you may touch me. It's pleasurable. Perhaps too pleasurable. But don't touch me any lower."

Anlin realized that stroking him was indeed pleasurable. Other than with Telm, she'd never consciously touched another human being. And this experience was nothing like caressing her son who had been all round, velvet smoothness as a baby and had grown into all sharp ribs and bony shoulders right before he'd been taken from her. Trailing her hands over Faulk was a very different experience. It made her feel both heavy and quivery, an odd sensation she'd never felt before.

"If you like to be touched, why wouldn't you like it everywhere?" She continued to run her fingers down over his abdomen until they bumped into his clenched hands, then she feathered her hand back up.

He gave a choppy exhale, the precursor of a laugh. "I would like to be touched everywhere, but if you pet me any lower, you'll discover just how much I like it, and I'm afraid it will frighten you away."

She returned her gaze to his face. "I'm very difficult to frighten," she said, running her hand back down, exerting pressure on his hands until he unclasped them, letting them fall to his side. She encountered his braies, the material damp and somewhat chilled. Within was the heavy bulge of his arousal. When she ran her fingers over it, he stiffened, an odd look ghosting over his impassive face and then quickly disappearing. She did it again, watching his expression. How odd. His staff was hard, ready for mating, and yet, she was still fully clothed.

She partially circled his arousal with her hand and moved it up and down. He could no longer keep a look of tension from his face. His breathing accelerated. Anlin marveled at this power that she seemed to have over him. Perhaps this was something magical in herself that she had never before discovered. If it was a spell, however, it seemed to affect her as well. She, too, was breathing more rapidly, and she felt a damp warmth between her legs.

"Enough," he said loudly, one of his hands covering hers with a vice-like grip. "Enough," said more softly. "I am not a man made of stone."

He certainly felt like he was made of stone, but she didn't want to say that. There had never been a stone that put off such heat, however. Waves of warmth seem to radiate from him. She looked at him expectantly.

"Touching is only good for so long unless I'm allowed to touch back," he said. "Would you stand there and let me touch you just as you have touched me, or would you, eh, go away?"

"I wouldn't run."

"No, I mean go away in your mind."

Anlin stood still for a moment, examining her own mind. The peaceful meadow did not beckon. She found that she very definitely wanted to stay in the here and now. "I won't go away."

He released her hand, which fell to her side, and raised his, softly stroking the side of her face with one finger. A comforting warmth spread out from his gentle touch. He pushed her damp hair back with both hands on either side of her face. His thumbs made lazy circles on her temples—the calluses from years of handling a sword slightly abrasive and soothing. She closed her eyes. She could hear the rain beating on the roof, the constant drip of water into puddles in the section of the barn where the roof was gone. Somewhere behind her, a horse shifted and blew softly through its nose. She felt herself relax. The world shrank to sounds and the feathering circles on her face.

The circles broadened, covering her cheeks and eventually trailing over her lips, making them tingle. She unconsciously licked them. Faulk made a humming sound that was almost a groan. She felt his lips cover hers, warm and surprisingly soft. She jerked back; her eyes flew open. He kept his hands on the sides of her face, but didn't hold her tightly, letting her move away from him.

"It's only a kiss," he said. "A different kind of touching."

His face was close, his green eyes vivid. *It's only a kiss, a different kind of touching.* She closed her eyes. She felt him lean back over her. His lips touched her again, moving slightly like a brush of thistle down. His tongue played along her lower lip. She relaxed her mouth and felt his tongue lave the inside of her lips. The sensation was peculiar and sent a shaft of warmth from her mouth to her midsection.

She had lied when she said that she wasn't easily frightened, since this frightened her. Or, more particularly, the feelings spiraling inside her were frightening. She felt she no longer had mastery of herself and hated the feeling. Hated it, yes, but she still wanted to continue the unique experience.

She did not pull away.

One of his hands drifted away to caress the side and the back of her neck. Then it flowed over her shoulder and down the side of her arm. It was a gentle stroke that spread fire in its wake. The hand shifted to her waist, hypnotically rubbing up and down. Then it moved up her rib cage to cup her breast from beneath. Her breasts felt tender and heavy and she wanted, she wanted... she wasn't sure what she wanted. But she knew she didn't want this gentle touching to stop.

His hand lifted her breast and his thumb rubbed over her nipple. She strained toward him instead of away. She allowed her tongue to brush his and then rubbed it on his inner lips. Her hands came up from where she'd held them at her sides and wrapped around his waist, pulling him tightly against her. She relished the feeling of his firm body. She moved against him so her tender breasts rubbed against his chest, the friction causing a yearning she did not recognize.

She should have felt disgusted to have a man pressing against her, but she did not. This was not just any man; this was Faulk, and that seemed to make all the difference. She splayed her hands across the ruin of his back, touching him as he touched her.

He suddenly thrust her away from him.

"Wha—?" She stopped as Faulk held his finger to his lips and looked behind her. She listened for whatever it was that had attracted his attention, but could hear nothing but the pounding rain, the dripping water, and their own ragged breathing. And then, behind a portion of derelict wall, there was a scrape of metal like a hoe encountering a stone.

She turned to look in the direction of the sound, following Faulk's gaze. But she could see nothing except dripping darkness beyond the weak circle of firelight. The metallic sound came again. Faulk grabbed her arm and flung her toward the other side of the barn. With the same movement, he reached to his stack of gear and retrieved his sword and scabbard. He pulled the sword loose from its covering and threw the scabbard to the side.

Simultaneously, a form appeared, a man, then two men, three, four. They materialized out of the darkness, two burnishing swords and two hefting pikes.

"Behind me," Faulk said, backing toward the far wall. "Stay behind me."

Anlin complied, but she pulled her knife from the sheath at her waist. Whoever these men were, they had not come to share a fire on a damp night.

The four men spread out, trying to encircle them. The two with pikes poked at Faulk but didn't come close enough to actually touch him. Faulk continued to move backwards until Anlin was nearly pressed against the wall.

Then he suddenly sprang forward, toward one of the pikemen, dodging the blade, flowing by the shaft. With a stroke almost too fast to see, he sliced into the man's side. The man screamed, dropped his pike, and crumpled. This all seemed to happen in the space of a heartbeat, and then Faulk was back where he had been standing directly in front of her.

"Kill the bastard," one of the remaining men said in Rennish. His voice sounded very much like Nerth's, but in the uncertain light, Anlin was unable to determine the identity of the speaker.

The three men rushed toward Faulk, leading with swords and pike. With a deep growl, Faulk brought the second pikeman to the ground. He ducked under the man's thrust and felled him with a blow across the legs. The attacker crashed to the ground, screaming for his fellows to help him. The two men with swords hesitated and then rushed Faulk in a coordinated effort.

What transpired looked to Anlin like a deadly

dance. Faulk's sword blurred as he moved to counter one stroke and then the other. Metal clanged, loud in the darkness. Men grunted and swore. But neither of the attackers was able to land a debilitating blow. Faulk wove between their lethal blades, forcing the man on the right to back up, stumbling. He immediately turned to the man on his left, stopping a sword stroke aimed at his head and deflecting it to the side. Faulk's recovery was faster than his opponent's. Faulk thrust directly into the man's midsection, bringing him to his knees, his sword dropping from a nerveless hand.

The fourth man seemed to think better of attacking Faulk on his own and turned to run. Faulk easily caught him and brought him down with a stroke between the shoulder and the neck. This man fell without a sound, blood spurting from his nearly severed neck.

Faulk spun to face the three men groaning or screaming on the ground, but none of them posed any threat. He walked by them, kicking any weapons away that might have been within reach, bending over each of them as he passed.

Anlin stood rooted, her knife in her hand. Faulk hadn't needed her help. It had all occurred so fast, she wasn't sure exactly how the rout had happened.

"Please go get the horses ready to travel," Faulk said, walking up to her. "We can't stay here now." She reached out and touched a line of blood that ran down his left shoulder. He winced. "The second pikeman got under my guard. It's nothing to worry about. It's only a scratch."

The line of freely flowing blood certainly looked like more than a scratch to Anlin. "It would be better if I bandaged that before we went anywhere."

"Now, Anlin, now! Get everything ready so we can leave."

"Why the haste? These men can't hurt us now." She looked over at the huddled forms of the three men who still lived. The one who had been screaming had stopped, but all three were now moaning.

"These men can't hurt us, but any who might be following them could."

"But why would these men attack us? We've had no trouble with all the other Rennish we've seen on the road. We've been easily taken for traders."

Faulk turned her face up to look at him. "One of these men is Nerth," he said. "I thought his avarice was such that he would just pretend he'd never seen us, or else pretend he had told us nothing about how to get to Ridgemere. It's my fault I so underestimated him. I thought that if he were bought, he'd stay bought.

"Evidently, his conscience got the better of him. I assume he recruited these other men in Chirlon. We can only hope he told no one else. But even then, we have to get out of here." He took her arm and moved her toward the horses. "I'll help you ready the horses before I take care of other matters."

"What other matters?" She came to a stop.

"You must realize I have to kill them. It's likely they

will die of the wounds they already have, but I can't take that chance. I have to be sure they can't send others on our trail, if they haven't done so already."

"Kill them? But you said one of them is Nerth."

"Do you have any strong feelings for Nerth?" Faulk's voice was harsh, as if it were forced out between clenched teeth.

"No, no special feelings." She whipped her head from side to side in denial. She really didn't care about Nerth, but she'd lived with him for years. She knew him. He wasn't just some faceless attacker in the dark. He had probably been good to her, if measured by his own standards. "But to kill them when there is no resistance…"

"Sweet Cheelum!" His voice held disgust. "Killing us was their goal when they came here. Or at least killing me. You they might have kept again as a slave. Or perhaps they would have used you and then killed you. Whatever their purpose was, they were willing to kill to keep us from going to Ridgemere, though why they think that is so important I cannot imagine."

Faulk stalked away from her and began loading the packhorses, his movements jerky and angry. Anlin followed and silently helped make things ready to leave. She even eventually helped Faulk with his mail hauberk, although he made an irritated comment about already having been caught with his dick out and accepted her aid without good grace. Finally, they were ready to ride out into the inclement night.

"Take the horses out of the barn," Faulk said. "I'll be along in a minute."

"Faulk?"

"Don't say anything else. I'll do what I have to do, but there is no joy in it. Just get the hell away."

Anlin mounted her horse and led the others out into the blustery darkness. It was going to be difficult to find their way. Fortunately, they could follow the major trail for some time, but it wasn't going to be easy to follow even a well-marked path in the blackness.

Faulk reappeared from the barn and mounted his horse without comment. They moved off at a slow pace, Anlin leading. The night was miserable. The rain eventually stopped, but heavy clouds still obscured the moon. After she nearly led them into a ravine, Faulk dismounted and went first on foot. Their progress was slow, but they kept moving, always moving away from four dead men in a derelict barn.

Anlin tried to divert her mind from the memory. She'd been worried that Faulk was not ruthless enough to do whatever was necessary to bring Telm home. Now she wondered what had prompted that concern. She didn't understand the man who could touch her so tenderly and then calmly kill three men who were no longer physical threats.

Anlin found herself nodding in the saddle. Exhaustion had begun to take its toll. She forced herself to stare into the dark, trying to stay awake if not alert. It would be easy to tumble from the horse and her worry kept her upright in the saddle, jerking awake every time her chin came to rest on her chest. She must have dozed, however, since she awoke with a start when her horse came to a stop.

A faint, pearl gray smudged the east, indicating the approach of dawn. Directly in front of her was an odd, round building with a conical, thatched roof. It sat adjacent to the trail and had a large corral surrounding a lean-to off to one side. The corral was empty and the building shuttered.

"Do you have any idea what this is?" Faulk asked.

Anlin tried to focus her blurry and gritty eyes. The building was in good repair, but it was like nothing she'd seen before. "It doesn't look much like a house or a barn," she said. "It looks more like some sort of meeting house."

"But nothing of religious significance? There's a religious feel to this place, although I don't know why."

"It's nothing I'm familiar with."

"Then let's see who's home." Faulk slipped his sword from its scabbard and pounded on the door. The sound reverberated in the early morning stillness, but no one came to answer the knock. Faulk tried the latch and discovered the door was unbarred. It swung open on silent hinges.

The interior was neat and well-scrubbed. Bunk beds, with linens and quilts carefully folded at the foot of each bed, radiated from the circular walls like the spokes of a wheel. There was a fire pit in the middle with a smoke hole above.

"Hello," Faulk called out loudly, a useless gesture since the interior was obviously empty. "Sweet Cheelum, real beds. Correction, real *dry* beds." Faulk turned toward her with a smile. "This is made to order. We're both done in and the horses can't go much further without rest. You can crawl into one of these real beds and get some sleep. I'll take the horses to the lean-to and rub them down. Then I'll keep watch while you sleep. I'll wake you in a while and you can keep watch."

He turned to move toward the door. "I'll take first watch," she said. "I've gotten some sleep and you've been walking."

"And because I've been walking I've got my blood moving. I'll wake you when I'm too tired to stand. You get some sleep."

The beds looked inviting. Anlin didn't think she would bother with the linens. Just wrapping a quilt around her and becoming horizontal seemed like a wonderful idea. But before she surrendered to sleep, she had to know the answer to a question that had been buzzing in her head all the long night. "Faulk, if I'd said that Nerth meant something to me, would you have not killed him?"

He just looked at her, silence stretching, then he said, "If you'd had an emotional attachment to the man, I would not have killed him."

Cheelum wept. She should have lied. She could have

saved Nerth's life with just a word.

"Nerth was nigh on to gutted," Faulk said. "There was no way he could have lived, but his dying would have been long and hard. Had you told me you felt something for him that you evidently cannot feel for me, I would not have given him the release I offered the others."

His face became so bleak he was almost unrecognizable. "I would have left him to die screaming. I would have left him to die watching the flies crawl over his exposed innards. It would have been a low and ignoble thing to do. I killed those men not only for our own safety, but also to eliminate all the suffering and pain they would have had to endure before their inevitable deaths. But if I'd thought Nerth had your affection, something you've withheld from me, then I probably would have left him to die in agony."

He ran his hands through his hair and gave her a smile that was more of a grimace. "The hell of it is—I'm not sure I could have left him to suffer. But I would have wanted to. And that's a blackness in myself that I don't enjoy contemplating."

He swung abruptly away from her and exited. She could hear him talking to the horses in a low tone and then the sound of the horses moving away. She wavered slightly on her feet. If she didn't lie down shortly, then she would fall down. Faulk was a puzzle she couldn't piece together and she decided she wouldn't even try. At least not today. At least not while her brain screamed for sleep.

She grabbed a quilt off the nearest bed, wrapped it around her, and tumbled into the lower bunk. She momentarily registered that she was hungry. Of course she was. She had eaten nothing since noon the day before. But she wasn't so hungry that she would get up and look for some food. The quilt smelled clean and faintly of some herb. It made her think of a bright meadow in the sun. It was a much happier thought than dead men in a barn. And then there was no thought as she fell headlong into sleep.

❧ 11 ❧

The touch on his shoulder brought him instantly awake. As he rolled to his feet, he remembered the bunk above him and ducked beneath its bottom support pole. Sun slanted through the shuttered windows, indicating the rain had stopped.

"It's okay," Anlin said quickly. "There's no emergency. It's about four hours passed dawn, and this is when you told me to awaken you."

Anlin looked at him warily and Faulk realized, as he'd come to his feet, he'd pulled his sword from the scabbard that had lain at his side all night. He now towered over her with a naked blade in his hand, ready to fight. He gave her a self-deprecating smile and slid his sword back in its scabbard.

"I slept like the dead," he said, quickly regretting his word choice when she frowned. "But the sleep did the trick. I'm no longer exhausted. Now I'm hungry."

She smiled then, her change of expression like the sun coming up, the plains and angles of her face filling with beauty. Her dark hair, fluffed out to dry, now came to her shoulders in a riot of spun silk. The white blaze, flowing back from her temple, reminded Faulk of a shaft of sunlight coming through a window into a dark room.

"The bread is getting a little stale," she said, "but we still have plenty of bread and cheese. It's over on the table by the door. I looked to see if there were any food stores here, but I couldn't find any."

Faulk rotated his shoulders, trying to take the tightness out of them. He'd slept in his hauberk, not wanting to be unprepared for any further surprises, and, while it didn't disturb his rest, it still led to awakening with stiff muscles. The wound made by the pike made itself known as he moved. He should strip and clean it before the cut became septic. His nose wrinkled at the slightly feral smell that surrounded him. More than just the wound needed cleaning. But if the conclusions he'd reached last night were correct, there was no time for such niceties. They would have a long ride today.

"You've had the opportunity to look around in daylight," he said, walking toward the table and the offered food. "What do you make of this place?"

"It's a way station of some sort," Anlin said. "There's room to sleep twenty-six people and plenty of fodder in the lean-to to feed that many horses. All seems to be in readiness for the arrival of some group. There haven't been any horses here for a while, though, or else everything has been meticulously cleaned. There's not a speck of manure in the corral that would indicate that someone came through here not long ago."

"I agree," Faulk said around a mouthful of cheese. The bread was a bit chewy, but the cheese was sharp and tangy. "Too bad whoever prepared the place didn't leave any 'fodder' for humans. A big smoked ham hanging from the rafters would be nice."

Anlin laughed, pushing her hair back from her face. "I'd have liked to have found a ham as well, but there is no food here. Believe me; I was very motivated to look carefully into every nook and cranny."

"I see you also spent your time locating where we are and where we plan to go." Faulk motioned to the map that Anlin had spread out on the table. The corners, which wanted to curl, were anchored with silver coins from the packs.

"Yes. I've been examining the map. I know exactly where Nerth said this mysterious Ridgemere should be and can make an informed guess as to where we are now. The only problem is that the trail we've been following isn't indicated on this map."

"Since the way is supposed to be secret, you wouldn't expect it to be."

"But it can't be all that much of a secret," she said. "The trail is too obvious, too much in use. We were able to follow the trail at night, even without moonlight. No one coming across it could miss it."

"Perhaps people don't just happen to come this way. We didn't pass any farms or steadings last night. The area around the trail is devoid of habitation."

"How can we be sure?" she asked. "It was raining and consequently, very dark."

"You're right, but in the darkness, we should have seen at least some strips of light that escaped around shutters. We should have smelled farm animals, but we didn't. Did you hear a dog bark? No, I think the Rennish have cleared all people from this path. It is secret only because they choose to think of it as such."

"Then, if it's not really a secret, why would those men have attacked us?"

"Because we're not supposed to be using this track. We're not husbands."

A look of quick comprehension crossed Anlin's face. "Yeah, that makes sense. This place was set up to house the husbands on their way to Ridgemere."

Faulk nodded his agreement. "And if this assumption is right, there should be another place like this one about a day's ride away. If we start soon, we'll be late in arriving, but it will give us a good place to stop and there should be fodder for the horses again"

"I think you're right," she said, beginning to roll up the map. "I'll go get the horses ready."

"No. Wait." He put his hand on her arm to stop her movement. "I want to get this whole husband business straight in my mind before we go on. Do all the men in Rennic have one of these sequestered wives?"

"No, only about half of them have wives. You know who they are because they're the ones with facial tattoos. Of course, all men hope they will be chosen to be a husband, since that's the only way that they can have true children. Any children born to slaves are simply that, slaves. They don't really count as people. I can't even think of one instance when a man acknowledged, or even kept, such a child."

Such an attitude was so foreign to Faulk's nature that he couldn't really understand it. It was hard enough to understand how a man could ignore his own child in Fallucian society, although Faulk was living proof that it happened. "How is one chosen for the role of husband if this is so important?"

"Selectors come through the various areas about twice a year. I was always locked up with the rest of the slaves when this happened, but I did get a glimpse of one once. The selector was a woman—that I could tell. I got the feeling she was old by the way she moved, but there was no way I could be sure since she wore a loose robe and her face was veiled. She was accorded every respect and met with the village headman for most of the day. After that time, some men were called in, and they later appeared grinning like maniacs and wearing new tattoos. There isn't a man in Rennic who doesn't wish for true progeny."

Faulk could well understand the desire for heirs, but this process sounded more than strange. Like everyone in Fallucia, he knew the Rennish were different, but he'd never imagined a culture so dissimilar to the one he knew lay just across an imaginary boundary. "Were all the men who owned you husbands?"

Anlin shook her head. "No, only Nerth had the facial tattoo and went twice a year to be with his wife. Gilpin, the first man who bought me, was fairly young, and I think he still hoped he would be selected. Martic, on the other hand, my third owner, had given up expecting to be chosen. Maybe that's what made him such a cruel man. Or maybe he was not selected because he was cruel to begin with. I don't know, but he was mean and embittered." She shivered. "Sweet Cheelum, I can't tell you how awful it makes me feel to revisit all this."

Faulk could well understand her aversion to this conversation. He thought he'd rather die than give someone else such power over him. He knew the questions he felt he still needed to have answered would make her even more uncomfortable, but he didn't see how they could be avoided.

"Even men who were husbands only saw their wives twice a year?" he asked.

"Yes, as far as I know."

"Then what did men, even ones with wives do for…" He stopped, considering how he was going to approach this. "I mean, were there taverns or something similar that had available women?"

"You mean whores?" She asked it without inflection. "There was no need for whores. Almost every man had a female slave who was used for that purpose."

"And all these female slaves were Fallucian?"

"Heavens no! Most of them are Rennish. If a girl

does not have the necessary magical qualifications to become a wife, she's sold. To be a woman in Rennic is to be either a wife or a slave."

"What a horrible choice." Faulk felt a flare of anger for these unknown women. "Of course, I guess that is wrong. The women never get a choice—they are chosen. Do you know how this happens?"

Anlin shook her head. "I have no idea. I'd guess that it occurs when girls are quite young. I've seen female Rennish slaves as young as about ten."

"What a peculiar way to live," Faulk said. "Without a slave, even a married man had no, eh…"

"Night comfort," Anlin supplied.

"Well, yeah. As I said, this way of life is very foreign to me. Well, it's the Rennish way of life, so I guess it should be foreign to me." He gave her a quick smile, but hesitated again, once more not sure how to broach the next subject. "Were all of the female slaves treated as you were? I mean, were there no men and their slaves who formed an emotional attachment? It would seem normal that this would happen."

Anlin's look of shocked horror was almost comical. "Not that I knew of or even heard of. I think it's because the laws and customs keep this from happening. Between a man and his slave, there is supposed to be only fornication. None of the touching like we did." She looked down, evidently embarrassed by the memory. "Martic touched me, but only to hit or hurt. That seemed to excite him."

Faulk didn't know how to respond to this. He'd known similar men, men who could only become aroused it they inflicted pain. No one country or culture was immune to this type of behavior, sick though Faulk considered it to be. As weird as the Rennish evidently were, the fact that they had chosen to withhold the honor of allowing such a man as Martic to take a wife was laudatory.

"Do Rennish men treat their wives in the same way?" he asked.

"I never met a wife, and I was hardly in the position to ask." Anger now flashed in her eyes.

It made sense to Faulk that wives would be treated differently. But even then, to see one's spouse only twice a year was unnatural. And if only wives lived in Ridgemere, then what was Anlin's son doing there? He couldn't see what it had to do with Telm's perhaps being tainted with Fallucian magic.

"I have no more questions," Faulk said before Anlin's anger could boil over. "I think we need to get moving. Assuming another way station exists, we'll probably not get there until after dark.

✢

Pleasant, rainless days passed. Each night another way station presented itself. The ride would have been enjoyable had Faulk not been constantly alert for hidden dangers. If this was the secret way to a hidden place, there should have been guards, or at the least, lookouts. But there were none in evidence. The whole area seemed to be bereft of any human presence.

The path continued to slowly climb. They passed large expanses of forests of towering pines interspersed with broad meadows that had never felt a plow. The husbandman in Faulk wondered at a people who could huddle in mean village like Chirlon and ignore the potential bounty of the land they passed. The Rennish made no sense.

How could two peoples live so close to each other and be so different? The customs Anlin had told him about were more than different, however. To Faulk they appeared distorted, sick. People were not meant to live this way, with husbands and wives separated and with most of the population simply breeding like animals whenever lust overtook them. Faulk had thought it would be horrible to live as Anlin had, but he decided being a man in this society wouldn't be an easy thing either. Even the men seemed to have very limited choices.

Not that Fallucia had been gifted with a perfect social order. There were great inequities in Fallucian society. The Lords of High Places ruled all those under them, and regardless of how hard a man worked, he could only improve his lot to a limited degree if he'd not been born a Lord.

For all the intermittent horrors of his childhood, Faulk had been lucky. Unlike solid fighting men like Kevin and Waylon, Faulk had been given a basic education. He could read and write, abilities often restricted to the noble class and to the clerks who served them.

With Lealand, Faulk had found a family, a place to belong. Lealand and Lady Patrice had often treated him more like a son than a server. Because of them, and yes, even because of that sick bastard Abbot Jezrel, he'd been given the means to rise in Fallucian society. His own ability and Anlin's approval had given him his much-desired land. He would never be a Lord. He would always be Philip Giffard's sworn man. But in this he could be satisfied.

His only fear was that the place he had attained would be jeopardized by the increasing capriciousness of King Fremmor. The mental deterioration of the king destabilized the whole country. It allowed the venal and corrupt like Edmund Tarn to take control. Tarn had too much power for someone like Faulk to ever take down, but revenge for what had happened to Lealand was a persistent daydream, a continuing but forlorn hope.

They arrived at the next, expected way station just as the sun was setting. The slanting light illuminated a set of buildings almost identical to those that they'd stayed in earlier.

Although everything here was larger, evidently built to accommodate more people, there was the same circular dormitory with its conical roof, the same lean-to, the same corral. An extra building had been added, however, a smaller circular structure that was attached to one side of the dormitory.

As always, Faulk and Anlin approached cautiously, but once again, they were the only ones there.

"I'll settle the horses," Faulk said. "I'm assuming this place will be furnished as the others were and that there will be plenty of feed available for the animals. Why don't you search for a surprise smoked ham hanging in the rafters?" With the mention of the imaginary ham, Faulk's stomach emitted a low growl.

Anlin's angular face broke into the sudden smile that made her look beautiful. "I'll get us another hare if the ham doesn't materialize."

Faulk grunted in response. Rabbit and hard cheese—again. Their menu was ever repetitive. He led the horses away, stripped off the saddles and packs, and pulled hay into the bin in the lean-to. All the horses pushed toward the food. Baring his teeth, Faulk's big gray took pride of place. "Greedy buggers, all of you," Faulk said, still trying to banish the vision of ham from his mind.

It took him three trips to get all the packs stowed in the dormitory. He then stripped off his hauberk, greatly relieved to be shed of the weight after a long day in the saddle. He saw no need to sleep in it again. He and Anlin seemed to be the only people in this entire area.

While Faulk finished his chores, Anlin assembled their less-than-exciting meal. It was, however, filling and made him appreciate Anlin's skill with a bow. As they ate, Anlin spread the map between them.

"Judging from the position of the stream and the shape of the big hill we passed not far back, I think we're about here." Her finger traced a spot on the map. "If Nerth told the truth, Ridgemere should be here." Her finger moved to a spot not too distant. "I'd guess about half a day's ride."

Faulk washed down a lump of cheese with water. "That close? Then I guess it makes sense that these buildings were designed to hold more people. Evidently men would be coming from all over, and this would be their last stop."

"I think your assumption is correct. This must be the final gathering place for husbands coming to Ridgemere, and because it is, I have a surprise to show you when you're done eating." Anlin gave him a shy smile that made his mid-section tighten. He wished their relationship could always be this relaxed. He felt a yawning hole in his life because of what they were missing.

He quickly finished his meal and followed Anlin's dancing steps to a door in the far wall. The lintel was heavily carved with various fruits surrounding a short phrase in Rennish. "What does that say?" he asked.

"It says 'Holy duties bring joy.'"

"I'd always felt these buildings had a religious significance. Is this a temple of some sort?"

She giggled. Anlin actually giggled. Amazing. "Maybe of some sort," she said, pushing the door open.

The smaller round room was decidedly odd, but it

didn't look like any temple Faulk had ever seen. A big metal cauldron, its sides much higher than its girth, rested in the middle of the room. Under it smoldered a fire that filled the room with an aromatic smoke before drifting though slits in the ceiling. Surrounding the cauldron in a wheel-spoke pattern that echoed the arrangement of the bunks in the larger room were large wooden troughs. It was like nothing Faulk had ever seen, and he was at a loss to figure out its use.

As if understanding his confusion, Anlin announced, "It's a bathhouse. A real bathhouse." Then she literally danced, weaving her way among the troughs, spinning and laughing.

"A bathhouse," Faulk repeated, still not fully comprehending. He was familiar with bathing, of course. This usually took place in a stream, but in the winter, a fat barrel could be laboriously filled with hot water. There the bather could squat and relish a good soak. In Faulk's case, the soak was generally not long in duration. He was seldom the first to use the barrel and the water was cooling. To fit, his chest was usually pressed against his folded legs and this was not a comfortable position for long.

"This is the only thing that I've missed about Rennic," Anlin said, her face flushed and her eyes sparkling. Seeing Faulk just standing there, she continued, "I started the fire while you were out with the horses so the water should be nice and hot." She then pulled up a sliding door that looked much like a sluice gate on a dam and water poured from the cauldron into one of the troughs. She raised another door and a second trough began to fill.

As steam slowly rose from both troughs, Anlin began undressing. She heeled off her boots, shucked her riding pants, and pulled her tunic over her head. She then stood there, completely and gloriously naked, watching the water flow. Faulk wasn't sure which surprised him more—the room or Anlin's behavior.

When the water approached the lip of the trough, she pushed the door back down and the water stopped. She then did the same with the second. She trailed her hand in the water and murmured, "Yes, yes." At this point, she seemed to become conscious of Faulk's just standing there.

"Undress and get in," she said. "The water is perfect."

Then, matching action to her words, she slipped over the side and into water. She completely submerged and then sat up, ringing the water from her hair, grinning like an idiot. She pushed back and leaned her head against the sloping end of the trough with a contented sigh. She could completely stretch out with room to spare. Her breasts broke the surface of the water like islands in a calm sea.

Faulk stood transfixed. He realized that other than that first, horrible night, he'd never seen Anlin completely unclothed, and it was a sight well worth the watching. He was amazed at her relaxed demeanor. He would have to ask her if the aroma from the smoke had some sort of soporific effect. If so, it might be a good idea to buy some of the substance to take back to White Ford.

"Are you just going to stand there like some hulking tree?" she asked, opening her eyes a slit.

"No." The word had to be forced out around a throat that felt constricted. He didn't want Anlin to see he was aroused. He wanted nothing to frighten her, nothing to make her think of the type of relationships she'd had here in Rennic. They seemed to have come to some sort of accommodation on this journey. She hadn't disappeared into her own mind during their touching. Faulk hoped that maybe, just maybe, he and Anlin could find something good between them with time.

Turning his back to her, he quickly stripped off his clothing and entered the trough and it was—wonderful! Unlike the barrels he was used to in Fallucian bathhouses, here he could lie on his back with his shoulders and neck braced by the back of the trough. The hot water could reach every one of his tired muscles. The now healing pike wound initially stung, but quickly became painless.

Faulk bent his knees and pulled his shoulders into the water. Ah, it was heaven. He would definitely have to look at the big cauldron and the sluice gates. The blacksmith at White Ford was quite talented and if Faulk could make decent enough drawings, the smith could probably build something similar. The idea of adding a bathhouse to his holding in Fallucia was very appealing. It was surprising that the primitive Rennish had come up with something his own countrymen hadn't thought of.

Anlin seemed to be dozing. She was short enough that she could have slipped below the water, but Faulk was sure she'd awaken if that happened, so he leaned his head back and joined her in completely relaxing. He wasn't sure if this was one of the "holy duties" mentioned on the doorframe, but it certainly brought joy.

Slowly the water began to cool. Faulk knew he should get out, but he felt practically boneless. With effort, he pulled himself to a sitting position, water sloshing around him. He was about to pull his legs under him when the voice behind him said, "You shouldn't be here."

Then everything happened at once. He swiveled toward the voice, Anlin screamed, and he thought *stupid, stupid* as he saw the blur of the log that connected with his temple and slipped him into blackness.

❧ 12 ❧

Anlin saw the movement from the corner of her eye. She screamed Faulk's name, but it was too late. As he started to rise from the trough, one of the four Rennish men who had sneaked up on them swung a large piece of wood and struck Faulk in the head. He immediately crumpled, sliding back into the water.

She attempted to get out of her own trough. Her foot slipped on the wooden bottom, which turned her leap into a lurching stumble. The Rennish man closest to her grabbed her and pulled her from the trough. He laughed at her slippery wetness and pulled her back tightly against him. "Look at the little fish I caught," he joked to the man nearest him.

Anlin feared that Faulk's head had slipped under the water. She struggled with her captor, calling out in Rennish, "Help him! He could drown. Help him!"

The man holding her nearly dropped her in his surprise that she spoke Rennish, but, responding to her plea, one of his companions grasped Faulk by the hair and pulled his head up. "We won't let him die, little fish.

Seerin Krisla will want to see both of you."

It took two of them to drag Faulk from the trough. They dumped him unceremoniously on the floor. He lay as if he were dead, but his chest moved as he took shallow breathes. Faulk at least lived. "I must help him," Anlin said, struggling to get away.

The man gripped her bruisingly. "He doesn't need your help. He'll wake up shortly with a sore head. There's nothing you can do for him until then."

The closest man nudged Faulk with his foot but got no response. "Why'd you have to hit him so hard, Soren?" he asked. "He's really heavy. How're we going to get him on a horse?"

"That's your problem," said the man holding Anlin. "I'll just take care of little fish." Then he started to move toward the door.

"Please, let me get dressed before I see this Seerin person." Soren, she thought. The man holding her was named Soren. And names in any culture had power. "Please, Soren." The man carrying her paused.

"She's right," said the man still poking at Faulk. "I don't think anyone will be impressed if we ride into Ridgemere with a naked female in tow. You know how the Seerin stress behaving properly before women. We don't need to cause any extra problems. We're going to have enough trouble trying to explain how two Fallucians got to the last guest house without our knowing."

Soren simply grunted, but he did slowly lower her

to the floor. He pushed her back until she leaned against one of the troughs. "Stay here and do not move. I'll bring you your clothes."

"Can't I see if my husband is all right?" Anlin moved in that direction.

He pushed her back with a swipe of his arm. Anlin was very conscious of her nakedness. "No! I said to stay where you are."

Anlin obeyed. With Faulk unconscious and possibly badly hurt, this wasn't the time to anger her captors. Faulk's total stillness worried her. Blood, oozed from the wound where he had been struck by the log and formed a sticky mass in his damp hair.

Soren dropped the pile of her clothing at her feet. "Here," he said. "Get dressed. But you needn't look for your knife." He smiled smugly. "I have it."

She instantly regretted the loss of the knife. It was the one she had used to kill Martic before her escape—the blade was so nicely sharp, slender, and flexible. Possession of the knife had made her feel more confident. It was a talisman that proved she had some control over her own destiny.

As Anlin slipped into her clothing, she tried to formulate some plan. The man said they would be taken to Ridgemere, which had been their intended destination, but she hadn't wanted to enter as a captive. Fortunately, none of the men treated her as if she were a Rennish slave. Her nakedness didn't excite them as it had her former owners. They seemed to see her as only some Fallucian woman. For the present, it would probably be best to assume the guise of traders and keep the search for her son to herself.

Two of the men had gone into the dormitory, intent on gathering up the belongings that Faulk had stacked there. From the excited tone of their indistinct voices, they had evidently discovered that many of the packs contained silver coins. Perhaps these men could be bribed.

With this in mind, Anlin took a careful look at her captors. All had the facial scars that indicated they were shamans, but they did not wear the normal, brown, shamanic robes. Instead, they were dressed in leather riding pants and loose, coarsely woven shirts. All were young and carried themselves in the manner of knights or men-at-arms. If there were a leader, she couldn't distinguish which he was.

"Are you shamans?" she asked Soren.

"No, little fish," he said. "We're Sentinels. We guard the paths to Ridgemere and answer only to the Seerin. We like to think we are more than shamans."

"But any shaman would tell you that we are less," said the man who was rolling Faulk up in a sheet that had been brought in from the dormitory. "We will have to put up with a good deal of derision from the shamans in residence in Ridgemere when we admit we were unable to sense your presence and didn't know you were here until we stumbled on your horses in the corral."

"Then don't admit it," Anlin said quickly. From his bitter tone, Anlin guessed the man wrapping Faulk was dissatisfied. If all the others shared his feelings, bribery seemed a real possibility. "I'm Anlin," she said, "and the injured man is my husband Faulk. We have come to trade with—" Sweet Cheelum, she hadn't thought this through. If they were traders they would have to trade with someone for something "—the Seerin," she continued, pulling the name or title from their conversation, hoping she'd guessed correctly.

"You're traders who are coming to Ridgemere to buy something from the Seerin?" Soren looked very skeptical.

"Yes, we've come into Rennic to trade. We have silver with us and could let you have a quarter of it if you'd just ride on and pretend you'd never come upon us. This way I could tend to my husband and then enter Ridgemere in a more dignified manner." Anlin tried to fill her voice with confidence.

The man bending over Faulk laughed. "We already have *all* your silver, little fish, so why would we want only a portion? And if this man is a trader, I'll dress in a gown the next time the husbands come and wait to be serviced. His shoulders are muscled like a man who habitually wears mail and his hands have the calluses of someone who wields a sword. I'm sure that Gerone and Cale have found both mail and a sword in the dormitory."

"Indeed, we did," came a voice from the door.

"There was a very nice sword and well-made mail. And packs of silver coins. I believe we've stumbled upon one of the Lords of High Places making an incursion into Rennic—an incursion to bribe someone to Fallucia's advantage. That could easily explain all the silver. Am I right, milady?" The man executed a surprisingly correct bow that still somehow conveyed sarcasm.

"She said they were traders who had come here to buy goods from the Seerin," Soren reported. The man who'd accused her of being a Fallucian agent broke into laughter that was echoed by the others.

Faulk had been completely wrapped in a sheet that had been tied tightly around him with linen strips. He looked like a corpse awaiting burial. Seeing that tightened Anlin's stomach more than the evident hostility all the Rennish were now projecting.

"I think you've come to spy and to buy information. You should have come up with a more plausible reason for being here, however. Any trader who knew what he was doing would have gone to Hightor. You could not have been here unless someone had already told you something you shouldn't know." Anlin had been looking for the leader of the group. With this speaker, she suspected she'd found him. She wished she knew if he were Gerone or Cale.

"We were lost in the rain." Anlin tried to stop the accusations with a partial truth. "We just came upon the track and followed it."

The leader crossed the room with quick strides and

hit her in the face, knocking her down. All the fear she'd known in Rennic came flooding back, the emotion more powerful for its having been absent for a time. Anlin sat on the bathhouse floor and tried to get her breath. She seemed to be smothering.

"Get that lying baggage on a horse," the leader said, motioning to Anlin. "I'll help load the man." Then, to her horror, he walked over and kicked Faulk in his shrouded head. "That should keep him out until we get to Ridgemere. Then he can explain to Seerin Krisla just what it is he plans to buy."

Anlin felt a sharp tug on her hair and stood to relieve the pain. Soren propelled her out into the night and the waiting horses. The men flopped Faulk over one of the packhorses like a sack of grain and tied his body to the saddle, where he hung unmoving. The forth Sentinel attempted to control an agitated Fiddian.

Fear curdled in Anlin's stomach and before she could mount, she emptied the contents of her stomach onto the ground. A return to servitude loomed before her. She had never felt so frightened and so alone.

≈•≪

Ridgemere was a surprise. They reached the city just as the sun broke above the mountains, and it was, indeed, a city. Compared to the squalid villages with which Anlin was familiar, Ridgemere might have existed in another country. Even Hightor, the large town everyone in Fallucia assumed was the country's capitol, could not compare. Straight, paved streets ran between rows of identical long, whitewashed buildings. Colorful, blooming flowers graced carefully tended gardens. Everything looked prosperous and, above all, clean.

The street they rode on terminated at a large paved circle. In the middle of the circle sat a huge version of the round dormitories she and Faulk had stopped at. Anlin realized that all the streets extended from this circle like the spokes of a wheel. The arrangement of both the beds in the dormitories and the troughs in the bathhouse had echoed the same pattern.

A veiled woman wearing a brown robe similar to that of a shaman met them before the main door as they clattered up. The man who had last kicked Faulk quickly dismounted and went to one knee before the woman. "Seerin," he said, bowing his head.

This behavior, a man subjugating himself in any way before a woman, was even more un-Rennish than Ridgemere itself was. Anlin could only stare in shock. In the ten years she had been in Rennic, other than the one Selector she'd spied, she had never seen a woman treated with anything other than disdain and contempt. Women were slaves, drudges, receptacles of lust to be used and ignored. But then, as she had told Faulk, she had never seen a wife—and Ridgemere was the home of all the wives. This was obviously a different world.

The man stood and conferred quietly with the veiled woman. Anlin was unable to make out what was being said, but the Sentinel appeared apologetic and the woman angry. With an exclamation of "Now," the woman turned and disappeared back into the building.

The man ran his hand through his hair in frustration and faced the still mounted Sentinels. "Take the man to the cells and bring the woman into the waiting room," he said. "I'm to report directly to Seerin Krisla." He then followed the veiled woman into the building.

Soren dismounted and unceremoniously hauled her from her horse. She only had a brief glimpse of Faulk's shrouded form still lying limply across the packhorse before she was dragged through the door.

A long and opulent hallway opened before her. The walls were hung with colorful tapestries depicting forest scenes. Anlin only had quick impressions of her surroundings, however, as her escort hurried her along the corridor until another hallway bisected it. This passage was narrower and lacked decoration. She was shoved into the first door they came to.

"Wait here," the man said before spinning on his heel and departing.

The room she entered could have been found in any manor house or castle in Fallucia with the exception that it was smaller, but it was equally well appointed. Two nicely carved chairs flanked a cold fireplace. On the right, a small table held a collection of pottery resplendent with an odd, iridescent blue glaze. A large window opened into a circular courtyard surrounded by a covered walkway.

Through this window, Anlin thought she heard the laughter and happy shouts of children, but when she looked out to investigate, none were in sight. There was some movement on the far side of the courtyard, but the angle of the rising sun left that area in deep shadow, and she was only able to make out a robed form, evidently either a shaman or one of these Seerin.

Anlin felt adrift. Nothing in her surroundings seemed consistent with the Rennic she knew. She had never heard of Seerin, although the veiled form reminded her of the Selector she had once glimpsed who came to choose those who would be honored as husbands. Perhaps these Seerin were female shamans. If so, they must wield their own form of power.

She heard the door open behind her and turned to face it. A veiled woman entered. She was obviously not the one who had spoken with the Sentinels being bulkier and slower moving. The woman stopped and stared, as if imprinting Anlin's image on her memory. Then she walked to one of the two chairs and sat down.

"Please be seated and we will talk," the woman said, motioning to the other chair. Her voice was both calm and commanding. Almost without thought, Anlin did as she was bid.

The woman detached her veil and let it fall to one side. Her face was as round as the moon in full, her eyes Rennish dark. She was definitely not young, but it was difficult to tell her age since corpulence had smoothed out any wrinkles and added extra chins. Anlin's first impression was of a benign grandmother or an inquisitive young babe. There was something unforgiving about the woman, however, that belied this initial supposition.

"I'm Seerin Krisla," the woman said, "and if you will allow me to touch you, we can eliminate a number of questions and erase your need for creative lies."

The Seerin stretched out her hand. Without Anlin willing it, her own hand joined with the Seerin's. Anlin felt a tingle run up her arm, more irritating than painful, as if a hundred flies crawled from her wrist to her shoulder. The woman held the contact for a breathless moment and then dropped Anlin's hand.

Seerin Krisla smiled, the look of the doting grandmother returning. "Thank you. That was an easy way to eliminate the basis of Sentinel Cale's fantastic tale. He would have it that you and your companion were Fallucian spies come to suborn someone here in Ridgemere, preferably a shaman."

She laughed although Anlin could not see the joke. "I sense nothing deceitful within you. I can find no unknown magical ability that would allow you to shield yourselves from the Sentinels' questing. On the contrary, I find you totally devoid of magic, an unusual occurrence for anyone in the upper classes of Fallucian society. Cale is correct in one assessment, however; you are from the family of a lord. There is no way that you have come into Rennic for trade. What is your purpose in coming to Ridgemere?"

Anlin wished she could conjure one of the creative lies the Seerin said she would have no need of, but nothing came to mind. The truth seemed the best approach. She and Faulk had come in good faith. They had not planned to kill or steal. They truly were here for trade. But before she could begin her explanation, her greatest worry burst from her lips. "Does my husband live?"

"Yes. I don't believe he has taken any permanent harm. The chief shaman currently interrogates him. It would be advantageous to both of you if you gave the same reasons for being here, however. Telling me the truth would be best."

Anlin realized she had told more of the truth than she'd anticipated with her question. Her first concern had been Faulk. Not Telm. Not the son of her heart. Not the purpose of their journey. But Faulk. There was an unreality to the realization.

"I am Anlin, daughter of Lord Philip Giffard, wife of Faulk of White Ford. For ten years, I was held in Rennic as a slave. During that time, I had a son, a son who was taken from me. My husband and I came to Rennic to find this son and to redeem him with the coin we carried. We were told that he was now in Ridgemere, and we paid someone to put us on the right course. So, your Sentinel was correct in his assumption that we had indeed bribed people, but that had not been our original intent. We wanted only to find my child."

"Your explanation brings up other questions,"

Seerin Krisla said. "How did you happen to be enslaved here when you obviously belong to the family of one of the Lords of High Places? It is our habit to ransom such people."

Anlin couldn't keep the bitterness from entering her words and she glared at the Seerin. "No one would believe me. My sister was ransomed, and I was abandoned. I do not have fond memories of my time here in Rennic."

Seerin Krisla dropped her eyes. "No, I would imagine your memories are not good ones." She shrugged. "But such is the lot of those whom the Goddess does not mark as wives. All women are made in her image, but not all are given the divine spark. Without this spark of magic, these women are nothing but husks, not worthy of consideration. They are only soulless beasts, but such women understand their place in the world.

"Since you are Fallucian, you lack this understanding. Perhaps on the next turn of the wheel you will be granted the boon of the Goddess's magical spark, but only if your life during this turn is exemplary. People are allotted a place in this life based on how they have lived previously. It is easy for us to tell which ones deserve praise and which disdain."

Her face took on a mournful cast. "But in Fallucia this truth has been forgotten. Instead, the Lords of High Places try to keep all the magic for themselves and a few of their retainers. The common people are never allowed the possibility of bettering their next life. Fallucia has lost the Wheel of the World and looks instead to the sky god you call Cheelum.

"We long ago realized that we could not save Fallucia from error. We have not the strength of numbers to overpower you. Our magic cannot overcome the Fallucian version that has become twisted from hoarding it within select families. All we Rennish can hope for is to hold enough power to be left in peace to worship the Goddess in truth."

"How can you say this?" Anlin asked heatedly. "Fallucia has never attacked Rennic. Instead, it is Rennic that raids along our borders. Yes, magic resides most often in the Baronial families, but I am a good example that this is not always the case."

"Yes, and the only man your family could find to mate with you was another who is bereft of magic. Is that not true?"

"No, it is not true," said Anlin, her anger rising. But a small voice whispered that there was truth in what the Seerin said. Anlin knew she would have not been a marital prize, that she would have married some lesser noble had she not been a captive in Rennic all those years. She often wondered if it was this lack of value that had left her to her fate instead of being ransomed or rescued.

But long ago the hurt had changed to anger. "How can you say that Fallucia is twisted when the Rennish treat half their population as 'soulless beasts,' when you separate husbands and wives and allow only limited visitation. This is a sickness. This is a nightmare existence." She found herself breathless. Fury beat in her veins for all that she had endured.

Seerin Krisla gave Anlin a benign smile. It was the look an indulgent mother gave a child who was throwing a tantrum. "You think our system supports a nightmare existence? Hardly. You think you are a wife, but does your husband come to you in prayerful joy or does he just desire to rut like a beast? All men will rut. It is the nature of the male."

"As the Rennish men I've known have proved," Anlin interjected with heat.

The Seerin chose to ignore her outburst. "But to join with one's wife, to fulfill a sacred duty to provide seed for a vessel into which a magical soul can reside, this is something far different from simple rutting. From childhood, Rennish males are trained to know the difference in these activities and to act accordingly. Men are supplied slaves to use to accommodate these base instincts and to keep their seed strong for a holy mating."

"You are sick to condone such behavior, much less to train men to behave in this manner." Anlin knew her anger and disgust were compelling her to give opinions she should keep to herself, but she seemed unable to control her speech.

"And now that you are a Fallucian wife, is your sexual congress so different from what you experienced in Rennic? I think not." The Seerin made her pronouncement with complete confidence of her correctness. "All rutting will produce children, but few will produce a vessel that can hold the divine spark. Such children generally come from those who are already blessed. That is why the wives live pampered lives in Ridgemere. That is why their husbands are carefully chosen. And that is why it is doubtful that any son of yours would be in this city."

"But I was told that he was here. I was told that he was *traked* and was brought to Ridgemere..." Anlin felt she was swimming against a powerful current, that her words made little impression on the Seerin.

"It is true that we bring those who have a glimmering of Fallucian magic here," Seerin Krisla said. "We do not want the odd spark scattered in our population. If this is indeed the case, your son would have been given some menial position," she suddenly smiled, "and if so, we would probably release him to you for the appropriate amount of money. We really don't want him. His removal to Ridgemere was a protective measure. What is your son's name?"

The seed of hope Anlin had long nourished began to bloom. "His name is Telm. At least I called him Telm. He was taken from me while I lived in Chirlon."

Seerin Krisla's complacent expression vanished to be replaced with one of surprise. "Your son is Telm? No, there must be some mistake."

"Why?" Do you know of him?"

"Of course, I know him, or, at least, I know of a boy named Telm. But I don't believe he is *your* son. He has just received his first mark. The youngest of the acolytes to do so. Callip says he is destined for much power. He cannot be yours."

"Is he about seven years old? My Telm would be that age. He has a birthmark in the shape of an oak leaf on the inside of his thigh." Anlin prayed to whatever god might be present, *Please let it be him. Please.*

The Seerin shook her head. "No, I do not think that this is possible. But I would know nothing of a birthmark. The boys are under the control of the Shamans. The Telm I know is being taught by the Chief Shaman, Callip."

"Where is he? Can I see him? I'm sure he would still know me."

"I can only hope that this is not the case." Seerin Krisla said. "But such a mystery needs to be unraveled for the good of our community. Callip is currently with the man you call husband, and Telm should be with him. Come!"

With surprising grace, the heavy woman stood and walked to the door. Anlin stayed right behind her.

Joy! *This* feeling was joy. Telm was here. It had nothing to do with what went on between men and women, regardless of how sure the Seerin was that this was the case.

❧ 13 ❧

Faulk realized he was cold. He reached for the blanket that must have slipped off. The clanking of metal on stone brought him to full awareness. He was lying on his stomach on a stone floor. He pushed himself to his hands and knees, the motion making his head pound and his stomach revolt. A chain attached to a shackle on his right wrist slithered noisily across the floor as he tried for better balance.

Memory came flooding back to him in disgusting detail. He remembered the bathhouse, remembered his lack of caution and preparedness. "Stupid, stupid," he muttered as he swayed on all fours, closing his eyes in an attempt to stop the world from spinning.

He stayed in this position for minutes, hours—time seemed both compressed and stretched. Finally, his stomach stilled and the shooting pain in his skull receded to a dull ache. His failure to anticipate what had happened filled him with shame. Anlin's scream still echoed in his mind. He was conscious of his nakedness, chained like an animal in a pit.

He suspected that coming to a full up-right position was beyond him, so he pushed back on his hands and rocked back on his legs until he was sitting with his legs jutting out in front of him.

It was then he saw the boy squatting at a distance.

"Are you chosen of the sky god?" the boy asked. The cadence was unusual, but the words were definitely Fallucian.

Faulk shook his head and squinted his eyes to better see the speaker in the gloom. The area Faulk sat in was barely illuminated by some guttering torches high up on the wall, but he could tell that the speaker was a boy, all bony legs and arms with a Rennish face, slightly misshapen. "There is no sky god," Faulk said, his voice grated like a rusty gate.

"There's Cheelum," the boy said.

"He's just God." Faulk could make no sense of this conversation. His head ached like he'd consumed an entire cask of ale. He wasn't in the mood for a theological debate.

The boy chuckled. "The Seerin are right. Fallucians have forgotten." The boy came to his feet with the speed of a released hare. He warily kept his distance from Faulk but walked in a circle around him. Faulk tracked the boy with his eyes, eventually having to turn his head and look over his shoulder.

"If you're not chosen by your God, then why are you so marked?"

Faulk realized the boy was referring to the scars

that crisscrossed his back. In different circumstances, Faulk would have found the boy's observations ironic. The abbot who had wielded the scourge that had disfigured his back had done so because Cheelum had *not* chosen him. "Could I have some water?" Faulk asked, speaking of a need rather than the former ridiculousness.

"Oh, yes," said the boy, who darted away. He returned with a wooden bowl that he placed on the ground at a distance.

Faulk assumed the bowl now sat within the range of his chain, but just barely. "I'm unable to stand. I can crawl, but that is without dignity. Could you bring the water closer?"

The boy took a cautious step toward him and pushed the bowl forward with his foot. He repeated this, always prepared for flight, until the water sat a long arm's length away. Then he shuffled back and again squatted, his bright eyes watching Faulk as a sparrow might watch a snake. Now that he was closer, Faulk could see that the boy's face was swollen on one side, his cheek puffed out around what looked to be a cut gone septic. Did the Rennic know nothing about the care of wounds? Even a small cut could kill if left unattended.

Faulk leaned forward and grasped the lip of the bowl. The movement brought the pain back to his head, but his first sip of water made it worth it. The finest wine had not tasted as sweet. He wondered how long he had been insensate. He was not hungry, but his thirst had been strong.

"How long have I been here?" he asked.

"Since early this morning. The Sentinels brought you and a woman to Ridgemere at first light this morning." A smile flickered on the boy's face, but it was slight and quickly gone, as if he knew not to stretch his swollen cheek. "The Seerin Krisla is very angry. I'm sorry that I was not there when she spoke with the Sentinels. The Sentinels are always so..." he stopped as if groping for the right word, "puffed up—like a toad. It would have been interesting to see Seerin Krisla flay them with her tongue. You should not have gotten so close without their knowing. Did you use the sky magic to hide you?"

"I have no magic," Faulk said. "Nor does the woman with me. Perhaps that is why you didn't notice us. Where is the woman now?"

"No sky magic?" the boy shook his head, looking disappointed. "The woman is with the Seerin, of course."

There was something about the way the boy held himself, the way he turned his head, that was familiar to Faulk. Suspicion grew. "How do you know Fallucian?"

The boy shrugged. "I've always known it. Callip makes me practice. He and I talk in Fallucian often, but it is good for me to talk to those who actually live there. I do it when the Lord comes to visit the Seerin. But he is not here, so now I've come to practice with you. I speak it well, don't I?" There was a great deal of pride evident in the last question. The Sentinels were not the only people capable of being puffed up.

Taking a chance, Faulk replied, "Yes, Telm, you speak Fallucian very well."

The boy shot to his feet and shuffled backwards. His eyes were wide with fear. "You *do* have the sky magic. You have stolen my name from my mind." He then turned and fled.

Faulk sat, occasionally taking a drink of water. He shivered. He should have asked for his clothes or, perhaps better yet, a quilt, before frightening the boy away. Of course, he hadn't expected that to happen. He hadn't foreseen consequences very well since he rode into this cursed country. He felt his lips twist up in dark humor. He hadn't even actually ridden in. He'd arrived pushed by a run-away horse. Anlin had accepted him as husband primarily to have a protector on this journey. He wondered if she felt cheated.

But at least he now knew that Telm was alive. He'd found the boy. Or, more accurately, the boy had found him. Faulk hoped that Anlin had seen him, for all the good that would do them. Whoever ran Ridgemere—the Seerin or the Sentinels or someone unknown—now had both of them and the silver they'd hoped to trade for Telm. He couldn't see the Rennish exchanging the boy for coin they already possessed. He couldn't see the three of them happily riding out of here and back into Fallucia.

Impotence ate at him. As much as he tried, he just couldn't retain control of his own fate. Some person or some happenstance always seemed to have a leash on him. He jerked at the physical chain that now bound him. He achieved nothing but a sore wrist for his efforts.

The boy was evidently not returning. Faulk was cold and his head still felt as if it were stuffed with a hive of bees, buzzing and stinging. He lay back down on the stone floor. He again wished he'd asked for a quilt, imagined pulling one around him. Perhaps he slept and woke and slept. Time continued to be elastic.

And then there were footsteps. He pushed himself back to a sitting position, found his head no longer spun, and staggered to his feet. He would be standing to meet whoever now came to view the animal chained in a pit.

It was a Rennish man dressed in a brown robe. He was slender and graying at the temples. Four parallel scar lines decorated each cheek and one crossed his forehead like a bolt of lightning. He stopped and observed Faulk in silence. Faulk felt the power of his scrutiny like a blow.

"The boy was wrong," the man finally said. "You are not *traked*."

"No," said Faulk. "I've no magic at all. If I had, I would not be naked and cold and chained."

The man raised his eyebrows. "That is not necessarily true, but I can do something about your being cold and naked. The chained part... well, we will see."

He turned and left, his footsteps echoing in the gloom. Faulk wavered on his feet, but was loath to sit down again, not wanting to be in a subordinate position. If the man didn't return quickly, however, Faulk suspected that he would fall down and it wouldn't matter. He was relieved to hear someone returning.

The man reappeared, followed by Telm. The man carried two stools, and the boy held a brown robe over one arm while his hand clutched boots that looked suspiciously like Faulk's own. Stopping some distance away, the man asked, "If the boy brings you clothes, will you injure him?"

"Of course not!" What type of person did they think him to be that they thought he might harm a child?

The man motioned Telm forward. The boy approached skittishly but placed the rough brown robe in Faulk's open hands and dropped the boots near his feet. Once the clothing was in his possession, however, Faulk saw an immediate problem. He shook his wrist, making the chair rattle. "I won't be able to get this on because of the shackle," he said.

The man smiled, the lines of his face folding into the habitual creases of someone who smiles often. "Poor planning on my part. Telm, give us more light."

"I, eh..." the boy looked uncertain.

"You've earned your first mark," the man said impatiently. "Do it!"

Telm's face became a mask of concentration—and the flames in the torches leaped up as if oil had been added to a lamp. Faulk was surprised. This was magic as practiced by only the most Talented of the Lords. He'd been told that the Rennish hated all magic. It all made no sense.

"Thank you," the man said. Then he turned to Faulk. "This is how it will be. I'll bring you this stool and release your wrist shackle so you can put your arm into the robe. Then I'll reattach the shackle. You will not attack me or make any attempt to escape. If you do, I will give you pain. Do you understand?"

"Yes," Faulk said, thinking that the man wasn't very big and should be easy to overpower. He regretted that to escape, he would probably have to knock Telm unconscious so the boy wouldn't call out when Faulk took him. Faulk didn't know where he was being kept and hadn't any weapons, but if he were free and had the boy, other possibilities might present themselves. He tried to relax his posture and appear non-combative.

The older man approached and placed the stool near Faulk's legs. He then reached for Faulk's wrist, and with what seemed to be the slightest touch, the clasp fell open. Faulk slowly pulled the sleeve of the robe onto his arm and then continued the motion more rapidly, powerfully striking the smaller man in the middle of his chest.

It had been Faulk's intent to follow up his first punch with another to the man's face. This never occurred. Instead of falling back and gasping for breath from the first blow, the man calmly grabbed Faulk's extended arm—and Faulk felt as if he were suddenly on fire. Invisible flames flashed up his arm and wrapped around his torso with excruciating pain. Faulk was unable to take enough breath to support the scream that was echoing in his head. He felt his skin crisp, his muscles contract.

The man almost gently released his arm, and Faulk collapsed to the floor, rolling himself into a ball and cradling his arm against his chest. He now relished the coldness of the stone floor that helped extinguish the flickering agony that still moved over him.

The man nudged Faulk with his foot. "Get up and put the rest of the robe on. Then sit on the stool. Stop being foolish." His voice sounded almost tired.

"Why would he try to attack you?" Telm quietly asked. "Did he not see your marks?"

"He doesn't know or understand." The man hooked the second stool with his foot and pulled it toward him. "Fallucian magic is corrupted sky magic and is tightly held by only a few families who call themselves the Lords of High Places. These families simultaneously brag of their abilities and disguise what they can really do. Fallucians are not honest enough to wear their Talents on their faces as we do."

The man settled down onto his stool with a soft sigh. "Come on Fallucian," he said. "What happened was painful but not really injurious. Pull yourself together."

As the man spoke, Faulk had been slowly getting to his feet and tying the front of his robe. It was easy for someone who had not felt the flaring pain of being burned to say that no damage had been done.

Remembered pain still flickered across Faulk's skin. There were no burns or blisters in evidence, however.

Faulk lowered himself onto the stool he'd been given and stared at the scarred Rennish face that was glaring at him. Telm crouched to one side, his expression only inquisitive.

"My name is Callip. I am the Chief Shaman in all of Rennic. This line," he motioned to the jagged scar across his forehead, "proclaims that I have power beyond all others. Only the foolish defy me. Tell me, Fallucian, are you a foolish man?"

"No." Faulk hated that this word came out as a croak. "I am Faulk of White Ford," he said more steadily, "and I am generally not a foolish man."

"Good. Then I will not need to replace your shackle."

The two men observed one another and the silence lengthened. Finally, Callip asked, "Why have you come to Rennic, and more especially, what has brought you to Ridgemere?"

"The boy," Faulk said, nodding toward Telm. "My lady wife and I have come to find her son Telm and return him to her. We have brought money to buy him."

"No," Telm moaned, the word stretched out as long as a breath. The boy paled, bringing the injury to his cheek into stark relief.

Simultaneously, Callip said, "Telm is not for sale. He is not a slave." He dropped a hand to the boy's shoulder in a movement that was both reassuring and possessive.

Anger surged through Faulk, extinguishing any of the residual tingling in his skin. He felt his muscles tighten. To have found the boy and then be thwarted called for direct action. He wanted to grab Telm and run, but he knew now that Callip was not a man to cross. Faulk was definitely *not* a foolish man. He could learn and learn quickly. He remained seated.

"Do you say this because you already have the silver we brought in your possession?" he asked. "You say that Telm is not a slave, and yet, just by looking at his face, I can see he's been abused. His mother and I can offer him a place in Fallucia where he will have opportunity and not be abused."

Callip barked a laugh. "No one would abuse Telm here. He has a place of honor among those who study to be a shaman. He is my own acolyte. He has recently won his first mark, unusual for one so young. His face was cut and the incision packed with clay to insure a proud scar. Many more will be added. He has somehow combined both Rennish earth magic and Fallucian sky magic. The day will come when he exceeds even me."

Callip brushed back the hair of the still pale boy, an affectionate gesture. Telm said something emphatic in Rennish that Faulk couldn't understand.

"What did he say?"

Callip looked somewhat embarrassed. "He asked that he not be sent away with a Fallucian whore."

Involuntarily, Faulk came to his feet. The stool fell over with a bang behind him. It took all his control not to strike Telm, but memory of the licking flames held him in place. "His mother is not a whore." With difficulty, he kept from shouting. "Against her will she was enslaved and forced to behave in a despicable way. The fault lies with you Rennish and your sick society, not with Anlin." He was trembling with his effort to control himself.

Callip, damn him, remained relaxed and seated. He sadly shook his head. "Our sick society didn't mark your back. I'm sure your scars were given to you in Fallucia. Obviously, you know a lot about abuse. You're completely a product of your own culture and from the appearance of your back, that isn't much to brag about. Fallucia is corrupt in every way. Your countrymen come here to Ridgemere to trade your country's secrets for bits and pieces of our magic, which they can then use against those in power in Fallucia. We, at least, don't harm our own."

"You don't harm your own? That's ridiculous. Most of your slaves are Rennish, not Fallucian. You unnaturally separate husbands and wives. The bulk of your people live in squalor, eking out a living that is barely at the subsistence level."

Faulk took a breath to continue his tirade, and Callip calmly inserted, "You're certainly not an expert on things Rennish. All you have done is ride though a small portion of the country, most of it on the forbidden way to Ridgemere. You know nothing."

Both men stilled at the sound of people

approaching. A woman dressed in the ubiquitous brown robe entered the circle of light. Directly behind her came Anlin. Faulk was relieved to see that she was in no way harmed. Anlin let her gaze roam over Faulk, but when her eyes came to rest on the boy, she stopped, transfixed.

As the women approached, Callip and Telm immediately came to their feet and just as quickly dropped to one knee with their heads bowed. "Seerin Krisla," Callip said.

Telm reached up and tugged on Faulk's hand, trying to draw him down as well. Faulk resisted the pull. He certainly wasn't going to bow. He looked the woman full in the face.

She didn't display the scars that evidently indicted magical power, but power seemed to emanate from her nonetheless. Her face was a smooth and round as a baby's. Her eyes sparkled with intelligence, and she observed Faulk carefully. She looked surprised by what she saw.

"You have your mother's eyes," the Seerin said to Faulk.

Faulk felt as if he'd been hit in the gut. His *mother's* eyes? No, that was wrong. Faulk had always been sure he looked like his father. He'd seen the same eyes in Abbot Jezrel's face, the same eyes that were awash with insanity as the man applied the scourge. If the abbot were not his father, then who was this unknown woman whose eyes he was supposed to have? And more importantly, how could this woman in Rennic have any information about his parentage at all?

"You have the better of me, milady," Faulk said with a slight bow of his head that might suggest some veneration if she chose to see it that way. "I don't know who my mother or father were, but I doubt that you would have this knowledge either."

She reached out and touched Faulk lightly on the temple. His flesh tingled where her fingers lay. "Anlin calls you Faulk, but I did not think you were our Faulk."

"*Your* Faulk? I'm not Rennish."

"Of course, you're not. You're Fallucian on both sides. Your mother was Lettice of Graymont. She came across the border to escape the wrath of her brother Jezrel, and when she indicated she had the Refuge Fees, the Sentinels brought her here. She had rejected the suitor her brother recommended and had found love with another man. When she arrived in Ridgemere, she was pregnant by her lover, who, unfortunately, had long been married to someone else. She believed her brother would kill her to erase the family shame. She was not the first high-born Fallucian woman to seek shelter here with the wives."

"Does my mother still live?" The whole scenario was so different from what Faulk believed that it seemed impossible. But it did explain why he resembled Abbot Jezrel. If what Seerin Krisla said was true, the man was his uncle. If his mother had fled Jezrel, however, Faulk couldn't understand why she would have sent her son to be raised by him.

"Your mother died shortly after your birth," the Seerin said. "When she arrived here, she was worn and frail from her journey and never fully recovered, although we gave her the best of care. One of our many mothers suckled you. By the time you were weaned, it was obvious your mother's powerful magical ability had passed you by, and there was no place for you at Ridgemere. We contacted your father, and he came for you. He should have told you this long ago."

"I was raised by Abbot Jezrel at Jarburgh Abbey," Faulk said. "From what you said, Abbot Jezrel must be my uncle."

Seerin Krisla abruptly turned away from Faulk and began pacing, nearly tripping over the kneeling Callip and Telm. "No, that can't be right. Lord Tarn came for you. He said he would raise you with his other sons, Euthic and Edmund. We would have never given you into the care of Jezrel."

"Well, that is what happened." Faulk choked the words out. His mind was racing. The late Lord Tarn had been his father? He shared a father with Euthic and Edmund Tarn? He knew both of them, as men rather than boys, but as bad as his life had been at Jarburgh, he suspected that had he been raised as a bastard son, with those two as his legitimate brothers, his life would have been worse.

Seerin Krisla continued her agitated pacing. "You should have not been taken to Jezrel. When your mother paid the Refuge Fee, assurances were given to her that if something happened to her, her child would be given to its father. When Lord Tarn came for you, he agreed to give you a good life."

She stopped and looked Faulk directly in the face. Her expression was one of sympathy overlaid with anger. Faulk hoped the sympathy was directed toward him and the anger elsewhere. While she lacked Callip's distinguishing scars, Faulk realized this woman was undoubtedly the shaman's equal in power.

"We did not cast you upon the wind," she said. "We honored our Refuge commitment and have monitored your life. We were told you had been knighted, that you were a trusted advisor first to Euthic, and after his death, to Edmund. We understood that you had been given a large holding and had married an heiress." The anger than had been shimmering suddenly burst through. "We've had a special relationship with the Tarns ever since you were given over to them. Are you telling me that all we've heard is a lie?"

"Much of what you've been told has come to pass," said Faulk, "but it had nothing to do with any of the Tarn family. If anything, they have made my life more difficult and were instrumental in destroying Philip Lealand, one of the best men I've ever known."

The Seerin said something in Rennish that brought Callip to his feet. The two of them then began an intense discussion, none of which was decipherable to Faulk, but which obviously became heated. Telm continued to kneel, but he looked up at the speakers, his expression bleak. He slowly shook his head back and forth in denial.

Faulk turned to Anlin to see if she could give him any clue about what was being said. She ignored Faulk and continued to gaze at the boy, her sober expression slowly turning to a smile.

From the moment she'd seen him, Anlin had known the boy was Telm. *Her Telm*. Oh, his face had lost the round look of a baby; it was angular and hinted at a handsomeness she had not anticipated. He was also much taller than she remembered, but the eyes were the ones that had looked into hers with such trust, the hair that curled around the shells of his ears was the same, and the way he held his head had not changed.

The angry discussion between the Shaman and the Seerin washed over her as she looked for one distinguishing characteristic after another. It was only when she noticed her son's concern that she paid attention to what the two Rennish were saying. And what she heard brought a smile to her lips.

Seerin Krisla and the Shaman were both angry with Lord Tarn. In the Seerin's case, furious would be a better description. On this issue, they were in accord. They differed on what to do about Telm, however.

"What happened to Faulk is a stain on our honor," the Seerin said. "I promised his mother he would be cared for. You've told me of the condition of his back. That was not care. That was the brutal legacy of a god-mad man whose very existence, it could be argued, can also be laid at our feet. I can think of no other recompense except to let him take the boy with him."

"Unacceptable!" The Shaman's voice rose in volume in counterpoint to the Seerin's measured tones. "It is unacceptable to pay for some past mistake, which was really not of our making, with the abandonment of Telm."

"He would not be abandoned. He would be given into his mother's care."

"And what makes you think that this care will be so different from that which was shown to your precious Faulk? The minute the Lords realize Telm's potential, they will seize him and attempt to corrupt his ability. This boy, grown to a man, is not a weapon I want to see turned against us."

"I do not see this happening," the Seerin said with infinite patience. "None of the Lords, or more importantly, their Talented women, have the ability to teach someone like Telm. Even you find Telm difficult to teach since Earth magic and Sky magic have been so entwined within him. They would simply be confused by him and would leave him alone."

"So, you counsel that Telm's amazing potential should be allowed to what? Molder? Run wild to whatever consequence?" Callip's voice held disgust.

"Some ability is already established. The boy will

always have that, and it will put him on the par with most of the most Talented in Fallucia. He will grow up as a Fallucian."

"Another improbability," the shaman said. "Will any in that benighted country ever look at him as anything other than Rennish? The cast of his features proclaims his mixed parentage. You would sentence Telm to a life of unhappiness and despair. For what purpose? To make amends for a mistake he had nothing to do with?"

"And we do not do that every day?" Seerin Krisla asked quietly. "We condemn many to unhappy lives. It is one of the responsibilities the Goddess places on us to balance our great ability. Your only problem here is that you personally know Telm. You like him. You see yourself in him. But personal considerations must be put aside when the honor of Rennic is involved."

"It is not Rennic's honor that is in question here. It is yours. You are the one who initially believed what you were told by Lord Tarn. You are the one who has continued to be hoodwinked by his son, the present Lord. You are asking Telm to pay the price of your mistakes."

"Callip, how dare you impugn my motives? It is I and the other Seerin who must act as Selectors, who are faced year in and year out with the hard decisions, who see the misery that lies beyond the gates of Ridgemere while you hide within." Seerin Krisla's volume had risen to match the Shaman's so the two were close to yelling at each other. As if she suddenly became conscious of their audience, she lowered her voice and said, "This is a discussion for another time. It is approaching mid-day, and I'm sure we all would like to eat."

She turned to a perplexed Faulk and said in Fallucian, "I will have decisions and apologies to make to you shortly, but for now, I will have someone guide you to one of the wives' rooms. There you and Anlin may rest. Food will be brought to you. I will meet with you before dark." Then she swept from the room.

"Come Telm," Callip said and moved to follow the Seerin.

Anlin reached out and stopped the boy as he attempted to brush by her. His shoulder felt bony under her hand. Did they not feed him well? He looked up at her through eyelashes that sparkled with tears. His cheek was inflamed where the scarring would take place. Telm's sweet, beautiful face had been mutilated. Tears filled her eyes also. "Do you know who I am?" she asked gently.

"You're the Fallucian slave who took care of me when I was a boy," Telm said without inflection.

His words hurt her, but she wanted to tell him that he was still a boy. She wanted to hug him. Instead she stayed frozen and said, "I'm your mother."

"So Callip has said." Then he tried to push past her. She tightened her grip and held him firm.

"Don't you remember how we used to cuddle in the bed? It was so warm and comfortable with you asleep in my arms. Don't you remember the red cloth ball I made you just before you were taken away? We would throw it back and forth in the yard."

Telm shifted from foot to foot and looked away from Anlin. "I remember all that. But now, I have my own bed, and the room has a brazier, so I'm never cold. And I've out-grown the need for baby toys. I have all I need."

Anlin released his shoulder, and he scuttled out of the room. This was not how she'd imaged her reunion with Telm. Her heart ached with love for him, and he seemed completely indifferent. No, this was worse than indifference. "He hates me," she said.

"What are you saying," Faulk asked from across the room. Anlin realized she had being speaking Rennish. In fact, mostly Rennish had been spoken since she walked into this cell. Faulk probably had no idea what was going on.

"That was Telm," she said. There was no reason to again express her fear that her son hated her. It was bad enough that she knew.

"Yes, I know. He was here when I regained consciousness."

"Oh, Sweet Cheelum, I didn't even ask how you were. I was worried when the Sentinels kept hitting you in the head to keep you unconscious. I was afraid you'd never wake up."

He smiled slightly. "Maybe I did take too many blows to the head. I have no idea who these Sentinels are, except that Telm seemed delighted they might be in trouble. Evidently there is some sort of friction between these Sentinels and the Shamans, and Telm identifies with the latter group."

"He does. He's the Chief Shaman's acolyte. And he hates the idea of leaving here and coming back to Fallucia with us. I think he, oh hell, I think he hates me as well," she forced out. And then the tears that had been threatening burst forth, along with great staccato sobs she couldn't control.

Even during her worst experiences as a slave, she had never felt this bereft of hope. She had had this dream, this unrealistic dream, of a happy life with the one person she loved unconditionally. But Telm didn't want her. He didn't want her at all.

Faulk was suddenly next to her, pulling her into his arms, her head nestled on his chest. The robe he wore felt scratchy and smelled odd, not like Faulk at all. But the solidness of the chest and the hand gently patting her back were all Faulk. Instead of feeling constrained by his arms, she felt sheltered. She laid her head against him and cried tears that had been building in her for years. When the torrent had finally ceased, she just absorbed his warmth.

They were standing thus when a Seerin came to get them. It may have been the woman who had originally met them when they'd arrived, but her veil was in place and it was impossible to tell. She led them up stone stairs and through a door into bright sunlight, and then across the circular road to one of the long, white buildings. An inscription over the door once again proclaimed, "Holy duties bring joy." But this was no bathhouse. They entered a long, wide hallway with heavy doors spaced at intervals along it.

Their guide stopped before one such door and entered it. "This is one of the wives' receiving rooms," the Seerin said. "Food and drink have been left for you on the chest. There is a lavatory through the door to the right. Seerin Krisla says for you to relax and refresh. Someone will come for you in a few hours."

Then she bowed to them slightly and left, closing the door firmly behind her.

Anlin looked around the chamber. It was opulent, perhaps bordering on decadent. A brassier sat in one corner, making the room comfortably warm. The same subtle aroma she had smelled in the bathhouse came from it. A large, thick tapestry, filled with a pattern of vines and leaves, lay on the floor.

The vine pattern was repeated in the heavily embroidered bed hangings that surrounded a massive bed. On the bed was a cover made of furs stitched into wide stripes of fawn and white. To one side was a round table with two cushioned chairs. Near it was a tall chest on which sat bowls and dishes of the same iridescent blue pottery that Anlin had seen in the waiting room where she had met with Seerin Krisla. And from these bowls issued tantalizing smells.

Anlin's stomach growled. "I'm eating before I do anything else." She looked at Faulk. "Don't you want some?"

"In a minute," he said. The one discordant item in the room had snagged his eyes. One of their packs lay near the door to the lavatory.

He walked over and squatting, opened the pack. "Only clothes," he said. "Some of yours and some of mine. Obviously repacked. But I could do with something clean." He shook out his good, green tunic. "Maybe this lavatory is a miniature bathhouse. I could use that as well." Carrying clothes in his hand, he disappeared through the door.

Anlin uncovered the bowls to find what looked like pieces of chicken covered in a savory sauce and some sort of fruit compote. Both steamed with enticing fragrances. She immediately filled a plate, sat at the table, and began to eat. The flavors were superb. She'd certainly never had anything like this the whole time she'd been in Rennic. Nor could she remember such interesting fare being offered at her father's well-supplied board.

She was well on her way to vanquishing her hunger when Faulk reappeared. His hair was damp, and he had on the moss-colored tunic he'd worn at their wedding. A razor must not have been included in their pack, however, since his face still wore a deep-red stubble.

"That place is amazing," he said, crossing the room. "It has the same basic set-up as the bathhouse, but on a smaller scale. There's a little cauldron with a spigot, and when you turn it, heated water flows out into a bowl.

It's really ingenious. And under the privy hole, there's running water, almost like an irrigation channel."

Anlin could feel his enthusiasm and delight. She had to smile at him. His enthusiasms always dealt with improvements he could make to White Ford. "And what took you so long in there was trying to figure out exactly how everything worked. Am I right?"

Faulk looked embarrassed. "Yeah, I thought it was something that could easily be added to White Ford. I can't imagine how the same country can have the hovels we saw in the countryside and villages and the luxuries that are here in Ridgemere. It's like two different worlds."

As if to prove his point, Faulk placed a Tremellian glass in front of her. Anlin knew how costly and fragile they were. "You forgot to get some wine," Faulk said and turned to fill a plate of his own.

"It is a different world," Anlin said, "and it must cost a great deal to support this luxury. This might be the cause of the poverty of the rest of the country."

Faulk seated himself and began to eat. "But why would they do such a thing? The Seerin and the Shamans could live very well without building a whole city around them."

"I think this entire place is designed so the Rennish can breed more powerful magic," she said.

Faulk nodded. "I've been on the receiving end of that powerful magic. Callip touched me and I thought I had burst into flame. But that makes no sense since we've long thought that the Rennish hated magic of all kind. And I can't figure out how they could 'breed' for magic anyway."

Anlin raised a cynical eyebrow. She was quite sure Faulk understood the concept of the breeding part. "Well, I think the rumor they hate all magic is just misdirection so Fallucians didn't look too closely at what is happening just over their borders. And I think they truly do hate Fallucian magic…"

"Sky magic is what Callip called it," Faulk said.

"Really? Sky magic? How strange."

"And they think their magic is earth magic, although it seems to me that magic is magic."

"Maybe that's because neither of us has *any* type of magic," Anlin said. "Maybe if you wield it, there is a difference. Whatever type of magic the Rennish possess, however, they're trying to strengthen it by mating those who have it. That's where the selected husbands and wives come from. They're chosen for their magical ability, and it's evidently the hope of the Seerin and the Shamans that the children of these pairings will have even more concentrated magical Talent."

Faulk started to laugh. "Then this whole elaborate set-up, the entire city of Ridgemere, is really just a brothel. Oh, Sweet Cheelum, the sign 'Holy duties bring joy' now makes sense." He continued to laugh until he had tears in his eyes.

Anlin failed to see what was so funny. There was nothing humorous in the attitudes of the Rennish. "The women here are wives," she said more tartly than she wanted. "If there are any whores in Rennic, they are the slaves who certainly never have such comfortable surroundings. I found the philosophy so calmly espoused by Seerin Krisla to be disgusting." Then she told Faulk everything she'd learned in her discussion with the Seerin and what she'd overheard of the argument in Faulk's cell.

By the time she finished, Faulk had pushed his plate away and had poured them both more wine. "Drink some wine," he said. "It's quite good and from what you overheard, it seems we may have reason to celebrate. I think if Seerin Krisla and Callip disagree, Krisla will prevail. She was the one standing when Callip was on his knee."

He raised his glass in a salute, but his face remained serious. "I don't understand why the Seerin feels she has been dishonored because I was given to my uncle instead of being raised by Lord Tarn. I suspect that life would have been even more onerous. And I wouldn't have been rescued by Lealand if I'd been with Tarn. I doubt the Seerin realizes that she's given me a real gift by telling me that Abbot Jezrel is not my father. That's what I've long believed. Not that the having Lord Tarn as my father seems much better. I never really knew him, but his sons, who, Sweet Cheelum, are my half-brothers, are not men I admire."

Faulk smiled into his wine glass. "At least Tarn wasn't afflicted with the madness that often goes with a surfeit of magic in Fallucian males. Abbot Jezrel, I realized when I was grown, was quite mad."

Anlin had no idea what the Tarns were like, but she doubted Faulk's life would have been worse with them. She'd seen the ruin of Faulk's back. "Seerin Krisla must have promised your mother you'd have an easy life and feels guilty that you didn't. She evidently felt a bond with your mother, who must have had a great deal of magical ability to impress Krisla."

"And since I had none, I was given away as worthless." Faulk sounded more resigned than bitter.

Anlin didn't correct him. To be thought worthless was bad enough, but to be considered soulless, as Seerin Krisla believed those without magic to be, was worse. Anlin looked forward to leaving this cursed country, especially if Telm, no matter how reluctant, accompanied her.

She felt she could bring Telm back to her side, given time. If he were with her in Fallucia, she could rekindle all the old feelings that had been between them. She would make a happy life for him. She would! And she now believed that she would be taking him home with her.

There was a soft knock. Anlin came to her feet, but Faulk went before her to open the door. The younger Seerin stood there. "Seerin Krisla sends word that she will not be able to meet with you until tomorrow morning. You should be ready to travel then. I will bring more food and anything that will add to your comfort."

Anlin felt the blood drain from her face. "They're not going to let Telm go with me, are they?" She gripped the edge of the table as if it kept her from sliding into a dark abyss.

"I am not privy to Seerin Krisla's decisions." The young woman said and began to close the door.

"More wine." Faulk's voice stopped her motion. "This wine is very good and I'd like more of it since we have no choice but to remain here."

"Of course," the woman said, fading back into the hallway.

Anlin looked at Faulk and rephrased the unanswerable question as a statement. "They're not going to let me have him."

"We don't know that. We have no idea what Seerin Krisla has decided. It's useless to worry about what might happen. We know we'll be leaving tomorrow, and there have been times when I wasn't sure even that would happen. I choose to believe Telm will be returned to you."

Anlin felt sick. She didn't share Faulk's optimism. They would leave tomorrow, and she and Faulk would be going alone. Telm, her child, her baby, would disappear forever. More scars would be added to his face, and he would become a man who could feel nothing but loathing for a Fallucian mother.

She would never know what happened to him. It was as if he'd been taken from her again, screaming "Mama, mama," as Nerth rode away. It hurt. It hurt so badly. She sat back down, folding around the incredible pain in her gut.

She felt Faulk's hands on her shoulders, pulling her upright in the chair. "Do not despair. It is a foolish knight who concedes the battle before it is even fought. We found Telm, and I wasn't sure even that would happen. You need to have confidence that he will return home with us."

Anlin shook her head in negation. In response, Faulk pressed the smooth, cool wine glass in her hand. "Drink some wine. Think of pleasant things. You're feeling down because you're tired. You didn't sleep last night since you were riding here."

"At least I rode. You were slung over a horse like a dead body."

"My point entirely." Faulk chuckled. "I've had a lot more sleep."

Anlin knew what he was doing. Faulk was trying to make her think of other things, and he was willing to make light of all that had happened to him to do so.

She couldn't find the energy to resist him. She drank her wine and listened to Faulk talk about inconsequential things, about the advisability of putting sheep in the upper pastures, about his plans to build stone walls around the White Ford manor to make it more secure. His voice rolled over her, filling the emptiness inside her. Until she surprised herself by yawning.

"Come, lie down. You should rest a while," Faulk

said, and she let him lead her to the huge bed. She was amazed by the softness of the fur cover that was spread on the bed. It felt like resting on a cloud—a cloud on which she slowly floated away.

❧ 15 ❧

Faulk ran his hand over the bed cover. He enjoyed the feeling of the lush fur. The differing texture of the two types that were used added to the sensual pleasure. The tawny stripes were made from red fox, fluffy and light, a whisper against his hand. The white stripes were some sort of weasel in winter coat, he wasn't sure what it was called, and that fur was tighter, slicker, but equally compelling. He wondered how many of these animals had lost their lives just to make this one covering. And it was possible that each room in this vast complex of buildings featured something similar upon the bed.

How much could all these furs have been sold for in Fallucia? Faulk guessed it would have been a substantial amount, coin that could have been put to use improving the lot of the general populace here in Rennic. Instead, they rested on a bed in Ridgemere where they could provide sensory delight for only a select few. Was this part of the joy that was promised if one did one's holy duty? Were the wives who awaited the twice-yearly arrival of their husbands also trained to aid in this joy?

Anlin had been told that men were trained from boyhood in proper behavior. And from her experience, that behavior consisted of sterile, unemotional, sexual gratification with a convenient body for most of the time. Faulk personally thought an active imagination and self-gratification would have been preferable, but he guessed the prevailing practice at least found something to do with extraneous, non-magical females. Rennish society was a rotten mess.

That the Rennish were breeding for improved magical ability was not so impossible, however. It explained much. To breed a warhorse, one did not put a large stallion to a pony and hope for the best. No, the bloodlines of expensive destriers carefully noted years of selective breeding—the stallion for size, the mare for temperament. Ridgemere was just some sort of reversed stud farm where the stallions were brought to the mares.

Faulk tried to imagine what it would be like to be one of the men who came here through the way stations. Did they gather in the same groups every time? Would friendships have been forged, the dormitories filled with jokes and innuendo? There would have undoubtedly been excitement, anticipation.

Sweet Cheelum, by the time the men exited the bathhouse, they would have been curried and caparisoned, probably already stiff as pokers, ready to do their holy duty. And then they would be brought to a sumptuous room like this one, be greeted by a smiling and willing wife.

No wonder Nerth had pointed to his husband's tattoo with such pride. Ridgemere was the only place in the entire Cheelum-cursed country of Rennic where any type of joy *could* be found. It certainly didn't offer any for women in the position Anlin had been in. Their lot was joyless by design.

His fingers left off stroking the fur and shifted to the inside of Anlin's arm. Her skin was equally soft. He actually found it more compelling. He ran his fingers from wrist to elbow, fascinated by how her muscles quivered under his touch. He must have tickled her, however, since she brought her carelessly thrown arm back closer to her body. He smiled at the grimace that flickered across her face. Even without all the artificial props, he could give her joy, if she would only let him.

The urge to unwrap her like a present and spread her naked on the soft fur was almost overwhelming. Everything in this room was designed to appeal to the senses, and the atmosphere alone was seductive. Faulk could feel it, but he suspected Anlin had noticed only that the room was comfortable. The desire to pull Anlin to him, to mold her body to his, became almost irresistible.

He resisted.

Rolling off the bed, he paced the room. He wondered if there were holes in the walls where the occupants could be observed. He certainly wouldn't let a stallion cover a prized mare without watching for problems. Would the Seerin and Shamans be any different?

Thinking of the possibility extinguished his budding ardor. He had no desire to provide prurient entertainment, especially when Anlin's behavior would only reinforce the prevailing attitude toward those who lacked magical Talent.

He sat at the table and poured more wine. It was very good. His head still ached from being previously abused, and he thought it wouldn't be that much worse in the morning if he now over-indulged. He'd managed to get Anlin to drink enough that she had fallen into an exhausted sleep. She hadn't even awakened when dinner arrived. Faulk decided it would be a brilliant idea if he were to do the same.

Success came about the same time that the flagon emptied. Faulk extinguished the candles and removed his tunic before lying down on the far side of the big bed from Anlin's slumbering form. The room had cooled some, but he thought it would still be more comfortable to be on top of the luxurious furs than under them.

He fell asleep stoking the cover's softness. He was saddened that all this sumptuousness was wasted. But in his dreams, this was otherwise. In his dreams, pleasure was given and received.

❧ • ❧

Faulk awoke with an arousal tenting his braies.

Anlin was walking across the room toward the lavatory. He rolled over on his stomach, trying to hide the embarrassing evidence of his night visions. It was unnecessary, however, since Anlin didn't look in his direction before entering the washroom and closing the door behind her.

He got off the bed and retrieved his good tunic. He planned to look as knightly as possible for the postponed meeting. He thought his opinions might be better heeded if he appeared more important. His head pounded from the combination of his wine consumption and his previous injury. The fur from the bed cover seemed to have transferred itself to his tongue while he slept. With luck, breakfast would be accompanied by ale.

Faulk was pleased he was decently dressed when someone knocked on the door. The enticing smell of hot bread announced the arrival of breakfast, thankfully complete with a flagon of ale. He was gratefully sipping from his cup when Anlin came in from the lavatory. In place of the nondescript clothing that she had favored since arriving in Rennic, she had on the same yellow tunic she'd worn to their wedding.

"You look quite elegant this morning," he said.

"I saw you'd changed into better clothes last evening and I thought I'd do the same to meet with Seerin Krisla this morning." She gave Faulk a deprecating smile. "I suspect I'm using clothing as a confidence aid."

"The same," Faulk said, unconsciously patting the embroidered nightpiper on his shoulder. "The bread's hot. I'll get some more in a moment." He got up and, carrying his ale cup, went to take his turn with the amazing facilities in the lavatory.

He'd just washed his face with an unusual, spicy smelling soap when he heard conversation from the adjoining room. He walked back into the bedroom wiping his face with a linen square.

"They want to see us now." Anlin's eyes were wide. All the worry and fear that had been present the night before was apparent in them.

"Good," Faulk said. "Then we'll be able to get an early start. Have you finished breakfast?"

Anlin nodded.

"Then we're ready to go." Faulk motioned for the Seerin to precede them and, taking Anlin's arm, they walked down the hallway.

The room they entered was identical in configuration to the one they had just left, but this one was furnished like a combination of an estate office and a refectory. Bookcases, filled with expensive leather covered volumes, lined one wall. Three long, narrow tables with adjacent benches took up the middle of the room.

Seerin Krisla sat at the end of one of the tables with an open window behind her. Faulk appreciated her positioning. It was always best to make your opponent look into the sun. The Seerin's placement also meant her expression would be difficult to read. To her right sat Callip and Telm. Faulk was surprised to see the boy. By Anlin's brief hesitation, he assumed Anlin was surprised as well.

"Please sit here," the Seerin said. She indicated the area to her left.

Faulk and Anlin slid onto the bench, Faulk taking the place next to Seerin Krisla and directly across from Callip. He thought if he could buffer Anlin from the two of them, he could in some way protect her.

"We have had many things to consider that are unknown to you," Seerin Krisla began. "Your sole concern is returning Telm to his mother's control. Ours encompasses much more. We have learned that we have been lied to, and acting on these lies, we may have caused a great deal of chaos. Yes, this chaos has been visited on our enemies, but the way these results have occurred is not what we intended.

"We realize you are not scholars," she continued, "although even Fallucian scholars have forgotten much of what transpired eight hundred years ago—"

"Eight hundred years go?" interjected Faulk. "What has all this to do..."

Anlin gripped his arm at the same time the Seerin said, "All will be made clear if you give me a chance to explain."

Faulk tried to contain his impatience. Next to him, Anlin was as tight as a strung bow. He didn't want the pressure to continue for hours in fear that she might break. "I beg your pardon," he said quietly.

The Seerin glared at him but continued. "Eight hundred years ago, all people worshipped the Duality—the God of the Sky and Goddess of the Earth—and all magic was one. This was right and proper. But more and more men began turning from the Goddess, thinking only women should be concerned with her works. These men followed the dictates of the Sky God, since they erroneously believed that using His spells and magic gave them greater power. They used only sky magic, prayed only to the Sky God, and eventually lost the goodness that is the Goddess and her specific magic.

"Unfortunately, those who were most attracted to what they perceived as the power of the Sky God were the most militaristic, the most violent, members of society. They came to imagine the worshipers of the Goddess, who followed the paths of kindness and pacifism, were in some way conspiring against them. In their arrogance, they saw the Wheel of the World as constricting and believed they could make themselves fit to be companions of their god in just one lifetime. They imagined earth magic was opposed to sky magic and attempted to stamp it out. The followers of the Goddess were persecuted and killed. Over just a few generations, most of Her worshipers had been pushed back into the mountainous areas, onto the unproductive land. But even here, the people of the Goddess were pursued until they cried, 'We have no magic. We hate all magic.' Believing themselves victorious, the followers of the Sky God became embroiled in their own affairs and learned to ignore those people who hid in the mountain fastness that was called Rennic. These conquerors proclaimed that the Sky God was the only God and that his name was Cheelum. And thus, the people of Fallucia lost the true path and have ever since abided in error."

"And all of this is true," Callip and Telm recited in unison.

With their pronouncement, Faulk realized he had just heard a catechism, a statement of belief that for the Rennish was unchallengeable. How much of the tale was actual truth was uncertain, but Faulk wondered why, after eight hundred years, anyone should even care. "I will accept the validity of what you say," Faulk said, "but I fail to see what any of this has to do with what is happening now."

"It has everything to do with it." Callip said, leaning slightly across the table in his earnestness. "The past has made our two countries what they now are. Fallucia has remained power-hungry and grasping. Fallucians seek to spread belief in their false god throughout the world and they seek to control all the peoples in it. We in Rennic are content in our isolation, but we know that our larger, more aggressive neighbor across the border covets what little we have.

"Over the centuries, we have contrived ways to protect ourselves. The Shamans have woven a pattern of spells over the entire country that repels the incursion into our thoughts and plans from scrying, since Fallucians excel in seeing visions in water or crystal. We have raised up a group of men with the ability to perceive Fallucian magic and have set them on our borders to resist any attack. We have structured our society so that our magic may be increased each generation. We only wish to remain free to follow the dictates of our hearts."

Seerin Krisla held up a hand to stop Callip. "It is an uncomfortable thing to admit fear, but we fear for our way of life and seek to protect it. Our intent is to defend and never attack. Within this last generation, however, we stumbled upon an offensive weapon—and now find that we have inadvertently unleashed it upon your country."

She stopped for a moment, and Faulk observed those who sat around the table. The Seerin looked uncomfortable, Callip appeared angry, and Telm simply exhibited awe. Most likely the boy had never before been included in such conversations. Anlin carefully studied her folded hands, her head down, as if all that was said could wash over her.

"I assume it is this weapon that is, in some way, linked to our retrieval of my wife's son," Faulk said

Callip's expression became grimmer and he nodded, but it was Seerin Krisla who spoke. "Centuries ago, it was discovered that wearing an amulet of polished Glafser allowed the Sentinels, the men who guard our borders, to more easily sense Fallucian magic. The stone somehow caused sky magic to double back on itself until, to the ears of the amulet wearer, the slightest heartbeat of sky magic became a pounding drum. We do not know how this works; only that it does. Perhaps the shield against Fallucian magic that has long been woven over Rennic has called some response from the very stones of this country. Whatever the reason, the men who wear Glafser can discern sky magic from a great distance and will fight to the last man to vanquish those who possess this magic."

"To the immediate concern, please, Seerin," Callip said. "There is no need to tell these people all our secrets."

"I'm only telling them what they need to know," Seerin Krisla replied tartly. "They need to know Glafser exists and that we intended it to be defensive." She turned and spoke more directly to Faulk. "It was when your mother came seeking sanctuary that we discovered Glafser could have a different use. She came upon me when I was in conference with one of the Sentinels. She took one look at the amulet freely displayed around his neck and collapsed.

"I feared the stone had had some negative, perhaps lethal, effect on her. When she revived, she said she'd been shocked to see that particular amulet since it was identical to one her brother Jezrel wore. She collapsed when she thought he'd come here to retrieve her."

"But Abbot Jezrel hadn't come to Rennic or sent the amulet?" Faulk asked.

"No," the Seerin said. "After their training, Sentinels

are each presented with an amulet. The design is distinctive, as is the stone. Glafser is a pale blue with red veins running through it. After seeing another amulet, Lettice remained positive it was identical to her brother's.

"The only way a Fallucian could be in possession of such an amulet would be if it were taken from a Sentinel killed in a border skirmish. When a Sentinel is killed, we mourn the man, but we've never given a thought to what happened to his possessions. According to your mother, these amulets are much prized in Fallucia since they are believed to magnify the magical power of the wearer."

"Which makes sense," Callip interjected, "since Glafser does much the same for us."

Seerin Krisla frowned at the interruption. "The important point is that a discussion with your mother indicated the men who had the stolen amulets all exhibited a tendency toward madness."

The Seerin sat back as if she had just explained something important, but for the life of him, Faulk couldn't figure out what it was. He could have told them that Abbot Jezrel was insane, amulet or not. He was sure this wasn't anything that Anlin, silent and tense beside him, had any interest in. "How does this problem with amulets lead you to return Telm to his mother?" he asked, hoping all of this was connected and Telm's return would be the outcome.

"This leads us to admitting that once we realized

the power of Glafser to create madness in the Lords of the High Places, we succumbed to the idea of spreading chaos among the leading Fallucian families." Callip said. "We gave various cloak pins and men's rings and amulets made from Glafser to a perceived ally for distribution."

"Sometimes, defense requires an offense to be successful," the Seerin said.

Callip now frowned at Seerin Krisla. "Not when it goes against the tenets that we live by. Not when it abrogates our vows of pacifism." He turned to look directly at Faulk. "And this is why I'll be returning with you to Fallucia. Since we've discovered our supposed ally is a liar and without honor, it is necessary to retrieve all the Glafser stones."

Faulk froze. Whatever he'd planned to say next fled his mind. Sweet Cheelum. He and Anlin couldn't drag a Rennish Shaman back with them to Fallucia. Faulk had been unsure of Anlin's half-Rennish son's reception, but he felt the boy would be insulated by both being at White Ford and being in the middle of his grandfather's much larger estate. The arrival of the Chief Shaman of Rennic to White Ford did not bode well, however. It did not take clairvoyance to see that harboring someone as magically powerful as Callip presented a substantial breach of security. Faulk hadn't forgotten the sensation of being burned alive. He hated to think of the havoc that Callip could cause.

"Who is your disreputable ally?" Anlin asked. Faulk

was surprised by her question. He'd thought she wasn't even following the discussion. But he knew the answer even before the Seerin spoke.

"Lord Tarn," she said. "We've given Glafser to Lord Tarn, both the older and the younger. They were to gift the stones to the Lords who ruled along the border. Our intention was to sow chaos in the area adjacent to Rennic, believing people who are poorly led are less likely to make incursions into another country. But we now suspect both of them used the stones for their own purposes, rather than ours."

Faulk was sure they had. Edmund Tarn had ambitions beyond his due, and his father had been no different. Faulk wondered if Edmund had even looked as high as kingship. Anlin's father, Philip Giffard, had expressed concern that Fallucia was becoming unstable as King Fremmor slid into madness. Faulk suspected that among the jewels the king cherished was a Glafser stone. The scars on his back seemed to tighten when he considered that without the influence of Glafser, even Abbot Jezrel's madness might have been mitigated. Faulk might not have had to spend his early life is misery. It was even possible his mother might not have had to flee.

"So, you'll be coming to Fallucia?" Anlin asked as if she thought this presented no problem. "Will Telm be coming too?"

"Yes," Callip said, and Faulk felt the tension leave Anlin's body. Of all the things that had been said, this was the most important to her. Perhaps the *only* topic of importance. She would have her son back.

"Callip and I have had a great deal of discussion about this," Seerin Krisla said, "and have come to a compromise." She looked at the shaman, who gave an almost imperceptible nod. "You both must agree to our conditions before you depart—or Telm will not be going with you."

Anlin gave a sharp cry and would have stood if Faulk hadn't placed a gentle hand on her shoulder. Her look of anguish cut him like a sword stroke.

"You must realize that Telm is reluctant to leave here," the Seerin quickly said. "This is a life he knows. This is a place where he's honored. But Callip has convinced me that Telm should experience what it would be like to live with his mother, to at least come to terms with the Fallucian side of his heritage. In Rennic, we would not allow a child with Talent to live with someone who did not possess the spark of magic. It would be a waste. But Callip has prevailed upon me to see that this is a special case."

"Consequently, Telm will go to this place where you live…" The Seerin looked expectantly at Faulk and Anlin.

"White Ford," Faulk supplied.

"Yes. Telm will go to White Ford. He will stay there through the winter. When the snow melts in the passes, however, it is Telm's right to choose whether he will remain or will return with Callip. Do you swear to abide by these conditions?"

"Yes, I do swear," Faulk said quickly. He was sure this was not everything Anlin wanted, but to his way of thinking, it was fair. While it didn't guarantee Telm would stay permanently, this would at least give Anlin time to know her son and to realize that life for someone of mixed heritage would be very difficult.

"Telm is still a child. How can he make a considered, intelligent decision?" Anlin continued to try to get everything she wanted, but Faulk knew it wouldn't work. One look at Telm's set face indicated she was alienating him from the beginning.

"Just agree," Faulk whispered.

"What? No!"

"Swear it is Telm's decision or leave empty-handed." Faulk no longer kept his voice low.

Anlin looked rebellious. Interestingly, the same expression echoed on Telm's face. Then she seemed to understand this was her one chance to get to know her son. Reluctantly she said, "I so swear."

"Good," said the Seerin. "Callip will be there to assure you keep your vow. The horses are being readied as we speak. You all can leave as soon as your personal baggage is assembled." Then Seerin Krisla stood and gestured with her hands that they should leave.

It seemed an abrupt departure, but Faulk didn't argue with its suddenness. He was anxious to get on the road and put Rennic behind him. He still worried about arriving in Fallucia with a Shaman and his acolyte but decided this was a concern for another day. Right now, he would retrieve the one pack that was in their room and make sure everything else they'd brought with them was accounted for. He would be obstinate if his mail and sword and big gray horse were not there. The packhorse that had carried the silver coins would be no loss. Faulk was sure it wouldn't be needed.

✌ 16 ✌

Oddly, Anlin thought leaving Rennic was more frightening than entering it. She had been uncomfortable returning to the place of her enslavement since it brought back memories that haunted her. But leaving meant she drew ever closer to having to face the destruction of a dream. When the trip ended, she could no longer pretend her son was going to be happy in her home. He would be there, but she was sure he would *not* be happy.

They traveled back the way she and Faulk had come, stopping at the empty way stations. When they left the secret trail, they found shelter with village shamans. Callip led the group. Telm came second, immediately followed by Anlin, who spent hours watching the stiff shoulders of the boy in front of her, wishing she could think of some way to reach him. She was trailed by both packhorses since the silver was returning with them. Callip had been adamant in his refusal of any funds that would indicate Telm was being bought.

An ever-vigilant Faulk brought up the rear. He was still not convinced Callip would guide them to the border without incident. Faulk seemed relieved when they by-passed the village of Chirlon. If anyone in the surrounding countryside connected the death or disappearance of Nerth and his friends with the arrival of two Fallucians in the area, nothing was said.

At this elevation, the mornings were now cool, reminding Anlin of how brief Rennish summers were. It would not be long before the trees began to blush red and orange and yellow, in sharp contrast to the deep green of the towering pines. There was a beauty to this harsh land, but Anlin was happy to be leaving it.

When she and Faulk talked at their nightly stops, it was obvious his mind was also attuned to the changing seasons. The time it had taken to get into Rennic added to their stay in Ridgemere and now the journey back to Fallucia had pushed them inexorably toward autumn. Faulk fretted about the harvest, which he was not there to oversee. He worried that all the dwellings and buildings he'd thought needed repair had not been made winter ready.

Faulk's mind had already returned to White Ford. Anlin's remained solidly fixed on the small, straight back that daily rode before her.

The last night before they came to the Tarsell River, they were housed with a local shaman. She and Faulk were taken to a small building at the rear of the garden, a hut that evidently was used as a guesthouse, while

Callip and Telm stayed in the main dwelling. It was the first time she and Faulk been alone since leaving the luxurious room at Ridgemere. This time the accommodations were not so elegant. The benches and bedstead were primitively constructed. The mattress crackled of straw-filling when Faulk sat on it.

"It's difficult to believe the Rennish can reconcile the difference in the way most of the people live in the countryside and the way the favored ones live at Ridgemere," Faulk said stretching his full length across the bed with a sigh. "I can see where the slaves are not in the position to rebel, but you'd think the men who aren't chosen as husbands would resist."

"Those without magic are convinced they are being punished for something they did in a past life, so they try to follow all the rules with diligence, which, they hope, will bump them up the ladder on the next turn of the wheel." Anlin spoke while pacing. She was tired but couldn't seem to settle.

"Sweet Cheelum, I'm almost glad I was raised by a crazy man. At least he thought I only had to get my life right one time around. I don't think I could plan for something beyond this." Faulk turned on his side and propped his head up with his hand. "You realize, though, that Telm is convinced of the rightness of Rennic thought."

"I know. I'm actually trying *not* to think about it. I keep hoping I'll be able to change his attitude once he lives with us, that he'll see how much more sense the

Fallucian lifestyle makes."

"I'm sorry Anlin, but I don't see that happening. Telm may be young, but he's smart. He's going to take one look at the villeins on the holding and ask how they're better off than the slaves in Rennic. He's going to see how carefully the magic-oriented Lords of High Places marry among themselves to consolidate both magic and land ownership, and then he'll want to know just how different that is from the Rennic version of selecting for specific husbands and wives. And if he asks me, I'm going to have to tell him the two systems really aren't that much different."

Anlin stopped short and glared at Faulk. "Well, I can certainly tell him the difference. Since I've been a slave, I can assure him that it is much better to be a villein at White Ford. Our people are free to choose whom they will marry, they are free to structure their lives within the bounds of the duties they owe you as their lord, and they're free to improve their lot through hard work and diligence."

"You've given the game away by using the phrase 'our people,'" he said. "That sure sounds like ownership."

A flare of anger pulsed through her. How dare Faulk compare the two systems? She'd lived through hell in Rennic and certainly knew the difference.

"And as far as the Lords' families only marrying one another," she said, "Telm only has to look at us to see that's wrong. You basically won my hand in a tournament when you were just..." Her voice trailed off. Faulk had swung up to sit on the side of the bed. He did not look happy.

"I was just some landless knight with no discernable lineage," he finished for her.

"That wasn't what I was going to say."

Faulk looked skeptical, then his face dissolved into a wry smile. "Well, if what Seerin Krisla said was true, and I have no reason to doubt her, I'm the product of a Graymont and Tarn union, albeit without marriage, and you can't find too many lords from higher places than those." He laughed. "I'd have held out for a larger holding if I'd known."

And a more favored bride, Anlin mentally added. She was realistic enough to realize what Faulk had gotten out of their marriage—and what he had not. She understood that he felt there was something lacking, but he didn't know how to fix whatever it was. He wanted more from her than she had to give.

If there was one thing that this trip had done, it was to make her realize she could *like* this man she'd taken to husband. While Faulk would see the mistakes he'd made in Rennic as faults, Anlin felt they had made him more human and not as forbidding.

He'd exhibited a sense of humor that had previously eluded her notice, and he had been unfailingly kind to her. Neither was a trait she'd thought she wanted when she decided to become the prize for the best fighter she could find, but she'd discovered they were both characteristics she favored.

She hoped Faulk wouldn't become distant again once they returned to White Ford. She enjoyed being around him. She wanted them to present a united front to Telm; she wanted to make the boy feel he could find a home with them.

She knew she lacked the skills the lady of the manor should possess, but she could learn them—she *would* learn them. It was only a matter of applying herself. But she suspected that Faulk found her lacking in areas other than housewifery.

"When we get back to White Ford, will you attempt to get an heir?" The words jumped out before she had time for thought.

Faulk looked surprised, but when he answered, his tone was level, almost casual. "Yes, of course. You know I want children of my body to eventually inherit the holding at White Ford. In this, I'm like most men. I'd like to think that what I build today will be enjoyed by following generations. And I made it clear from the beginning that Telm does not fulfill my requirements for an heir."

"I wasn't thinking about Telm," she said. "I wasn't trying to put him forward. I was thinking about…"

"Ah, your concern is about the process of getting these heirs."

"Yes." She was embarrassed and not sure where to go next with the topic. "I liked the touching."

His face brightened, his look almost boyish. "You

did? Good. That's good. Eh, would you like to try it again?"

In answer, she walked to where he sat on the edge of the bed. She ran her fingers along the side of his jaw. He hadn't shaved in days and his cheeks were bristly with a short, dark red beard. It was almost soft to the touch. She liked the way his beard felt differently on her fingertips depending on whether she stroked up or down. She also liked the way Faulk leaned into her hand, eyes closed, as if he were a cat who enjoyed being petted.

"If you sat on the bed, it would be easier for me to touch you, too," Faulk said. Anlin noticed his hands were gripping the edge of the mattress. She sat. His hands immediately came up and stroked her face as she was stroking his. She smiled when she realized she too had closed her eyes and was leaning into his hand. He loosened the tie that held her still-short hair at the back of her neck and rubbed her temples with his thumbs. Strange, she hadn't realized it would feel so good to have her hair hanging loose.

"I despair that my hair will ever make a decent matron's braid." She murmured the thought, then realized that it didn't make much sense.

But Faulk seemed to follow her slightly skewed logic. He ran his fingers through her hair and said, "It's lovely, you know. Soft and thick. Much nicer than pulled back tightly into a braid. And your white blaze. I love your blaze." He held her head steady with a hand on either side, leaned forward, and kissed the area of her forehead directly below the streak in her hair. She tried to jerk back, knowing how ugly the scar was. Martic had told her over and over how disgusting it looked.

"No, stay. Stay," Faulk said, holding her head firmly. And then he kissed her lips, softly, as if she had been touched by a windblown leaf. Her lips wanted to do something under his, she wasn't sure what, but the feeling was nice. He feathered kisses across her cheeks, her nose, her eyelids. "Do you know why people close their eyes when they kiss?" he asked. "It's because without sight, the touching feels so much better, and kissing is just another form of touching. Would you like me to blow out the candles and make the room completely dark? Then when we touch it will feel better whether we close our eyes or not."

"Yes," she said. Anlin had no fear of the dark. The things that men had done to her had always been in the light so they could see her, watch her. The things Faulk did weren't so scary. He wanted to touch, not mate, and it was nice. Yes, it would be nice in the dark.

Faulk got up and, moving around the room, extinguished the three candles that had been burning. Now there was only a faint, rosy glow from the brazier. She felt more than saw him return. His weight sagged the straw mattress and pulled her toward him. He moved further back on the bed, behind her, his warm hands on her shoulders, kneading muscles she hadn't realized were so tight and knotted. He massaged down her spine, around her shoulder blades, over the tops of her shoulders and along the sides of her neck. It was wonderful. She began to feel boneless.

"Lay back and I'll massage your front." Faulk's voice sounded strangely hoarse.

Being totally relaxed, she did so. Faulk rubbed her temples, then ran his fingers down the sides of her neck and the front of her shoulders. When his talented hands descended to her breasts, she stiffened. The hand she put up to stop him met with warm flesh. At some time since the candles had been snuffed, Faulk had shed his tunic.

"I'd like it if you touched me in return," he said, and the hand with which she'd intended to restrain him could not be stopped from stroking his chest. She marveled at the symphony of textures—smooth skin, crisp hair, hard muscle. Her fingers brushed his taut male nipple and it seemed like he stopped breathing. He reciprocated, drawing his fingers around and over her breasts, teasing the sensitive peaks. Her breathing also became erratic.

He changed his position and loomed above her. He slowly lowered his head until his lips were again on hers. The pressure was stronger; his tongue licked along her lower lip. She relaxed her mouth and his tongue slid in, the motion causing an odd reaction in her midsection. She felt him tug at her tunic, but the garment, secure beneath her, didn't budge. Finally, he broke his breathless kiss. "Let's take this off," he said. "It will feel so much better touching flesh to flesh."

And there in the darkness, when all was sensation and the touching felt so good, she eased her body up so Faulk could pull her tunic from her. The air was cool on her body, but, before she could react, Faulk's hands were doing wonderful things. She arched to seat her breasts more fully in his palms. Then his mouth replaced his hands, and he was licking and sucking. She had held Telm to her breasts when he was a baby, but the feeling had been nothing like this heart-stopping sensation. She was unable to control the movement of her body and she writhed against Faulk, relishing the feeling of his hard warmth.

He ran a hand lower, over the core of her. She bucked against the pressure and moaned. An affirmation or negation, even Anlin wasn't sure. She was both frightened and exhilarated. Dampness pooled between her legs. "Stay with me, Anlin mine," Faulk murmured. "Please stay with me." His hand was within her drawers, stroking the hair at the apex of her thighs. She felt a spiraling tightness, a hunger for something she did not know.

"Spread your legs, love. It's touching, only touching." Unable to resist his compelling caresses, unconsciously seeking a release from the pressure building within, she did as he asked. His fingers traced along her cleft, back and forth. She wanted, needed. His finger entered her, slick, easy, without pain. He thumbed her nub and brought her hips off the mattress, wanting more. The knot inside her pulled tighter and tighter until suddenly, without warning, she shattered into a thousand pieces—pieces that flashed and sparkled, more beautiful than the sun catching dew on the grass.

When the pieces of herself reassembled, Anlin was pulled firmly against Faulk, their bodies sweat-slicked, his lips marking sweet patterns on her face. "What?" she asked, still dazed and incoherent.

"I think you've just found the joy that comes from holy duty." There was laughter in Faulk's voice, as if what had just happened had found an answering delight in him. "And it can be better, much better. Will you let me make it better? Will you stay with me?"

Anlin wanted to tell him she definitely didn't plan to disappear into her mind, not if she could have the same experience again, but her brain didn't seem to be connected to her mouth. There was no way the experience could have been better, but she was willing to try if Faulk wanted. "Yes," she managed to say.

He rolled slightly to the side, untied his braies, and slid out of them. When he again pulled her against him, she could feel his arousal rubbing against her leg. She stiffened and pulled back. "No, stay, stay."

He took her hand and placed it on the distended portion of his body that she had always considered a man's cruel weapon. But this experience was totally different. Instead of being repulsed, she found Faulk's arousal fascinating. The texture was like velvet. The heat of him seemed to burn into her hand. Faulk moved her hand, trailing her fingers up and down his shaft. "It's touching, only touching," he said in a choked voice. "There's nothing to be frightened of."

And she wasn't afraid. This was part of Faulk, and he would never hurt her. She wondered if her stroking was as pleasant for him as his had been for her. His breathing seemed to keep time with the movement of her hand. He nudged her over on her back and began petting her as she stoked him.

The pounding on the door was loud, insistent. "Faulk!" Callip's voice. "Faulk, I need you now."

He rolled from her and stood in one motion. She could not see in the dark, but she heard his sword leave its scabbard. He opened the door a crack, sheltering his body behind the stout wood. Light from a torch shown through the narrow opening. "The boy's gone," Callip said. "I didn't anticipate his running off, but he has. I need you to retrieve him."

"Do you know where he's gone?" Faulk asked.

"Of course. He's not far and is on foot. I can sense his magic like a flare in the darkness."

"Then why in the hell do I need to go after him?"

"Please, Faulk. Telm is afraid. I could tell he was, but I thought he could control it. He's afraid to leave Rennic. He's sure that if he does, you will never let him return, regardless of what you've sworn. I need you to get him and reassure him. If I go, he will never be sure you are honorable enough to do as you've agreed. He needs your assurance."

"Oh, hell." Faulk let the door come open a little more. Callip appeared in the blaze from the torch, his face rigid with concern. "All right," Faulk said. "Give me a moment."

He came back into the room, silhouetted against the light. "You heard?" he asked as he dressed.

"Please bring him back," Anlin said. "If you must tie him up to bring him back, do it. Maybe if I talked to him, told him how much I want him at White Ford..."

"I'll bring him back, but I sure as hell won't tie him up. Sweet Cheelum, being tied and forced is what he fears the most. Those damned Seerin and Shamans have spent the past four years convincing Telm that anyone who lives across the border is evil, that Fallucians are without honor and cannot be trusted. They've done such a good job of it that the boy is scared to death. He's run away like a skittish horse, and I'll coax him back, not force him."

Then he walked out, saying, "Lead the way," to Callip, and closed the door behind him. She heard the two men speaking and then nothing. Anlin was left alone in the dark. Her body still hummed with delight and confusion. This was not how such a night should have ended. She should not be left alone with all her uncertainties and regrets.

When she'd set her plan to bring Telm back to Fallucia into motion, her greatest hope had been that he was still alive. It had never occurred to her that he might not *want* to come with her. She had imaged him despised and mistreated, a slave in need of freeing. She lived with the vision of him throwing his arms around her and crying "mother" when he first saw her, confident that here was the one human in all the world who loved her, and whom she loved, unconditionally.

But Anlin's dream was just that—a dream. Nothing had happened as she'd anticipated. Never had she considered that Telm would be comfortable and happy, that he would have taken on the values of his mother's captors.

Whatever memories he had of his first three years of life had been replaced by a tale told by others. She'd become the Fallucian whore who took care of him. Even at three, he possibly realized he was a slave as she was a slave and that his life was precarious. Now he'd found a place of comfort, and he could see a fulfilling life before him, a life that did not include Anlin.

He was no longer her sweet little baby. He was no longer the little boy who had screamed and clung to her leg when he was taken from her. He was not now, and perhaps never had been, the smiling image she'd held in her mind through the years of torment after he'd disappeared. And since the Telm she'd remembered and had expected to find again was gone, Anlin was as bereft as she would have been had she discovered he'd died.

Faulk and Callip would bring him back, of that she had no doubt. But she was much less certain what the future would hold. He'd been trained to hate her and her kind, and she could not see a way around that. He was just a boy, only seven years old. Perhaps she could change his attitudes. That was her hope and she must cling to it.

When they got to White Ford, all Telm's fears would be laid to rest. She had to believe that. But as she sat alone in the dark, this belief was tenuous.

Even in the uncertain light of dusk, White Ford was the most beautiful place Faulk had ever seen. It was now home. It was now his. The fields had been harvested and a few strips already plowed in anticipation of winter wheat. The manor house itself looked sturdy and protective as it huddled next to the Milk River. And once they'd arrived at his demesne, the people had greeted him with enthusiasm. They became somewhat more subdued when they realized that two Rennish rode with him and Anlin, but still seemed glad that they had returned.

After Rennic, the prosperity of his holding was all the more evident. The people were well fed and clothed, the fields cared for, the livestock fat and sleek. But above all, White Ford was peaceful. This, Faulk hoped, would stay the same.

But he feared chaos might soon overtake them. Callip was a person of importance in Rennic, and he brought news of a corruption in Fallucia that could shake the country apart. Lord Tarn was spreading madness and using the instability it caused for his own gain. But who would believe it? And more importantly, whom did Faulk trust to do anything about it?

A tentative relationship between him and Anlin was also beginning to grow, and he needed to spend time on its nourishment if it was to come to bloom. The problem was that he didn't have that time. He owed a duty to Lord Philip Giffard and to the country as a whole. The effort to retrieve all the Glafser amulets and to punish those who sought to gain from their use took precedence over his own happiness.

And then, of course, there was Telm.

Telm was a problem Faulk did not need, but which was firmly his to resolve. Anlin would be devastated when the boy left—and Faulk was sure this was the only eventual outcome. He could see the coming winter as one of constant tension as Anlin tried vainly to forge chains of affection with a boy who had already discarded her care.

Faulk felt like he, at least, had come to an accommodation with the boy. There was stubbornness in Telm, a tendency to strike out before he himself took a blow, that Faulk found familiar. He'd never imagined he'd find similarities in himself and the half-Rennish boy, but he had.

When he had run away, Telm had traveled further than even Callip had anticipated. With the Shaman's help, Faulk had tracked Telm to a dense forest on a direct line from where they had stopped for the night and the then distant Ridgemere. It was as if the boy had a map in his mind that showed the shortest way to reach his goal. Faulk had literally treed him, since Telm had climbed into the high branches of a pine to escape Faulk's notice.

Faulk had barely been able to make out a boy-shape in the darker silhouette of the limbs against the murky gray sky of the false dawn. "Are you done being an idiot?" Faulk called up to the branches.

He was greeted with silence.

"There is no need to pretend you're not there," Faulk said almost conversationally. "I can see you."

"No, you can't. You have no magic." Telm's defiant voice echoed down.

"Which means you can't *sense* me. But I can *see* you just fine with my normal, unimpressive human eyes." Faulk's big gray shifted under him and Faulk loosened the reins so the horse could browse. "Callip has evidently taught you to underestimate anyone with abilities different than your own. This could prove to be a fatal mistake as you grow older."

There was no movement or sound from above. The big horse contentedly grabbed chunks of grass and chewed, the activity making the bridle rattle. After some moments, Telm asked, "Are you just going to sit there forever?"

"Yes." Then silence.

"That's a big horse."

"Yes." Then silence.

"If you brought that big horse over by the tree, could you reach up and help me get down?"

Faulk fought to hold back laughter. "Of course." He did as he was asked, and then watched as Telm swung from the lowest branch to grasp onto the tree trunk. The lowest branch was very far up. Faulk could only guess at how the boy had gotten to his perch. In the dark of night, with his arms and legs wrapped around the trunk, Telm must have shinnied up. But in the weak light of dawn, looking down, the ground would have seemed impossibly far below.

Faulk stretched to his full height and waited until Telm had come close enough to grab. Then he'd grasped the boy around the waist and swung him into the saddle in front of him. He was surprised at how little Telm weighed, evidently a product of Anlin's slimness and his father's shorter, Rennish stature. He tried to remember who Anlin had said the boy's father was, but then decided it made no difference. Telm's father had probably wanted him as much as Lord Tarn had wanted Faulk.

Telm's robe rucked up as he straddled the horse, exposing thin legs covered with a myriad of scratches and abrasions. Faulk looked pointedly at Telm's legs and said, "I guess a robe is not the best clothing for climbing trees."

"No. It's also no good for getting in and out of brambles." Telm gripped the pommel as the horse began to move. Faulk had noted that Telm rode stiffly and in opposition to the motion of his horse. He would guess the boy didn't have much opportunity for riding in Ridgemere. "Are you going to tell Callip?" the boy asked in a soft voice.

"There's no need," Faulk said. "He's the one who told me that you'd run away."

"No, I mean tell him that I got up a tree that I couldn't get down from. Callip always lectures me on my lack of planning."

As if any seven-year-old had much foresight, Faulk thought. "I'll not mention it if you can explain why you ran away. Callip seems to think you're afraid." Faulk felt a sudden rigidity in the boy's body. Seven-year-olds also didn't like to be thought of as being afraid, even if they were.

"I just didn't want to go," Telm said. "I didn't want to have to go live with that woman."

"I assume you mean your mother."

"So Callip says."

"Well, you only have to stay until next spring, and Callip will be nearby. Then if you don't like it, you can go back to Ridgemere. Both your mother and I have sworn to this, and we are honorable people."

Telm was quiet for a while, then he turned to look up at Faulk, a serious expression on his face. "Are you really married to that woman? I mean, is she really a wife?"

"Yes, I'm married to your mother." Faulk stressed the last two words. "In Fallucia, husbands don't wear tattoos to show their status."

"But you're both, eh, without Talent," Telm said. Faulk wondered what word the boy had originally considered before he edited his speech to say 'without Talent.' "Seerin Krisla says that such people shouldn't breed." The last came out in a rush.

Faulk had to bite back the comment that he wasn't doing so well with the breeding part. This was not the time when he wanted to be out in the woods looking for a wayward boy. Instead he said, "It's a good thing that Anlin did, don't you think, or you would not be here."

The boy fidgeted. Faulk thought they might have come to the crux of the problem. Faulk realized Telm was embarrassed that Anlin was his mother. Not only was she Fallucian, she was also without magical ability, and, consequently, deemed to be worthless. Telm would be much more comfortable if Anlin were simply "that woman."

"Your mother has worried about you for years," Faulk said. "The obstacles she had to overcome to go back to Rennic to look for you were formidable." And then he told the boy as much as Anlin had ever told him, perhaps embellishing some parts a bit, but mostly sticking to the truth. Faulk wasn't sure it would make that much difference, but at least it seemed to give Telm something to think about.

He then went on to describe White Ford and discuss his plans for improvements. He dropped in all sorts of facts he thought would appeal to a boy, such as the Milk

River got its name because it ran through chalk cliffs and the resulting water was a murky white. He wanted Telm to be interested in the place he was going.

When they returned, Callip and Anlin waited with almost identical looks of concern. Faulk wondered if either of them recognized they loved the boy equally. But he didn't ask such a question. This was the day they would cross the bridge over the Tarsell, and Faulk was occupied with steeling himself for that occurrence. If he never again had to cross a suspension bridge, he would be happy.

Even after he'd accomplished the task, he felt the same way. But he also felt a great deal of relief.

They met some of the local Lord's men-at-arms on the Fallucian side of the border. There was no difficulty since they knew both Faulk and Anlin. If the patrollers thought they were returning with two Rennish prisoners, Faulk did not disabuse them of the idea. But he also knew he would not be able to tarry more than a day after arriving home before reporting to his liege lord—or Lord Giffard would come to him. Rumor could outstrip the speed of a horse.

And so, as the small cavalcade rode into White Ford, Faulk felt the sweet emotion of homecoming. He savored it, for all its brevity.

Warned of their arrival, the staff in the manor had prepared a gala meal. They had also readied a cell for the rumored prisoners and were surprised when they were asked to prepare two rooms in the guest wing instead. This guaranteed that everyone who was not infirm would be at the evening meal. The presence of two Rennish at White Ford was considered the wonder of the decade.

Faulk could have stopped the homecoming celebration. He could have pleaded exhaustion. He could have demanded privacy. But he knew it was better to meet the curiosity of the holding's villeins and freemen head on. If they lacked facts, the speculation would be more fantastical than the truth. It would be better to be open about the two Rennish who would reside at White Ford for at least the winter

The occasion certainly was not without discomfort. Surrounded by the loud and raucous local inhabitants, Faulk watched Telm become increasingly withdrawn—and watched Anlin fret about it. He introduced both newcomers with a toast, welcoming the son of his lady wife and the Chief Shaman of Rennic. Telm's identity made him even more of a curiosity, but at least the boy would be known and not have to answer more questions later. Faulk noticed Telm's eyes were very wide and that he made a number of asides to Callip in Rennish.

Faulk stopped the flow of ale well before the meal ended. Pleading fatigue from their trip, he then nearly pushed all the visitors out of the doors. He enlisted Kevin and Waylon to aid in this herding procedure. When the hall had been sufficiently cleared, Faulk stopped Waylon's departure.

"I have to go to Giffard's Crest tomorrow and may be gone for a few days," he told his man-at-arms. "When I return, I'd like a list of boys on the fief who are between six and eight. The type of boy that one might consider as a page. Lively but not a bully. Hettle the reeve has a likely looking boy, but I don't really know what he's like. I want you to investigate and make recommendations. I'm looking for companions for Lady Anlin's son."

Waylon paled, the freckles sprinkled across his homely face standing out more distinctly. "I didn't ask you to fight a horde of Rennish single handed, man," Faulk said clapping Waylon on the shoulder. "I'm just looking for friends for one boy."

"But how am I to figure out what kind of boys will do? I don't want to disappoint you, Faulk, but, eh, well..." Waylon took a deep breath, "What I mean is, you say the boy is Lady Anlin's son. I have to believe that. I mean, who would want to make up that kind of story? The kid sure looks all Rennish to me—dark, short, with those strange black eyes. And he's already got one of those things." Waylon drew a line on his cheek with a finger. "I mean, what does a boy like that want to do?"

"Run around and get into mischief, I supposed. The things you did when you were seven or eight."

Waylon looked dubious. "I'm not sure I'm the man to do this. Maybe Kevin could do better."

"Kevin has other duties. You'll do just fine." Then Faulk realized one of Waylon's difficulties. "Hettle has a fair hand, and he can make up the list when you get the names."

Waylon looked somewhat relieved. The man-at-arms' lack of letters had been part of the problem, but it was something Faulk could address by arranging for the priest to tutor both Waylon and Kev.

Faulk realized, however, this was not the entire problem, which lay in Telm's parentage.

He could order that friends for Telm be provided, and boys would appear. He was lord here and none on the holding would gainsay him. He worried these boys wouldn't be the true companions he envisioned, however. He hoped to alleviate Telm's loneliness; he thought if the boy had friends, he would find it easier to stay at White Ford. He wanted the child to be happy here for Anlin's sake.

But what if Telm was too different to find acceptance here? When Faulk looked at Telm, he saw just a boy. A boy with a Rennish cast to his looks, that was true, but still just a boy. He hoped others would do the same, but that might turn out to be a wish more than a fact.

And if he'd answered Waylon honestly, Faulk would have admitted he wasn't sure what seven-year-olds did for enjoyment anyway. He knew what *he'd* wanted to do at seven—he'd dreamed of riding a horse or catching frogs or just running for the sheer joy of it, but he'd not been allowed to do these things at Jarburgh. There all had been study and prayer and the lash.

He ran his fingers through his hair. This was not a problem that would be solved on this night. He saw that Hettle lingered and suspected the man needed to confer with him on estate business. And then Faulk needed to think of how best to present the facts about the damaging use of the Rennish amulets to Lord Giffard and perhaps formulate some plan about how to combat the rot that was settling into Fallucia because of them.

The most pressing need for the night, however, had already retired to their chamber. Anlin. His wife. His wife who seemed to like touching. She hadn't gone away into her mind three nights ago. There was much to build on there. Faulk found that he was smiling when he went to join the waiting reeve.

Hettle had reported the harvest had been good nearly before Faulk had dismounted. So now he presented Faulk with a litany of minor irritants. The only item that required much discussion was whether to purchase a second plow team. There was a likely pair of oxen being offered at Hannon's Height. The price was good because the present owner was loathed to feed the beasts over the winter. Hettle was also concerned that fodder for the oxen might prove costlier than waiting to purchase a similar team in the spring.

"But the plowman likes this pair?" Faulk asked.

"Yes," said the reeve. "He said they were young and strong and in good condition." Hettle looked somewhat embarrassed. "I think part of their allure is that they are both white and well-matched. The plowman pronounced them handsome."

Faulk laughed. "There's nothing bad about having something nice to look at while you're doing your work. If you're sure we have the extra grain, then I think we should buy at this price."

"Very good, sir." Hettle looked pleased. Evidently, even the pinch-faced reeve thought a matched white team would look good in the green fields. Faulk considered asking him about his middle son but decided that since he had given this chore to Waylon, he had to have the confidence the man-at-arms would fulfill his request.

"Well, goodnight then," Faulk said.

With the reeve's departure, only a few serving women were left in the hall, and it seemed that most of their work had been done. All the tables had been put away along the walls and the fire had been banked in the central fireplace. Faulk now had time to go up to his solar and plan his approach to Lord Giffard on the morrow.

As Faulk mounted the stairs, he decided the first obstacle would be to get Giffard to accept what Callip told him was the truth. It would be normal for Giffard to be suspicious, to assume that Callip was trying to plant false information to cause dissention within Fallucia. Faulk and Anlin only knew what they had been told but had believed what had been said because of the reaction of Seerin Krisla. Philip Giffard hadn't been there to see the Seerin's shock.

What they needed was to find an amulet, particularly one in the possession of a noble who behaved erratically. A number of the Lords of High Places would have to be convinced of the plot before anyone could go to the King and demand to see *his* amulet.

Faulk needed to make a list of the things that could be considered proof and where to find them. To do so, he needed to go to his office instead of his chamber. He turned to go back down the stairs, then changed his mind.

Since he was already at the solar door, he might as well go in and see if Anlin was sleeping. Faulk smiled at his own mental equivocation. It wasn't as if going back down the stairs presented a hardship. He had to admit he didn't want to hole up in his office—thinking of problems and solutions and making lists.

He wanted to see his wife. He wanted to feel the silky texture of her skin.

He was, therefore, disappointed when she wasn't waiting for him in the solar. The flanking chairs on either side of the fireplace were empty. He crossed to the chamber door and peered in. The faint glow from the fireplace in that room showed a lump in the bed that could only be Anlin. She had come up and gone to bed.

It made sense. She was probably both physically and mentally exhausted. He didn't want to wake her. Duty it would be then. Lists awaited him. He backed away from the door.

"Faulk, is that you?"

She was not asleep. He mentally crumpled pages of lists. "It better be," he said and walked further into the room. "I thought you might be asleep."

"Too many things on my mind," she said.

"I can appreciate that. I feel like I'm doing three things at once, or at least I should be." He stripped off his tunic, laid it over a chest, and began to release the points of his hose. "I gave Hettle permission to buy another plow team. They're both white and well matched. I think it bothered Hettle that the plowman thinks they're pretty."

He was rambling. He knew he was rambling, but suddenly he was afraid he had been too optimistic. What if Anlin's acquiesce to touching didn't mean she was ready to accept him fully as her husband? He now had a better appreciation of the horrors she'd lived through in Rennic, but he hoped what he offered wasn't something Anlin would even find comparable.

Should he remove his drawers? In the light from the fire she could probably see that he was aroused. He'd gotten an erection walking the stairs. His thoughts made him randy as a goat. Would the physical evidence of what he had in mind scare her? Would it make her turn inward again?

He was being ridiculous. He always slept in the nude. Sweet Cheelum, she was his wife after all. He jerked his draws down, left them lying on the floor, and walked over to the bed. He turned back the bedcover and slid in. The sheets were chill against his skin. The hand that stroked his thigh was warm. For a moment, he forgot to breathe.

"Your leg is nice to touch," Anlin said. "The hairs are soft and tickle, and I can feel your muscles move under my hand."

Faulk decided to breathe again. Anlin had no idea what he wanted to move under her hand. He rolled onto his side and looked down at her. She wore a small, secret smile. Amazing—Anlin in bed with him and smiling. He leaned over and kissed that smile. Her free hand came up and traced his ear. His stroked down her side, finding only smooth warm flesh, his touch unimpeded by a nightgown.

Breathing again became problematic. He wanted to bury himself in her. He wanted to make her cry out in ecstasy. But most of all he wanted her to stay here, in the present, and not disappear into some shadowy place in her mind. Slow, he told himself. Keep it slow.

Continuing to kiss her, Faulk slid his arm under Anlin and, rolling, pulled her on top of him. She made a squeaking sound at the change of position, but then relaxed atop him. He ran his hand up and down her spine. "Sit up and straddle me," he said. "Then you can touch me wherever you want."

He felt her hesitate—and then comply. The flickering light highlighted her proud breasts now available to his greedy hands and mouth. He touched her and she touched him until they both panted. She unconsciously rubbed back and forth across his straining arousal until he thought he would spill without ever being inside her.

"Take me in you." he groaned, raising her hips up slightly with his hands.

For a second, her face took on a vacant expression, and he feared he'd lost her. But then her hand touched him, bringing his erection to the hot, slick entrance to her core. At first, the angle was wrong; then he was suddenly sheathed. He made some sort of incoherent sound and rocked her hips with his hands. The secret smile again appeared on her lips and she found her own rhythm. She leaned over, sweat-slicked, and rode him.

In that moment, Faulk knew the Rennish ideas were in error. One life was enough to know such joy.

𝓣𝓱𝓮 𝔀𝓲𝓷𝓭 𝓫𝓵𝓮𝔀 𝓲𝓷 𝓯𝓲𝓽𝓯𝓾𝓵 𝓰𝓾𝓼𝓽𝓼 and carried a hint of rain. Anlin was glad she wore her cloak. The tight weave stopped the wind and could repel the rain if it came. She was especially thankful for the deep hood, which hid her face from those around her. She had badgered Faulk to be included in the group going to see her father. It was a serious mission and everyone wore sober expressions. Everyone except Anlin, who could not keep from smiling.

She had walked this earth for nearly twenty-three years, and today was the first day she had realized her power. It was a heady feeling.

She had understood she lacked magical ability when she was quite young and knew this deficit caused her parents pain. Her years of captivity in Rennic had been ones of utter powerlessness. Even this morning, she thought she was going to be relegated to the sidelines once again when important decisions were made.

"I appreciate all your arguments," Faulk had said,

"but there's no need for you to go to Giffard's Crest. This isn't a social visit. I'm going to try to convince your father that Lord Tarn and his henchmen are causing the madness that is destabilizing the country. And, assuming I'm successful, we'll have to come up with some response." Unsaid was the sub-text that she would be in the way.

"But I was there and heard what the Seerin said. I can add weight to whatever you say," Anlin said.

"Callip is going. He will give all of the facts from the Rennish point of view."

"But I would like Telm to meet his grandfather. I want to give Telm a feeling of continuity, to see that he is part of a family here."

"Please, Anlin, let it go. This is not a good time for you and Telm to visit." Faulk gave her a stern look she knew masked his worry. He had been up before dawn making lists of the salient points he wanted to cover with her father. Faulk was a great believer in lists.

He'd also dressed in his moss green tunic, something Anlin knew he wore when he needed confidence. It was his only good article of clothing. She felt that she'd let him down by not making him a new tunic, but her skill with the needle was such that she'd never be able to embroider the nightpiper emblem that graced his left shoulder.

Without thought, her hand brushed over Faulk's talisman, touching the fine stitches that formed the bird, feeling the hard contours of his chest beneath. And with the catalyst of this touch, Anlin found her power.

Faulk's irritated expression relaxed; the corners of his mouth turned up. Anlin stepped closer, placed her other hand on his right shoulder, and raised her head. Faulk pulled her to him and kissed her, his lips at first gentle and then more demanding. Her fingers tangled in the russet curls at the nape of his neck. Her breasts pressed tightly to his chest. She could feel the heat of him, smell the spicy fragrance of the soap he used to shave. Evidence of his ardor nudged her abdomen.

He was remembering the night just past, Anlin could tell. She certainly was. Faulk had taught her much about touching and the wonders that could follow. She had never known such explosive feelings existed. She'd never known her body could join with a man with such joy. She didn't know if what they had done in bed had been a revelation to Faulk, as it had been to her, but she knew he'd liked it. Yes, he'd liked it very much.

"I would miss you tonight if I were not with you," she whispered. "Now that we've found such accord, I'd hate for us to be parted."

Her earlier arguments had been considered and logical, but this was the argument with power, the one that had bent Faulk to her will. And so, she now rode to her father's keep—hiding her satisfied smile deep within her hood.

She wished she knew of some way to reach Telm as well, but he still kept a distance between them. He rode at Callip's side, indifferent to Anlin, but still pleased to be included, evidently curious to see one of Fallucia's High Places. She wanted to show him all the locations that had delighted her as a child—the high window from which all of the Giffard demesne spread like a living map, the dark mystery of the mews and its rustling falcons, the large kitchen with its perpetual bustle and tantalizing smells. She wanted to share with him her youthful experiences of exploration. He clung to Callip like a burr, however, his face taking on a look of polite boredom when she spoke to him.

They had been climbing for some time, Giffard's Crest rising above them. The wind freshened, and it was with relief that they reached the busy bailey. Amid the excited calls, ostlers came forward to take their horses. Callip and Telm elicited stares, but the looks were more curious than hostile.

Her father, Lord Giffard, awaited them at the top of the stairs to the hall. He looked more drawn than the last time Anlin had seen him, as if some of his vigor had departed with the heat of summer.

"Daughter," he said, taking her hands and then turning to greet the others. Anlin knew no more emotional welcome would be forthcoming. Since her initial return from Rennic, they had been separated by her feelings of betrayal and her father's feelings of guilt.

Lord Giffard clasped Faulk's forearm, keeping him from kneeling. It was a singular display of respect for the man who had won her. Her father was obviously pleased with Faulk's tenure at White Ford. He seemed less certain of what ceremony Callip required, both men silently appraising one another. Lord Giffard finally settled for a shallow bow. Callip echoed the motion.

Lord Giffard acknowledged Telm not at all. He looked over the boy as if he did not exist. Anlin felt irritation at the slight. As they proceeded into the hall, she walked next to her father. She plucked at his sleeve to get his attention.

"I don't think you had the opportunity to meet my son Telm," she said, keeping her voice level with difficulty.

Her father gave her a bland look. "I'm glad you were able to find him since that seemed so important to you. I'm pleased that he lives, but I would have been satisfied if he had not returned with you. It has not been a Giffard tradition to acknowledge bastards. We care for them and try to give them a decent life, but we do not claim them as our own. I don't know what you want of me, Anlin."

How had she expected her father to behave? Had she really thought that he would clasp the boy to his breast and proclaim him his grandson? Well, maybe in the same dream where Telm was still the little boy who had been taken from her instead of the stranger he'd become. In the harsh light of reality, Anlin knew this would never happen.

"Civility is not acknowledgement," she said, knowing that civility might be the best that she could hope for.

Her father turned away to call for mulled wine to chase away the visitors' chill. Anlin schooled her features to the frozen mask she had perfected. She must have been less successful in hiding her emotions than she imagined, however, since it was Faulk and not one of the servers, who brought her a cup of wine, curled her fingers around the warm metal, and murmured that all would be well. Perhaps she'd given away more about herself than she thought in the warm darkness of their chamber.

Her father's comments had left her to wonder what other Giffard bastards might exist. Had her father sired children on some women other than her mother? She thought her brother Roland a better candidate. She well knew his attitude toward women and suspected Roland thought their best place was on their back. Lord Tarn supposedly took responsibility for his bastard Faulk, and look how poorly that was done. Anlin wondered if all the Lords of High Places scattered their seed without consequence.

She glanced over to where Faulk conferred with her father, both men speaking in low tones. Her father's expression changed from interested to confused to incredulous. Faulk's face reflected only earnestness. "I think we four should go into my solar where we may be more private to discuss what Faulk has just old me," Lord Giffard said to the hall at large.

Anlin stood, understanding why her father would not want to discuss the madness caused by the amulets in front of the boy. There was no way that Lord Giffard could know Telm had already heard all the damning information. Then her father motioned for her to remain seated.

"We four," he said, indicating her brother Roland, who had entered unremarked and now surveyed the room with fever bright eyes. If her father looked as if the change of season had leached something out of him, Roland looked as if the cold weather had lit a fire within him.

Ignoring her father's gesture, she said, "I'm fully conversant with the issue and may have something to add." She walked toward the stairs leading to the solar, half expecting her father to physically stop her, but he let her precede him from the room and up the stairs.

A fire glowed in the fireplace and the room was pleasantly warm. The last time she had been here was to meet Faulk after the tournament. He had seemed so forbidding then, the cruel, ruthless man she thought she needed. Now his kindness seemed to define him, but she knew the consummate warrior still resided in him. He made her feel safe and cosseted. It was strange she hadn't realized how fulfilling such emotions could be.

The men filed in behind her and made their way to a table next to the fireplace. Her father sat on a chair at the head, as was his right. Faulk sat next to Callip on the bench to Lord Giffard's left which left the bench on the right for Roland and herself. Her brother glared at her as if he wanted to forbid her participation, but he remained silent.

"Sir Faulk says you're the Chief Shaman in Rennic," Lord Giffard said to Callip, "and that you speak with the authority of the rulers of that country."

"To be accurate, I *am* one of the rulers," Callip said with a deprecating smile. "Rennic is ruled by a council composed of Shamans and Seerin and our authority comes from the Goddess."

Callip sat back as if he had just explained everything there was to know about Rennic while Lord Giffard looked totally perplexed. "I'm not sure I follow."

"Well, eight hundred years ago," Callip began. Anlin saw hours of theological discussion to follow, undoubtedly concluding with how all those in Fallucia had been living in error. She started to interrupt when Faulk placed a quelling hand on Callip's arm.

"We really don't have the time to go into all the background, Callip," Faulk said. "We just need to put the facts before Lord Giffard so he can make some suggestions as to how we're to proceed. The most important point is that the Rennish have discovered a gemstone that aids them in their magic. This same stone has an injurious effect of Fallucians, however, and a number of the stones have been given to various Lords in this country."

Anlin could almost see Faulk mentally checking off points on his list. But before he could continue, Roland interjected, "What a load of crap! Everyone knows the Rennish have no magic, that they actually hate magic.

There is no way they would need something to aid them with Talent they don't possess."

"As I started to say," Callip gave Faulk a quelling look, "hundreds of years ago, the Rennish were a persecuted minority who had a different magic system from that currently practiced in Fallucia. To avoid total annihilation, we Rennish pretended that we had no magical ability. But we do. It is different from yours, but it is no less effective. Those who are very powerful practitioners are rare, however. So, to protect our borders, we've given our Sentinels amulets of Glafser. This stone amplifies Fallucian magic, so any incursion into our country is more easily discovered."

"Oh, now you have magic, do you? I'm certainly scared." Roland made a disdainful grimace.

"Quiet Roland," Lord Giffard said. "I would hear this." Then he turned to Callip. "If this stone, this Glafser, is able to amplify the type of magic that is used in Fallucia, in what way would that be harmful? I can see why you wouldn't want us to increase the magical ability in Fallucia, but I don't see why *we* should fear it."

"It causes insanity," said Faulk. "How often have we said that magical Talent in Fallucian males leads to madness? The catalyst for this mental deterioration is Glafser."

"Imagine you're in a cave," Callip said. "If you yell, the sound will rebound off the rock around you, causing an echo. Now, in the physical world, this echo diminishes. In the realm of magic, however, Glafser

282 • Hannah Meredith

makes these echoes repeat themselves over and over until the Fallucian who wears the stone can't hear his own thoughts. All is eradicated by the loud thunder of magic in his head." Callip moved his graceful hands as he spoke, seeming to build a cave and echoes in the air in front of him. Anlin wondered if this ability to make one visualize what the speaker described was part of Rennish magic.

"You've spoken to me of your concern with the deterioration of King Fremmor," Faulk said to Lord Giffard. "You've worried about the destabilization of the country and have commented on how some of the Lords are consolidating power at the expense of others."

"And you believe this Glafser is doing this?" Anlin's father asked.

"Yes," said Faulk and Callip simultaneously.

"But if this is the case, then who is selling this stone to Fallucian nobles?"

"A few of the amulets worn by our Sentinels were taken as prizes when our forces were defeated," Callip said. "But for many years, we in Rennic have had a special relationship with the Lords of Tarn. Currently, that lord is Edmund. He has warned us of Fallucian interest in taking over Rennic and bringing our country into the Fallucian kingdom. To combat this threat, we have given Lord Tarn amulets and other jewelry to distribute to those whose insanity would most affect your country."

"Lord Tarn?" her father asked. "I find this

impossible to believe. The man is ambitious, but I can't see him harming the whole country, laying us open to an invasion from Rennic." Lord Giffard shook his head. "No, this is too farfetched."

"It's true," said Anlin, entering the conversation for the first time. "Seerin Krisla admitted this to us when she discovered she'd been lied to about Faulk's upbringing. They thought Faulk had been taken to be raised by his father, Lord Tarn, and instead he was put in the care of his uncle—a man whose madness would indicate he was an early recipient of Glafser."

"This is absurd!" Roland yelled, standing up and shoving the bench back so quickly he nearly knocked Anlin to the ground. 'My poor damaged sister would believe anyone who told her the hedge-knight she married to is of noble blood, so she's willing to swallow this whole ridiculous tale. And you're right, Father. Lord Tarn wouldn't do anything to endanger Fallucia. But it makes very good sense the Rennish would make up a story to stop Fallucians from using something that would enhance our power. Now that we know they, too, have magic, it's obvious we need to improve our abilities to combat them."

"How can you say those things?" Anlin asked. "I was there and I can tell you what the Seerin and Callip said was the truth."

"Truth?" Roland shouted as he paced the room, throwing his hands about as he spoke. "How could you recognize the truth, and why would you think the

Rennish were telling it? From what you said and what our father has told me, you spread your legs for plenty of them. As far as we know, this scar-faced monkey you brought back from Rennic was one of your favorite lovers, and you'd want us to believe anything he says."

He quit pacing and leaned over Anlin so closely she could feel spittle on her face. "And don't think that I can't figure out what you're trying to do. You want to replace me with your mongrel bastard. You think to take all of Giffard's Crest as your own. Why else would you be parading him around? Why else would your supposed husband put up with the living proof that you'd been rutting with Rennish men for years? You want to prejudice our father against me."

Anlin looked at her brother in shock. Why was he saying all these hateful things? She knew he'd always felt she and her sister Sybil had more of their parents' affection. He's also been jealous that she'd gotten her way about having a tournament when she'd come home, but the things he was saying were crazy. Her own thoughts stopped her for a moment. Roland did sound crazy. He sounded insane.

"Roland," she said, trying to keep her tone reasonable, "why do you keep touching your chest? What do you wear under your tunic? Do you have an amulet?"

"Of course, I have an amulet," Roland screamed. "Anyone with any sense would have one. We Fallucians need to strengthen our magic before the Rennish attack.

And I need to prove my worth to our father. Our father who always favored the perfect Sybil and always gave you the benefit of the doubt because you were without Talent. While I, the son and heir, always had to scramble for the crumbs. Well, I'll not take the crumbs now. I'll have it all. King Fremmor will see me as one of his preeminent nobles. I'll—"

"Stop!" Lord Giffard shouted. Then he modulated his tone and said, "You're not making sense, Roland. You need to sit down and show me your wonderful amulet. I need to see what the stone is like that can give you so much power."

"Oh, *now* you recognize my power, do you? It's about time you saw me for the man I am. I reached my majority last year, and you've yet to suggest a possible wife for me, you've yet to give me the responsibilities you've given this jumped up man-at-arms who has nothing to recommend him except that he's fucking my sister. So, I'm proud to show you my amulet. You should see how I've planned for the future." And then Roland sat back down and drew the amulet from beneath his tunic.

"It's impressive," Lord Giffard said, leaning forward to take the disc in his hand. "The stone is unique. Where did you get it?"

Roland looked like a proud little boy. His face shown as it had when he'd flown his first hawk, the expression one of wonder and accomplishment. "Sir Charl of Shorely gave it to me. He knew I was worthy of the honor. He knows I think he should have won Anlin and White Ford at the tournament. Faulk only beat him by cheating, but I've promised him that I'll see this mistake corrected after those who have the real power take over Fallucia."

Lord Giffard held the amulet tightly, and evidently gave Faulk some signal, because Faulk leaped over the table in one movement. His fist met with Roland's chin, and her brother crumpled to the ground. Callip sat calmly as if he had some prescience that told him how everything would play out.

"I would not have believed it had I not seen it," her father said. "I know he's been acting erratically, but I thought it was just youthful over-enthusiasm. I had no idea madness was stalking him."

"Give me the amulet," Callip said, "and in a while, he will become more normal."

"He won't completely return to the way he was?" It was the question of a concerned parent.

"I wish I could promise that," Callip said, "but we don't know how long the effect of Glafser lasts on Fallucians. I'm sorry."

"The more important question," said Faulk, "is what we are going to do with the knowledge."

Lord Giffard sat straighter, pulling the aura of a Lord of High Places around him. Anlin could tell he was worried about her brother, but he also accepted that he had other responsibilities—responsibilities that affected the whole country and not just his family.

"I now see that King Fremmor has been corrupted in this same way," Lord Giffard said. "It's both frightening and reassuring to know the madness many of us thought was inbred has been caused by an outside influence. But I don't think we're in the position to ride to the king and confront him. We also cannot accuse Lord Tarn without more knights under our banner. We will need to figure out whom we can approach and hope to assemble a force that can intimidate Tarn and his allies." He turned toward Callip. "Can we expect help from Rennic in this quest?"

Callip looked uncomfortable. "We can only act defensively. It is our pledge to the Goddess."

"You can only act defensively?"

"Yes."

Lord Giffard laughed. "I think this means you've been protecting yourself from our potential attack, and we're been protecting ourselves from yours, and neither of us was really interested in invading the other."

"But for eight hundred years," Callip began.

"Leave it," said Anlin. "Just assume that both Rennic and Fallucia have been working from the wrong assumptions. At least you can promise that Rennic will not attack divided Fallucian forces."

"By the Goddess, Rennic would never do such a thing!" Callip looked offended.

"Then we need to plan what we'll do next," Faulk said. He'd tied Roland's hands and feet and pulled him over to the side of the room. "If you'll get me paper and ink, I'll make a list of what we need to do."

Anlin smiled. If all the world were to fall into chaos, she was quite sure that Faulk would make lists. There was something reassuring about that.

❧ 19 ❧

For the first time in memory, Faulk hated to leave for a battle. Fighting was what he did. It was what he was good at. Being a knight gave him status, and his honor demanded he follow his liege lord. It was not as if he had a premonition of disaster. No, as embarrassing as it was, Faulk simply didn't want to leave his wife.

He wasn't sure how this weakness, this need, had come to be. Perhaps it was that the awakening of Anlin's desire had been so long in coming. Perhaps it was that once awakened, he'd never known anything like it. Or, most probably, he was just a besotted fool. Sweet Cheelum, he was satisfied just to watch her sleep, her lengthening hair spread over the pillow, the white blaze catching the firelight like lightening across the night sky, her arm thrown over her head with the relaxation of an innocent child.

Yes, he was besotted. And he was a fool.

He turned away from his sleeping wife before his hand could reach out of its own volition and stroke the softness of her cheek, follow the line of her jaw down the length of her neck until his fingers brushed the lush fullness of her breasts, caressing them until the nipples pebbled under his palm and she woke. If he did, she would reach for him, arms wide, asking for the pressure of his body, encircling him as he buried himself in her sweetness.

He felt himself grow hard. He hadn't been this randy since he was a youth who had just discovered the wonders that were women. But this time there was only one woman who would do. Anlin. His wife. Yes, he definitely was a fool.

He picked up his new surcoat from the chest. Anlin had been working on it for most of the three moon turnings since their return from Rennic. Faulk had dutifully stood with his arms held out from his sides while Anlin and her maid Hilmar pinned and cut and discussed. Then he had pretended not to notice Anlin's dashing from the solar at his approach, the fabric clutched in her hands. Finally, yesterday, she'd presented it to him, pride sparkling in her face.

He suspected Hilmar had done a good deal of the actual sewing of the garment. He knew Anlin's talents didn't include needlework. But he was sure Anlin herself had carefully embroidered the nightpiper on the front.

The bird looked perhaps thinner and a little more falcon-like than it should, and the actual stitches were somewhat uneven and lumpy, but these deficiencies were obliterated by the love that had created the badge.

For a badge it decidedly was—the identifier of a landed knight. It had taken him a few minutes to figure out the purpose of the wide line of mixed blue and white threads that crossed on a slight diagonal beneath the nightpiper. The realization had embarrassingly brought tears to his eyes. It was the White Ford as it was viewed from the solar window—or perhaps as seen by a bird in flight. The combined images proclaimed him to be Sir Faulk, the Nightpiper of White Ford. He would wear the surcoat over his mail with pride.

He carried the surcoat with him to the hall where Kevin and Waylon were waiting to help him into his mail, which shone from a fresh sanding. The care of a knight's equipment and weapons was usually the responsibility of a squire, but lacking one, the men-at-arms did that duty.

"Is this the marvelous new surcoat that Hilmar has been talking about for weeks?" Waylon asked as he dropped it over the mail.

Faulk suspected Waylon had spent the previous night in Hilmar's bed and probably knew more about the effort that went into the making than Faulk did. Both of the men-at-arms had shown an interest in the fresh-faced Hilmar, but to everyone's surprise, she had favored tall, thin Waylon.

"Yes, I feel quite resplendent. Please thank Hilmar for her work," Faulk said.

Waylon gave Faulk a toothy grin. "You're supposed to think Anlin sewed every stitch herself."

"And that's what I think."

"Smart man," said Kevin. "I knew there was some reason we've sworn to you." He handed Faulk his sword and helm. "Callip's with the horses in the courtyard if you're ready."

Faulk recognized anticipation and eagerness in both men. They were like hunting hounds straining at their leashes when game had been sighted. More than one man-at-arms had found knight's spurs at the end of a battle. Faulk himself had. For Kevin and Waylon, the coming battle represented opportunity. Faulk suddenly felt very old.

There was no need to explain again that this time they were taking the battle to the king, not fighting for him. The punishment for such a breach of allegiance could be great if they were not successful.

Through Lord Giffard's auspices, Faulk and Callip had talked to the majority of the Lords of High Places, at least to those who didn't exhibit an onset of madness or who weren't known to be part of the cabal Tarn controlled.

Lord Giffard's group seized any amulet that was found and tuned it over to Callip. Lord Mariet, whose lands encompassed much of the eastern coast, found two stones newly received by his chief retainers. The prospect of further proliferation brought many of those Lords who wavered into line.

A petition, asking that all amulets or other jewelry made of the strange blue and red-laced stone be turned over to the Rennish shaman, had been sent to King Fremmor. The Lords also made clear their concern that the stones were having a detrimental effect on the Kingdom.

The King's response—or more probably the response of Tarn and his friends who kept the King in thrall—was to declare the concerned Lords to be in rebellion and to ready their own forces. Lord Giffard and his allies had no option but to plan an attack upon the King himself. The results of this battle would shape Fallucia for years to come. It was a fight none in the supposedly rebel contingent particularly wanted, but it was one that had been forced on them.

Faulk pulled a heavy, fur cape around him and slid on fur-lined gloves. He was thankful the warm clothing had been part of a ransom from a past tournament. He wished his men-at-arms didn't have to make do with wool capes, but there would be men on both sides who didn't have even that. A campaign in winter was a hardship on all involved.

They walked out of the hall and into the courtyard. Torches illuminated the small group that would be White Ford's addition to Lord Giffard's troops. These were most of the men who owed arms duty to the fief. A few would be left for protection of the manor, but if the battle should go against them, White Ford would be forfeit.

Lord Giffard, a proclaimed King's man, now rode against his King. Faulk remembered when Lord Philip

294 • Hannah Meredith

Lealand had done the same. He devotedly prayed the outcome would be different this time.

Fiddian, Faulk's big gray gelding, steamed in the pre-dawn cold. Callip sat nearby on a smaller bay. The only concession to the weather the shaman had made was to add trousers under his ubiquitous robe. He sat in the blustery wind as if the cold did not affect him. Possibly it did not. Faulk well remembered the feeling of being burned alive that had been caused by Callip's touch. It was not something the two men spoke of, although Faulk noted that the only weapons Callip carried into battle were his hands.

Faulk swung into the saddle, at ease with the weight of mail and fur. The horse boy released his hold on the bridle, and the gray danced, impatient to be away. Faulk steadied him and checked to see that everyone in his small cavalcade was ready to leave.

He heard his name called. Anlin's voice. He swiveled toward the solar window. Anlin stood there, backlit by candles, her nightgown a slash of white, her hair a dark nimbus around her head and shoulders.

"Travel within Cheelum's smile," she called, raising her hand.

It was a traditional farewell. It was proper. Why did Faulk wish that it were more? He knew she'd awakened to find him gone and had crossed the chill chamber and solar to come bid him good-bye. It would have to be enough. He raised his hand to return her salute and to put his group into motion.

He allowed himself one glance back at Anlin's figure glowing in the window. Sweet Cheelum, he hated to leave his wife.

There was the slightest hint of lighter gray to the east, but all was darkness away from the torches. Callip rode up next to him. The rest of his troop followed at a respectful distance. Fiddian worried at the bit, but Faulk kept him at a sedate pace. It would be irresponsible to arrive at the gathering point with blown mounts.

They traveled through the village, the soft clatter of metal that is peculiar to mounted warriors echoing between the buildings. Did the sound make those within the dwellings feel secure or threatened? Faulk devotedly hoped no other troop of men would come to threaten his village, his people.

"I would ask you a personal question," Callip said, his face indistinguishable in the darkness. "And because it is personal, I will take no offense if you choose not to answer, just as I hope you find no offense in my asking."

"Ask," said Faulk.

"Do you care for Anlin?"

"She is my wife."

Callip gave a cough. "In Rennic, that might have been an answer, since husbands are conditioned to bond with their wives, but, from what I've seen of Fallucia, this is not necessarily the case."

"That is true," Faulk said. "Men marry to get property. They marry to get children to inherit that property. There is no need for affection between spouses. It is nice if it happens, however." He hoped that Callip didn't hear the wistfulness in the last statement.

"Then you *do* care for Anlin. I had thought as much, but it goes against long held beliefs. Neither you nor Anlin has the least glimmer of magic. There should be no bonding possible—but somehow it has happened. It's most curious. This would not occur in Rennic."

"Of course, it wouldn't. Do you have any idea how Anlin was treated in Rennic? Are you ignorant of what men do with their female slaves? With their night comfort?" Faulk felt anger simmer in his veins, as hot and potent as the invisible flames that Callip had made dance on his skin.

Faulk had tried to keep the anger at Anlin's treatment in Rennic tucked away. He'd told himself that Callip was not directly responsible, that what had happened to Anlin was caused by centuries of fear and misconceptions, all wrapped neatly in a distorted religious philosophy.

Perhaps the fact that he already missed his wife brought the anger closer to the surface. He looked at the shadowed figure riding next to him. "Anlin was twelve years old when she was captured and sold as a slave. A child! She was continually raped by her owners. She was degraded in every way possible. There was never any tenderness, any concern. Men used her as a receptacle for their lust, and that was all."

He shook his head in an effort to erase the disgusting images from his mind. "Sweet Cheelum, do you not know what occurred? The men stroked themselves to readiness and then mounted her. I take greater care to ready my mares when I breed them. In Anlin's case, there was never any touching, never any kissing, never any emotional content that makes mating among humans an act of love instead of a bestial copulation."

"Faulk, is there a problem?" Kevin's voice came from behind him. In his anger, Faulk had let his voice rise. He hoped the men-at-arms had heard only the volume and not the content.

"No, just a heated discussion." Faulk tried to project the sound of a laugh. "All is well."

Callip remained silent beside him. It was just as well. Faulk couldn't imagine what sort of excuses the shaman could offer for the abomination that was life in Rennic for those without magical ability. He would never tell anyone of the damage that had been done to Anlin. Callip may know what happened, but he obviously didn't know the cost to the participants.

Not that life seemed much better for those who were gifted. To see your wife only twice a year, to live perpetually apart, would not be something desirable. And what of those women, those wives, who lived sequestered in Ridgemere? They were nothing more than walking wombs in which to plant the next generation of, hopefully, magically Talented children.

No, he couldn't think of any excuse that Callip could offer, although if the man began with "Eight hundred years ago," Faulk would knock him from his horse.

"I am sorry for your anger, Faulk," Callip said softly. "And yes, I am well acquainted with what occurs between men and their female slaves. It is part of a shaman's duties to train young boys in proper behavior. And most men do behave as they have been trained. Occasionally, a man thinks he forms a bond with his slave, even though he knows that no emotional attachment is truly possible."

Callip suddenly stopped talking and seemed to become absorbed with a twist in his reins. When Faulk made no comment, he continued, "This attachment is a particular problem with men who themselves lack magical ability. They frequently care for the children of their union with a slave since they will never have any true children from a marriage. When this happens, the woman and any children are taken and sold elsewhere."

Faulk wished he could see Callip's expression. His tone seemed regretful. As if regret could cover the horror of what he'd just said.

"Since I've been here in Fallucia and have gotten to know you and Anlin, I've come to think we might be mistaken in our belief that true bonding is impossible for those without Talent. I feel you and your wife have formed a bond that is like the one experienced by husbands and wives in Rennic. I assume you experience enjoyment in copulation beyond that of ordinary release and that even Anlin finds the act fulfilling. Am I correct in my assumption?"

Faulk's initial reaction was to tell Callip to go to hell. Whatever happened between him and Anlin was no one's business, particularly not a Rennish shaman. But Faulk also felt some responsibility to all those faceless people who lived in the hell that had been created by the Seerin and Shamans' misconceptions.

"I would like to think Anlin and I have formed what you call a true bond." That, at least, was Faulk's wish, but he wasn't going to voice his doubts that Anlin had only found physical gratification.

Callip said nothing more. They moved through the awakening dawn. The pale, gray light touched the frost on each blade of dry grass and bare twig, turning the mundane landscape into something beautiful. Faulk was lost in his own thoughts and was surprised when Callip again began to speak.

"It is very difficult for a man to admit he has lived in error. It is even more difficult for a whole society to do so. But since coming to Fallucia, I'm beginning to think this is the case. It is bitter to have one's certainties shattered."

Callip twisted in his saddle, letting his horse choose his own way, and looked directly at Faulk. "I have never had much association with those who haven't the divine spark of magic. There was no need for me to know such people. They really aren't fully human. They're making retribution for mistakes in past lives in so they may find a more complete existence in the next. I know you object to these ideas, but they are tenets I have held sacred. To me, these are unassailable truths.

"But now I see things that I would have thought impossible. And if I am wrong in some aspects of my belief, I must ask where else I, and the teachings I follow, have been in error."

Faulk sought for words to express his thoughts. He began to understand why so many of Callip's explanations began with *Eight hundred years ago*. So much of what everyone believed to be true was based on the past.

"As a young boy, I was raised by Abbot Jezrel." Faulk said. "Seerin Krisla says he is my uncle. The relationship has no significance for me except as an explanation that much of the anger directed toward me might have really been anger with my mother. You believe he was the recipient of an amulet and had been made mad. Again, the only significance of this is how badly he beat me. A saner man would have stopped before such extensive damage was done.

"But above all of this was the fact that Abbot Jezrel *thought* he was right. He truly believed he was helping me, that regardless of the agony he visited on me, he was in some way offering me a better life."

"An amulet had made him mad—" Callip began.

Faulk cut him off. "You have seen the statues of Cheelum in our temples. You believe we are wrong in our beliefs. You think Cheelum is really some powerful god of the sky instead of the smiling god with open arms who is depicted. In this, you share the madness of my uncle. When the Abbot looked at the statues, he saw a grimacing god who held humanity away with straight, locked arms. He believed Cheelum planned eternal punishment for those who did not hear his voice and heed it. The Abbot was willing to punish me now to save me from worse punishment eternally. He did evil for what he thought was good.

"I think all of the wrongs you're doing are for reasons you believe are for the good—and I can't wrap my mind around any of these reasons. Are you really breeding people to have greater magical ability? If so, you must make those without magic seem to be less than human. How else can you excuse your behavior toward them?"

The sky had lightened enough that Callip's face was visible. He looked thoughtful. There was no evidence of anger or irritation.

"Rennish with even limited Talent are conscious of those around them who have been similarly gifted," the shaman said. "They can *see*, for lack of a better term, those with magical ability. The greater the Talent, the easier it is *to see* and *be seen*. We are, to a certain degree, blind to people who have no magic. They are like rocks and trees and cows and crows. Present, but not something that intrudes on our consciousness. It is our belief that these people are without souls due to evil they have done in past lives."

Faulk wondered what Callip would do if he started mooing or cawing. But the man had never exhibited much humor, so instead he said, "Well, as one who has just been declared soulless and given the same value as a cow, I think you can see why I don't find your beliefs appealing. You might want to consider that in the coming battle, it will be me and invisible people like my men-at-arms who will protect your back."

Callip nodded. "Do you think magic in Fallucia has been increasing or decreasing over the years?" he asked, seemly veering from the topic at hand.

Faulk shrugged. He couldn't see how this was germane to their previous discussion. "I have no idea. The only thing I'm sure of is that I have never had any."

"Since I've been here, I've come to realize that Fallucian magic has been decreasing, dramatically."

"If that's the case, then Rennic should have even less to worry about. If your magic is superior, then Fallucia isn't much of a threat. You can let people live normally instead of trying to improve the magical ability in your country"

Callip squinted into the rising sun so he could look directly at Faulk. "Rennish magic has also been decreasing for centuries. We had no idea that the same had been happening in Fallucia. What is some of the strongest magic that you've seen practiced?"

"Other than Abbot Jezrel talking directly to Cheelum, you mean?" Sarcasm was obvious in Faulk's voice.

"Yes, I mean magic where the results can be seen."

"Well, I've known some women who can scry and

view things that are happening at a distance. And there are some powerful healers. I had a friend who took a mortal wound and two healers frantically worked on him, and he lived when he shouldn't."

"I'm assuming these healers were women."

"Certainly, more women than men have magical Talent in Fallucia. It's to be expected."

"But what of the men's abilities?" Callip asked. "Males tend to have martial magic."

The times that Faulk had seen men demonstrate magical abilities were few. Men tended to keep their Talent secret. Most often, the threat of retaliation replaced magic's actual use.

"I've seen men conjure flame to light candles or fires," he said. "There are some who can sense the movement of prey animals, which is an aid in hunting. I've been told that most of the Lords can do the same with men, that they would know if an ambush was laid and things like that. But I've never been where that has been shown. I've heard tales about whole armies being laid waste by a mighty wave made of the wind, but I've never seen that either."

"You've seen nothing but clever tricks," Callip said, "because the use of Great Magic is gone from Fallucia, just as it has mostly disappeared from Rennic. The men who lead this country are called the Lords of High Places, and they all, indeed, make their homes on the highest point in their demesnes. There is a reason for this. Ages ago, the Lords of Fallucia could throw thunderbolts and call the wind, and this was more easily done from a height. But they can do this no more. The amulets were so readily accepted because they gave men the illusion of increased power.

"Even in Rennic," the shaman continued, "our principle towns are built at higher elevations, the better to defend against the Fallucian threat. But Rennish magic has always been defensive. It has mostly been manipulation of the mind more than manipulation of physical reality. I am currently the strongest practitioner of Rennish magic, and I know I have only a small portion of the Talent my ancestors had."

"And where does this put Telm?" Faulk asked.

The shaman's normally austere face settled into a look that could only be affection. "Ah, Telm. Now there is an aberration. He is mixed blood, child of a mother without any Talent and a father who is a candidate to be a husband but has yet to be chosen since his abilities are not particularly strong. Telm should not exist. But he does. And I believe for the first time in generations, we have found someone who will do Great Magic.

"Perhaps the Goddess has sent Telm to both our countries, since it is both countries that have been losing magical ability, and both countries that have imagined their enemies across the border have remained strong. We Rennish have structured our society to defend against a threat that does not exist. We were sure of our direction. We were sure we followed the dictates of the Goddess. And I fear we were wrong.

When certainties are removed, all that is left is emptiness." Callip managed to wrap a feeling of desolation into that last word.

"I will do what I can to aid your cause since madmen are dangerous, whichever side of the border they live on," the shaman continued. "But I wish you had never come to Rennic. I wish I had never learned how the amulets were being used. I wish I had never followed you to this cursed country. It is much more comfortable to live with your errors than to have to confront them."

To Faulk's surprise, Callip tightly reined in his horse and dropped back behind him, leaving Faulk to ride alone. He was even more surprised at how upset the shaman seemed to be. Up until now, Callip had been a haven of calm. But Faulk understood how the removal of certainties could leave one teetering on the edge of an abyss.

The lessening of magic was a revelation to Faulk, however. But it was not one that caused him alarm. It simply meant the world was becoming more heavily populated with people who were like himself, people for whom daily, physical existence was all there was.

He could barely wait to tell Anlin. She had long felt the lack of magic as a deficiency, as something that her family expected of her and she could not provide. While it might be true neither of them had as much as a trace of magic, it now seemed those who were magically gifted had only a flicker. A flicker that was growing dimmer with each passing year.

In what Callip viewed as a disaster, Faulk saw hope. Perhaps within just a few generations, everyone would be judged by his willingness to work and achieve instead of by some innate ability. It somehow seemed fairer to Faulk. And if he could help bring this new world into existence, it was something worth fighting for.

The snow floated to the ground like large, lazy feathers. Accumulating rapidly, it soon formed a white blanket that covered fields, roofs, and trees with equal thickness. There was not a breath of wind. The world was cocooned in silence. The familiar view from the solar window now seemed foreign, otherworldly. At another time, Anlin would have enjoyed the beauty of the first snowfall. Today, however, it brought only worry.

Anlin did not need to be a tactician to know that snow would hamper an invading army while it would favor those already in place. And her heart rode on a gray horse with an army of invasion.

No, not invasion, she told herself, an army of rescue, for the forces with which Faulk rode were attempting to rescue a king, perhaps a whole kingdom, from madness. Noble intentions did not guarantee success, however, and she feared the snow would hamper the Lords who went to restore Fallucia to its rightful path.

She closed the shutters against the cold and the

eerie light of white snow reflecting gray sky. The solar was at once darker and friendlier, the glow of the candles and the flickering of the fire making her feel sheltered and secure. Was this the day when the forces would meet? Would blood stain the pristine snow?

She would not think of that. She would remember Faulk in the courtyard, mounted and strong, the knight who had claimed her with his prowess. She could see again his face, bright in the light from the torches, turned toward her, his arm raised in farewell. Did he hunger for battle? Did he delight in the company of men and the opportunity to use the skills for which he'd been trained? She had watched him until long after the group had been lost in the darkness.

He had worn his new surcoat, her gift of time and effort. If the embroidery was less neatly done than that on his old one, if the image of the nightpiper had not turned out exactly as she had hoped, he'd still seemed pleased. While it was true that Hilmar had done most of the assembly of the garment, the design and the embroidery had been all hers.

She'd drawn the pattern of the nightpiper with all the skill she'd used in making maps, but she was never completely satisfied with the results. Perhaps if she'd had more time, she could have produced a finished product she found more perfect, but once King Fremmor had rejected all overtures, the need for action had become immediate.

Anlin wished she'd had the magic of some of the

women in the ancient tales who could weave protection spells into their stitches. But a bird with a slightly crooked wing was all she could manage. She hoped the love that had motivated every stitch would have some effect.

Anlin was quite sure she loved Faulk. At least that emotion seemed best to describe what she felt. She cared for his happiness and wanted only what was the good for him. She delighted in his touch, a revelation, since earlier, she couldn't have imagined she would desire any man. And desire him she did—the touch of his hands as they roamed her most secret places, the feel of his lips as they wandered over her body, the way his thrusts cast her into a world of sparkling beauty, the sound of her name on his lips as he too found his release.

She missed him. Sweet Cheelum, how she missed him. The bed seemed empty, although his scent still lingered on the sheets, tantalizing her with memory. This was all so new to her, such a momentous surprise. She wondered if their physical unions were as special for Faulk as they were for her. Her talks with Hilmar, as they worked on the surcoat together, had not been reassuring.

Anlin had been surprised at how freely Hilmar talked of bed matters, but from what her maid said, it seemed that such discussions were frequent among women. Since Anlin had never participated in this type of conversation, the topics covered were both fascinating and uncomfortable.

"Faulk looks good in this color," Hilmar had said, "but I imagine he looks even better in nothing at all."

Anlin was not pleased to think her maid imagined Faulk naked. She found this ironic since when they had first married, she'd thought Faulk might find Hilmar pleasing and actually hoped he would gratify his base needs with her maid and leave Anlin unmolested. Her attitude had certainly changed. But she was not going to tell Hilmar just how wonderful Faulk appeared when he wore nothing at all. Anlin wasn't going to admit that the sight made her mouth dry and the place between her legs wet.

Hilmar was not loath to have such a discussion, however. Over measuring and cutting and stitching, Hilmar had blithely compared the attributes and prowess of both Kevin and Waylon, obviously enjoying her bouts abed with both men.

"I've settled on Waylon," Hilmar announced. "He's not so good looking as Kevin, but he cares more for my gratification than his own. Of course, it doesn't hurt that Cheelum granted him the equipment to see the job done well. Not that Kevin is lacking, mind you, but there's just something to be said about a giving man like Waylon. Kevin seems to be mostly pound, pound, snuggle, snore."

Anlin listened in fascination, although afterwards she found it difficult to look at either of the men-at-arms without blushing. She probably knew more about them than she wanted to know. But it also made her wonder about Faulk. Could he make just any woman he was with feel like he made her feel? Was her experience unique? And more importantly, could Faulk have been equally satisfied with someone else?

The insecurity, which her newfound happiness had kept at bay, took on greater immediacy now that Faulk was gone. She worried that she only filled the Fallucian version of night comfort for Faulk. She had no way of telling if his heart, as well as his wonderfully hard body, was engaged. And if he never returned, she would never know. The emptiness she felt because of his absence would become permanent.

But she would not think of that. She would erase that worry from her mind. She would keep busy. It had snowed. She would go play with Telm in the snow. All children loved to build snow castles and throw snowballs, and Telm seemed to spend too little time being a child.

Her relationship with her son had improved, although it could not be described as close. In honesty, it probably never would be. Telm had become someone very different from her little boy in the four years they'd been separated.

Anlin now realized it was impossible to go back and retrieve the past. Telm looked to Callip for support, understanding, and even discipline. Telm saw Anlin as someone extraneous and unimportant. At least enough progress had been made that he now acknowledged she was his mother and no longer seemed upset by the fact.

But there was nothing that either she or Faulk could do to make Telm fit into the pattern of White Ford. Not that Faulk hadn't tried. Bless the man; he certainly had tried.

Faulk had produced a horse, a graceful bay mare with a narrow white stripe down her nose and three white stockings, that he said was to be Telm's very own. He took the boy riding with him, making gentle corrections, so that Telm no longer looked like a stiff poker jutting from the back of a horse. Telm seemed to enjoy these times. Faulk's only comment was that the boy was not a born horseman but took good care of his mare.

Three boys were brought to the manor from the village to play with Telm. Faulk deposited the boys, Telm, a number of wooden games, and a puppy in the hall and had dragged a hovering Anlin away, stating that boys had to find their own method of getting along.

A rather nice chessboard had been broken. The boys had left, one with a split lip and another with a bloody nose. Telm, rather proudly sporting a blackening eye, would only say that he had not liked what the boys said and that Faulk had told him he didn't have to put up with any disrespect. Only the puppy, now strangely named Dragon, had remained.

Telm spent several hours each day closeted with Callip, their doings secret and mysterious. Once Telm had brought her a now-dented silver cup that Faulk had won in a tournament, apologizing for the dent, saying only that he hadn't been able to sustain the levitation.

She realized Telm was more Callip's than hers, and she knew of no way to change this.

But playing in the snow was something any boy would enjoy, even with Anlin, whom he now at least called Lady to her face and the Lady Anlin when speaking to others. It was an improvement over "that woman." She suspected there had initially been some terms that were even less complimentary. Faulk would never say, although there was a time when Telm had first arrived that she had seen the normally mild-mannered Faulk hit the boy hard enough for the blow to knock him to the ground.

The idea of playing in the pristine whiteness appealed to Anlin as well. She found her steps as she descended the stairs were lighter than they had been since Faulk had left. Telm had been at loose ends with Callip gone and should welcome a diversion. Anlin also enjoyed the fact that she would have to compete with neither Faulk nor Callip for her son's time.

Telm wasn't in the hall or in his room, however. Anlin wondered if he had found some haunts with which she was unfamiliar. She was relieved when one of the serving women told her that she'd seen Telm and the puppy going in the direction of the barn. Telm had probably gone to check on his horse, responsibility sitting rather heavily on one so young.

It was no surprise he had taken Dragon with him.

Telm and the puppy were seldom parted. The young, lop-eared hound tended to jump up and snag the bottom of Anlin's tunics with his sharp little claws. He also had an unfortunate habit of piddling on her feet in his excitement, but Anlin appreciated the beast because he made Telm laugh. It was a sound too seldom heard. Smiling, Anlin put on her heavy boots and wrapped up well, adding her cloak as a final layer against what she envisioned as an assault of snowballs.

The footsteps of her son and the leaping pattern of the puppy's feet were evident in the fresh snow. She wished there were some way to preserve them, so she could take them out and look at them whenever she wanted once Telm was gone. But she would just have to compile good memories against that bleak day.

She reached down and packed a snowball. She smiled. Nothing would draw out an opponent faster than an attack. Telm would be unable to resist.

She entered the barn and stopped just inside the door while she waited for her eyes to adjust to the darkness of the interior after the brilliance of the snow. The place smelled of horses and cows and hay, a not unpleasant scent that tickled the nose. "Telm," she called.

There was a rustling sound from the area where the horses were kept, but Telm didn't answer her. Had he seen her stop and make the snowball? Was he hiding and waiting to pounce before she could loose her white weapon? If she could catch him unawares skulking behind a stall, her missile couldn't miss. She moved stealthily through the gloom in the direction of the sound.

Her foot nudged something on the ground. Looking down, she saw the puppy, lying on its side, its continual motion stilled. She reached down and touched him. "Dragon," she said softly as if she feared waking him. The dog still lived, his heartbeat rapid under her hand, but he did not move.

Her head came up in alarm, glad the interior seemed less dark and she could make out what lay around her. Thankfully, the boy was not similarly felled, but she did not see him. She suddenly remembered the dented silver cup, but she could not imagine Telm would have tried any magic on his beloved hound.

"Telm, where are you?" Her voice was more strident.

"He's here." A man-sized shape appeared from one of the stalls and moved toward her. She finally recognized her brother Roland hauling a struggling Telm toward her from the gloom.

"What are you doing here?" she asked. With effort, she managed not to back away from Roland's approach. She had not seen him since they had taken his amulet from him and had hoped his sanity would return. The wild look in his eyes would indicate otherwise.

"I've come to retrieve a bitch's mongrel pup," he said, dropping the wiggling Telm at his feet and stilling him by placing a foot on his chest. Anlin realized the boy was gagged and bound. "I'd planned to take him back to Giffard's Crest and then send you a note that you could come and get him. But you've saved me the effort by your timely arrival."

"What do you want, Roland?" She carefully kept her voice level.

"Why, I simply want my due. I want our father to realize that *I'm* the important one. I'm sick of constantly hearing the praises of either a dead sister or the husband of the sluttish living one. I can vanquish a ghost over time, so I thought I might arrange for you to join our sister. Without you, your irritating husband has no claim to White Ford and will tumble back into the mire from whence he came."

"If your complaint is with me, then there is no need for you to hold the boy."

"Ah, yes, the boy." He smiled without humor. "I do have the boy, don't I? And since you've pointed out that I really don't need him, I might as well lean forward and see how long it takes his ribs to snap. You haven't whelped a very sturdy pup, Anlin, but that's what comes from indiscriminate breeding with all those scar-faced Rennish."

He leaned forward, as if to put his full weight on Telm's narrow chest, and Anlin reacted. She launched herself across the prone boy and jammed the snowball clutched in her hand into Roland's face. It wasn't much of a weapon, but it was all that she had.

It was probably surprise alone that drove the big

man backwards, away from his captive. Anlin's momentum carried her by him and into the edge of the stall, driving the air from her lungs. He was on her in a second.

Holding her hair, he jerked her upright and toward him. Anlin didn't resist his pull. Instead she came toward him, arms windmilling, willing to strike him anywhere she could. In the process she tried to push him farther from Telm. Her hand caught Roland's face, her finger nails digging grooves in his cheeks and seeking his eyes. She wished she had her knife, lost in Rennic. The narrow, flexible blade had dispatched one hateful man and could have done so again. But Anlin hadn't thought she needed any knife in a snowball fight.

Roland grunted and, with his hand fisted, struck her in the face. She tried to stay on her feet, her vision edged with black. She tasted blood in her mouth. Her legs felt unsteady, but she went toward him once again, not running from a man anymore. She knew his greater weight and strength gave him the advantage, but she would not run.

Despite her intentions, Roland knocked her to the ground with a blow to her mid-section. He knelt on her hips and grabbed her around the neck, choking her and banging her head on the floor in time with his words. "I'll have what is mine. I'll have what is mine."

She flailed her hands at him in an effort to reach his face, but he straightened his arms and she could not get to him. She struggled, trying to throw him from her body, trying to loosen his hands from her neck. She couldn't breathe. Panic filled her. She did not want to die. Now that she had something to live for, she did not want to die.

Then he suddenly released her, jerking back and screaming as if he were in pain, hitting at his tunic that was inexplicably smoldering. The most she could do was try to scoot away from him on the floor, the scene before her making no sense. Telm appeared behind Roland, his face a mask of concentration. His eyes were squinted; his brows were drawn together.

Roland's tunic burst into flames, licking up around his face, igniting his hair. He screamed, the sound high and wavering, and stumbled toward the door. He looked like a living torch. When he exited the barn, he lurched into a wobbly run, but did not get very far before collapsing into the snow. The flames extinguished and steam rose around him.

The intense expression disappeared from Telm's face. He shook his head as if awakening from a nightmare, and he suddenly looked like a frightened boy. He rushed to where Anlin partially sat on the floor.

"Mother, are you all right?" he frantically asked.

"Yes," she said, her voice sounding strange and raspy. Her throat had been injured and she had difficulty speaking. She was also choked with emotion. Telm had called her mother.

"We should get back to the manor," Telm said. "It's possible there are others." He extended his hands to help Anlin to her feet. She doubted he could actually aid her to rise, but she gave him her hands. Rope still encircled his wrists, the ends charred and dangling.

Anlin got to her feet. "How did you do that? Burn the rope and set Sir Roland's clothing afire?"

Telm looked embarrassed, as if he'd been caught doing something he'd been forbidden to do. "I can call fire. Anyone who has earned his first mark can do that. I can just do it better than most."

Anlin should have known that magic was involved, but Telm was so often just a normal little boy that it was easy to forget he had phenomenal ability. "Dragon has been hurt," she said, walking to where the little dog lay. "Can you help him?"

The boy's face fell, and he squatted next to the puppy. He ran a hand over the hound's tan hide and fondled one his floppy ears. He looked at Anlin with tears in his eyes. "I can do nothing," he said, stricken. "I haven't this Talent."

Anlin knelt next to her son. She too placed a hand on the puppy's warm side. She could feel the pup's heart beating erratically, but it was beating.

"The man kicked him," Telm said.

"I guessed as much." She continued to stroke the little animal. "I'm not sure I can make him well, but if we take him back to the hall, I'll do what I can. When I was very young, I used to take injured birds and small animals to my nurse to be healed. I watched what she did, which was mostly to keep the animals warm and to dribble water into their mouths. Some of them lived. But, you have to know, Telm, that some of them did not. I have no magic."

"I know," said the boy, "but I trust you to do what is right regardless."

His confidence buoyed her, and she gently picked up the little hound. He made a slight whimper when she cradled him against her.

She briefly detoured on their journey to the manor to stop where her brother lay in the snow. His face was a blackened crust. It looked like a piece of meat left too long on the spit. Strange mewing sounds came from his ruined mouth. His raw hands clutched the air over and over. She did not imagine he could live and thought it would be the best if he did not.

"I hope he dies," Telm said, almost echoing her thought, but with a darker intent.

"I suspect he will. But we must send people back to get him and bring him into the hall. I'll treat him as well as I know how. To not help him in any way that I can would be immoral. Then it will be up to Cheelum's mercy whether he lives or dies, but we must do all we can."

"He's evil," Telm said.

"No, he's mad."

Her son looked directly at her, his eyes suddenly very, very old. "I suspect that it's the same thing."

They hurried back to the hall. Their arrival and brief description of what had happened stirred up an ant's nest of activity. Some ran to the village and others went to bring Roland in on a sheet. They laid her brother on one of the trestle tables. If any noticed that Anlin's first concern was the puppy, none commented.

When she made her way to Roland, he was surrounded by white-faced people, but none had touched him. He was the heir to the Lord of Giffard's Crest. He was to have been one of the Lords of High Places. But now he was only part man and part crisped meat. Hettle had arrived in his position as reeve, but he was no help. Rather he was part of the problem having deposited his breakfast on the hall's floor.

The cook was the most efficient, wisely bringing a jar of the ointment that was used on burns from the kitchen fire. Anlin surveyed the wreck of flesh that had been her brother and didn't know where to start. Besides his blackened and blistered face, his torso was a mass of burns, many of which had charred pieces of his tunic attached. Anlin was sure the material should be removed, but her first attempt at pulling one of the pieces free changed Roland's mewing to a ghostly wail. She decided to cause him no more pain than he already felt.

Anlin knew of no true cure; she suspected the most talented healer would know of none. Some degree of comfort was all she could provide. She spread the cook's ointment over the burned area and covered him lightly with a roll of fine linen from which she had planned to make some chemises. She told one of the sturdier serving women to try to wring water from a cloth into his mouth and then walked away to sit on a bench, asking for ale to sooth the pain in her own throat.

Roland was her brother. She recalled him running after her, chubby legs pumping, wanting to be part of whatever activity she was involved in. But, as a child, she had wanted to tag after her older sister Sibyl. When she and Sibyl had gone to Hannon Heights for fostering, they'd left Roland behind without a thought, to do whatever little boys were supposed to do. Anlin had not seen Roland again until her return from Rennic, and then she had been too absorbed in her own bitterness and anger to take much note of him except in irritation.

She should feel a greater sadness that her brother lay dying, but all she could summon was a dull regret.

"How did this happen?" Hettle asked, coming to stand before her. He was still pale but otherwise improved.

"Roland tried to kill me, and he would have succeeded had Telm not acted and saved me."

"But how was Sir Roland so badly burned?" the reeve persisted. "Nothing in the barn has been burned."

"Suffice it to say that Telm saved me. That is enough." Anlin felt very tired.

"Was it magic?"

She just nodded. Whatever was said would only cause people to fear Telm. She was not sure that even now Hettle did not ease away from the boy. "Come up to my solar," she said to Telm. "There is nothing more we can do here."

Her son fell into step next to her. As they walked across the hall, she ruffled the boy's hair and he looked up at her with liquid eyes. No matter what horrors this day had encompassed, Telm had called her mother. To her mind, there had been more gain than loss.

❧ 21 ❧

Faulk stared across the snow-covered field at the host ranged against them. "Why would they come here to meet us?" he asked in disbelief. "If they'd stayed in the Eyrie, we would have had to besiege them, but in this weather, we couldn't have sustained a siege for very long. The Eyrie is unconquerable. Their actions make no sense."

"Of course, their actions make no sense." Philip Giffard said from beside him. "If any of the Lords who ride with us ever doubted the truth of our accusations, this behavior proves our point. The king is quite mad, since only a madman would leave an unassailable position to fight on a plain and put his men at risk."

The rising sun reflected off the snow with blinding brilliance, but it was easy to see the banners of those who fought with King Fremmor. Over half of the Lords of High Places had come in answer to the king's request for arms. Faulk wondered if most were corrupted by the amulets or if they simply felt that honor required them to fulfill their oath to the king. It was this latter group that Faulk was most uncomfortable fighting.

Although the king called them rebels and oath-breakers, most of the men who had come here in opposition to the king felt they were honor-bound to do so, that the protection of the country outweighed their previous pledges. It was a dire thing when men of honor fought one another for what each felt was right.

Lord Giffard held the central position on the rebel's lines. Since most of the others had come because of his persuasion, he commanded the force. It was a reluctant command, however, as was evident when he said, "I wish this could have been avoided."

"As do we all," said Faulk.

They had assumed they would have to scale the heights that led to the king's stronghold, the Eyrie, and lay siege to the huge castle. Plans had not been made for a frontal attack against another massed force. Messengers had been frantically dashing up and down the line trying to coordinate the impending attack. There would be no subtlety, no feints, just a straight dash toward the opposing line. It would be like an expanded melee, but this was no tournament and the effect would be much deadlier.

Faulk was surprised to see a small group of about a dozen men ride out in front of the King's lines. "Do you think they want to parley?" Lord Giffard asked, hope sharp in his voice.

"I don't see the banners of any of the leaders out front," Faulk said. "It doesn't look like the forward riders are any of the Lords allied with the King."

"Then what are they doing?" Giffard squinted into the white glare of sun and snow.

Faulk did the same. The distant activity seemed purposeless. The horsemen had formed a semicircle and appeared to be doing nothing more than sitting there, each with his hands raised toward the opposing force. The snow between the two armies glimmered with a suggestion of movement.

"Magic!" exclaimed Callip to Faulk's right. "They're using magic."

Faulk had fought in small skirmishes and had been at Lealand's side in the larger battle against Montcliff, but never had he fought against someone wielding magic. Its very lack in previous encounters supported Callip's contention that magic was declining. But if that were the case, why was it being used now?

The snow between the two forces seemed to gather itself into a long, humped ridge. It looked like a wave on the ocean and like a wave, it flowed toward the rebel lines with ever increasing speed. It broke right before the front lines, scattering snow over the entire group.

A noise, that had been a whisper just a moment before, now screamed through Faulk's mind. It was a cacophony of sound that brought indescribable pain. Faulk couldn't think. He could only react to the sound and the pain. Involuntarily, his hands came up to either side of his helm, as if to shelter his ears. Around him, all the attackers reacted similarly. Some fell from their horses. Some threw their helmets off, holding their heads and screaming. Horses, reacting to contradicting signals from their riders, moved in erratic directions, jostling into each other, rearing and kicking.

Through the din and the agony that battered his brain, Faulk realized that someone was pulling at his arm. With difficulty, he focused on Callip, who seemed unaffected by the shattering blast of magic. The smaller man continued to jerk on his arm, his face looking earnest, his mouth moving with words that Faulk was unable to hear.

Callip suddenly gripped the nasal of his helm, pulling Faulk's head down toward him, pushing his fingers into Faulk's face. The painful roaring subsided. It was still present, but not at a level that was incapacitating. Callip's voice filtered through the noise.

"I need more height," the shaman said. "Help me to stand on the front of your saddle and support me there."

No sooner were the words uttered than Callip was clambering onto the saddle in front of Faulk. Callip was festooned with amulets. All the stones that had been collected now swung from his neck, his shoulders, and even his wrists. Some of them banged against Faulk's helm as the shaman pushed himself to his feet, feet that were resting partially on the saddle and partially on Faulk's thighs. Although short of stature, Callip was not a small man and his weight pressed down uncomfortably. Nonetheless, Faulk braced Callip's legs and held him steady.

Callip began a push-away motion, such as a man might make if he were tangled in his bed linens and in the throes of a nightmare. The shaman repeated this motion over and over. True hearing returned to Faulk. He could make out the cries of those around him. And he could tell those cries were lessening, as if everyone felt relief.

The wave of blowing snow seemed to reverse and flow toward the opposing line.

Faulk could tell when it struck. The dozen horsemen in front of the line were the first affected. Almost as one, they collapsed, fell from their mounts, and writhed on the ground. Others in the line were similarly affected. Some fell. Others clutched their heads. And a few even fled.

"Attack! Attack now!" Lord Giffard called. His troops had recovered sufficiently so that many of them surged forward with their leader. Faulk tensed to follow.

"No! Stay here," cried Callip. "You have to support me until the deed is done."

Faulk understood that he needed to hold his position, that he needed to keep Callip raised high. Although this was necessary and was of greater aid to the cause of victory than his actually fighting, Faulk was chagrinned when the other horsemen surged forward without him. It took all his skill to keep Fiddian from joining the attack.

And so, during the greatest battle that had been seen in Fallucia in centuries, Faulk, the proud

Nightpiper of White Ford, was a spectator instead of a participant. He watched as his forces swept across the snow-covered field and crashed into the opposing line. There were pockets of violent resistance, but whole sections of the line simply dissolved before the onrushing rebels. As if they remembered they fought countrymen, most of the rebels seemed satisfied to knock their opponents down and capture them. With a limited amount of bloodshed, the King's forces were quickly overwhelmed.

The clash of arms abruptly stopped and silence drifted over the plain. Callip collapsed on top of Faulk, nearly driving him from the saddle. Callip hung head down like a doll that had lost most of its stuffing. Faulk managed to get the shaman upright, but the man's head flopped limply and his eyes were rolled back in his head.

"Callip," Faulk said, gently patting the man on the cheek. "Are you injured?" Faulk feared the shaman had given his life to thwart the King's magicians. To his relief, Callip moaned and attempted to sit up.

"Easy," Faulk said, steadying the smaller man.

Callip clutched Faulk and pulled his head close. "The citadel, you need to take the citadel or all could still be lost." The shaman's voice was weak but his words were distinct. Faulk looked up at the King's Eyrie, which sat atop a mount that thrust out of the plain. If King Fremmor and some of his supporters made it to the Eyrie, the rebels could still be faced with a difficult siege.

"Boy," Faulk shouted at a passing squire. "Get help for this man. He's saved us all." The squire looked doubtful but left toward the rear of the line and soon returned with two stout men-at-arms and a healer. Faulk eased Callip into waiting hands and again stressed the Rennish shaman had countered the magic that could easily have overwhelmed their force. On a day when battle fever was raging, it was important that all recognized allies from enemies. The scarred, Rennish face could bring out the wrong reaction if Faulk did not make Callip's position plain.

Finally given his head, Faulk's big gray was quickly in motion. He galloped across the field, the snow pounded smooth by all the passing feet. When Faulk reached the King's lines, he found Lord Giffard busy with organizing the disposition of prisoners and the dead. The rebels' victory looked to be complete. Faulk felt faintly embarrassed that his sword had never left its scabbard.

Faulk pulled his gelding up next to Giffard. "Is the King in custody?"

"Dead," Lord Giffard said. "The King lies among the dead. Whatever spell our friend Callip cast primarily affected those who wore amulets. The twelve who threw magic at us are all dead. From the looks of their chests, their amulets exploded; it's a bloody mess. Others scattered among the line suffered the same fate. The King had no wounds but was lifeless."

Lord Giffard's tone was level and matter-of-fact, but something about his expression told Faulk that his liege lord regretted what had happened to the king he was sworn to protect. Even if it was best for the country, the results were still uncomfortable to a man of honor. Faulk primarily felt relief, since, if the King were dead, then there was no worry that the struggle would continue.

"And Lord Tarn?" Faulk asked. "Is he among the dead or captured?" Tarn was the supplier of the amulets and the puppet-master for the impaired King. His whereabouts was of vital importance.

Lord Giffard looked momentarily confused. "Sweet Cheelum, I haven't seen him or those knights sworn to him in either group. How could I miss the fact that none of them were here?"

Faulk looked up at where the Eyrie hovered above the plain. In the confusion of battle, it would have been possible for a small group of men to leave the fighting and to begin their ascent of the mount without most people noticing. "Who's next in line for the Fallucian throne? Is it King Fremmor's son Thaddeus?"

"Certainly," said Lord Giffard. "But he's just a boy. The actual ruling of the country will have to be done by advisors until he comes of age."

"Where is he?"

Giffard followed Faulk's eyes to stare at the Eyrie as well. "He'd be in the castle. King Fremmor was insane, but he wasn't mad enough to bring his young heir to the battle."

"I need some men and I need them now! If Edmund Tarn has taken physical control of Prince Thaddeus, then we're nearly back to where we started."

Faulk saw realization of the impending threat flash across Lord Giffard's face. He immediately started calling for men to follow Faulk. Faulk didn't wait for them to gather, however. He spurred his big gelding toward the mount.

He heard hooves pounding behind him and glanced back to see Kevin following closely behind. Others also moved to join him, but they were further back. Since Faulk's horse had not been involved in the initial attack, he was fresher and ready to gallop. By the time Faulk had begun the ascent, the rest of the knights had dropped even farther behind. As the road became steeper, Faulk leaned forward and urged Fiddian to greater effort. He feared he would arrive at the citadel only to find the portcullis dropped and the young heir and his mother trapped inside with Tarn.

When he crested the top of the mount, Faulk was relieved to see the gate open and the portcullis still raised, but a lone knight barred the way. He recognized the black and silver surcoat of Sir Charl of Shorely, Tarn's sworn man and the knight Faulk had defeated to secure Anlin's hand. He reined in his lathered horse and looked at the powerful knight.

"It's over, Sir Charl," Faulk said. "You've lost the battle. There's no need to continue to fight. We're both

Fallucians and we both want what is best for our country. Stand aside."

"You'll not pass," Charl said holding his sword in front of him. "Lord Tarn has gone to secure the prince. We'll not let you rebels get control of him and bend him to become a Rennish puppet."

Faulk looked for signs of the madness the amulets caused but saw only belligerence. "Lord Tarn is the one who would make a puppet of the young prince, just as he did with King Fremmor. We want only to see our country strongly ruled. Prince Thaddeus has nothing to fear from me or any who came against his father, this I swear."

"I am not such a fool that I would listen to the oath of a man who brings a Rennish shaman and his cursed Rennish magic against us. But you didn't bring your wizard with you, did you, and so now you must rely on yourself. Do you dare fight me, Sir Faulk?"

Without question, Faulk dared. He had bested Sir Charl before. But a protracted battle at the gate would give Edmund Tarn time to take control of the prince and perhaps to rally the Eyrie's defenders. Time was not something Faulk had.

He briefly wondered if he could simply ride Charl down, but Fiddian was spent and to expose his flagging gray to Charl's lethal sword did not seem a fair recompense for the animal's years of service.

Faulk slipped from the saddle and unsheathed his sword.

The two men met as they had nearly a year before, but this time life, and not a fief, was riding on the outcome. Metal clanged against metal as Faulk countered Charl's initial stroke. There was no padding on the blades today. There were no referees to determine the winner. This time, each cut of both men's swords was intended to either maim or kill. Charl's longer reach was countered by Faulk's speed. Faulk felt he could eventually wear the man down, but that would take time, and time was Faulk's enemy as much as the armed knight who opposed him.

Faulk managed to get through Charl's guard and land a powerful blow on the man's side. Charl's mail kept the blade from biting flesh, but Faulk felt something give and suspected he'd broken a few of his opponent's ribs. Charl seemed to favor that side as the two men continued to circle. Intent as he was on the knight before him, Faulk still heard the arrival of another rider and recognized Kevin as the man-at-arms joined him in the fight.

Facing two opponents, Charl was forced to give ground. The bailey now stood open before Faulk. "Take him, Kevin," he called and sprinted around Charl. Faulk hoped he hadn't doomed his man-at-arms by leaving him to fight the seasoned knight alone. Securing the prince was the highest priority, however, and he had sparred with Kevin enough to think his retainer had a good chance of victory.

Faulk ran across the bailey. It was treacherously

slick where milling feet had compressed the snow into ice, however, and speed had to be tempered with caution. Out in the open, as he was, Faulk expected to be challenged, but the entire fortress was eerily vacant. Fremmor had evidently stripped the castle of all its guards, taking them with him to meet the rebel force. Madness upon madness to leave his wife and heir undefended.

The great hall sprawled along one side of the curtain wall. Having no idea where he could find Edmund Tarn, Faulk decided to start there. It too was empty, although Faulk heard surreptitious sounds through one of the side doors. He followed the noise and found two frightened maids trying to hide behind sacks of grain in a storage room.

"The prince, do you know where the prince is?" Faulk asked.

The two young women did nothing but quake and shake their heads.

"I'm here to help the queen and the prince, but I need to know where they are. If you don't tell me, then both of them could be badly hurt by a madman." Faulk removed his helm in an effort to look less threatening.

"The queen is generally in the solar," one of the women said, ducking her head as if she anticipated a blow.

"My thanks." Faulk immediately hurried across the large hall, his boots echoing in the empty room. He was almost to the top of the stairs when he heard a woman's raised voice. He had evidently come to the right place.

The scene that greeted Faulk when he entered the solar was not one that he had anticipated. A woman he presumed to be the queen sheltered a small boy behind her and held Edmund Tarn at bay with a fireplace poker. The woman's face was a mask of fury. If this was the prince's mother, Faulk hoped the boy would inherit the bravery of his dam.

"Tarn," Faulk called, "I don't think the lady is interested in giving her son into your care."

Edmund quickly turned toward Faulk, freeing his sword from its scabbard as he did so. He suddenly laughed. "Ah, Faulk. Ever-smiling Cheelum has seen fit to answer your prayers. You've wanted to fight me ever since Philip Lealand died. You guessed I had something to do with it, but you never could prove it. And you're too *honorable* to come after me on a supposition or in the dark of night with a knife in the back. Just like Lealand, you are so predictable. But your being here now is a matter of luck and not planning."

As he spoke, Tarn circled toward Faulk and flexed the wrist that held his sword from side to side. "I'm sorry you weren't there to see Lealand hang like the thief we claimed him to be. Such an ignominious death... but quite interesting to watch. He jerked around on the end of the rope for quite some time and shit himself. I think his wife found it entertaining too. Alas, she too did not live out the day, and I forgot to ask if she'd found the hanging enjoyable." Tarn smiled at the memory.

Faulk understood that Edmund was trying to anger him, to get him to rush in without caution. But even knowing this was the case, Faulk had to steel himself to keep from responding to Tarn's taunts.

"But I was there," Faulk said. "I was part of the faceless crowd—the *silent* crowd who were impotent to effect change but recognized injustice when they saw it. Lord Lealand and Lady Patrice were noble and honorable to the end, whereas your behavior only shows your internal rot."

Tarn struck then, stabbing his sword forward with amazing swiftness for so tall a man. Faulk managed to swivel to the side, Tarn's blade flashing just inches from Faulk's torso. Faulk continued to turn, bringing his sword down on Edmund's unprotected left shoulder. The blade was deflected by the mail, but Tarn grunted and fell back.

"I think you've had too much soft living and not enough training," Faulk said. "To leave yourself so open is the sign of an amateur."

"I was training while you were on your knees trying to satisfy the crazed abbot we left you with. My father thought it was quite a joke that you would get to make restitution for what your uncle thought were the sins of your mother. It was my father that planted you in your mother's belly." The last was said with a snarl, but the look faded when Faulk did not react to what Tarn thought was a revelation. "You knew!"

"I knew," Faulk said. "But the fact we share a sire is

not something I want to brag about. Others have always made it plain that I sprang from the lesser orders. When I discovered it was *your* father who had rutted with my mother, I knew my origins were lower than even I had expected."

Tarn was not so impervious to insult as Faulk had been. He rushed in with little finesse, slashing and jabbing like a madman. Faulk met him blow for blow. The solar rang with the sound of their swords. Despite Faulk's taunting words, the two men were evenly matched. Edmund had brute strength and height while Faulk had superior speed and skill. They labored from one end of the solar to the other, knocking over tables and chairs as they circled the room. Neither could find the advantage, although both tried to land high strokes that were aimed at their opponent's unprotected head.

Soon harsh breathing punctuated the less frequent clanging of metal on metal. Faulk's shoulders and arms burned with fatigue. His gambeson was damp and sweat ran stingingly into his eyes. Tarn must have felt similarly tired, for he intensified his strokes and thrusts in an effort to bring the fight to a conclusion.

Faulk caught one of the powerful blows on his sword and angled it so the blades slid together until the two men pushed against each other, hilt to hilt. Faulk, with the advantage of leverage, forced Edmund back suddenly, breaking the contact. Tarn gathered himself and swung powerfully for Faulk's head. Faulk ducked the blow and, in a pattern like the one he'd used to vanquish Charl at the tournament, brought his blade across Tarn's unprotected knees. Faulk felt the give of flesh, felt the blade bite deep. Like grain scythed in the field, Edmund Tarn toppled with a scream.

Faulk immediately positioned himself above the prone man, holding him down with a foot on his chest. Faulk's blood-edged blade hovered at Tarn's throat. Tarn, his own sword forgotten, pushed both hands against the blade of Faulk's sword.

"Truce," Edmund gasped.

"Truce? I think not." Faulk laughed without humor. "I owe you for Lealand. I owe you for the misery of my childhood. I owe you for what you tried to do to Fallucia. And the bill has come due." Faulk then shifted his weight and drove the point home.

Faulk watched almost disinterestedly as Tarn flopped like a landed fish, making odd, gurgling sounds. He observed the man as the light faded from his eyes. And he felt nothing. No satisfaction. No release. No completion.

Tired. He was tired. And he wanted to go home. Home to White Ford. Home to Anlin.

He pulled his sword from the carcass that had been Edmund Tarn and cleaned it on a piece of tapestry that lay on the floor. Sliding his sword into its scabbard, he slowly turned and walked from the room. The queen and her son had fled during his fight. He wished them well in the future, but really didn't care all that much.

All he cared about was going home.

❧ 22 ❧

Snow came and thawed, came and thawed, and finally came to stay. Mud that had mired the roads froze into miniature peaks and valleys and would remain that way until spring. The Milk River took on a thin coat of ice that thickened every day, hiding the movement of the water under a white cloak from the most recent snowfall.

And still Faulk did not return.

Anlin watched the coals shift in the central fire pit in the hall. Glowing castles formed and disappeared with each gust of wind that eddied around the large room and escaped up the smoke hole. She would be warmer in the solar or bedchamber with the double fireplaces, but she wanted to be quickly available if there was a messenger or word that Faulk and his two men-at-arms were approaching.

No, there weren't two men-at-arms now. Kevin had been knighted. He was Sir Kevin now. One of the vagaries of war. Waylon had been badly wounded, but he would be returning to White Ford just as he had left it, as a man-at-arms.

Part of Faulk's delay was waiting for Waylon to be able to travel. Hilmar fretted because she couldn't be with the man she loved when he was injured. Anlin knew her maid's wait was worse than her own, but this did little to speed these long, cold days of anticipation.

Somewhere beyond the shuttered windows, Anlin heard Telm's quick, choppy laughter and an answering bark from Dragon. The hound was rapidly growing into the promise of his feet and ears. He stayed active, undeterred by one rear leg that hadn't functioned properly since his brush with death. The two would be gamboling in the snow.

At least Telm had the dog. The human inhabitants of the fief avoided contact with the boy as much as possible. While the full story of Roland's death would never be told, enough could be surmised that people feared Telm and whatever unearthly power he possessed.

Even Callip had been disconcerted when he heard of what had happened.

The Rennish shaman had returned to White Ford shortly after the battle on the plain before the King's Eyrie. He brought news of victory, although Callip himself looked as if he'd been on the losing side. His skin had been sallow, his eyes dull, and his behavior listless. He had slowly returned to his normal vigor, but even now, he seemed to look inward.

He had evidently made friends with the priest in

charge of the Eyrie's extensive library, since royal heralds would periodically brave the roads to deliver brief and unsatisfying letters from Faulk and mysterious packets of scrolls for Callip. The shaman spent any time he wasn't working with Telm hunched over these parchments, occasionally asking her what a Fallucian word meant. Anlin wasn't sure what he was reading, but she often had never heard the words Callip recited.

Anlin bent back over her small embroidery stand and continued work on a complex picture of White Ford she was making for Telm. As much as the knowledge hurt, she knew her son would be leaving with Callip in the spring. Before leaving Ridgemere, she'd agreed it was Telm's choice whether to stay in Fallucia or return to Rennic, and her mother's heart knew he would never be happy here. Also, Callip had to return and Telm needed his tutelage. But, hopefully, they would both come back to Fallucia every two years to meet with the King's Council. All parties had agreed it would alleviate suspicion in both countries to know what the other was doing.

Anlin had become engrossed in getting the roofline of the manor right and so was surprised when Telm dashed in shouting, "They come!"

Telm was immediately followed by the miller's middle boy, who was red-faced and panting from his run from the village. "Papa sent me," the boy said, casting an irritated glance at Telm, who had stolen his thunder. "He saw Sir Faulk and his party approaching from the top of the mill."

Joy leaped up inside Anlin. She wanted to rush into the courtyard, but she made herself take time to praise the boy and his father for their timely report. Thanks cost nothing and did much to keep White Ford running smoothly. And then she could wait no longer. She met Hilmar coming down the stairs, dressed for the outside with Anlin's heavy cloak in her arms.

"Finally," both women said almost simultaneously, then they looked at each other and laughed. Anlin was not the only person filled with joy.

By the time the cavalcade arrived, the entire household was ranged on the steps, with Anlin and Telm at the front. Anlin had the impression the group clattering into the courtyard was larger than the one that had left, but once her eyes fell on the big gray horse and its rider, that was all she could see. Faulk, so straight and powerful in the saddle. Faulk, wrapped in a luxurious fur cape she had never seen before—and smiling wide enough to break his face.

She managed to maintain her dignity until a horse boy had come forward to take Fiddian and Faulk was swinging from the saddle—and then she ran. Laughing, he grabbed her and swung her around. The mail under his fine cape was cold, but his lips were warm, so warm the chill that had settled over her when he'd left began to dissolve like frost in the sun. He smelled of cold and horse and something distinctly Faulk. He tasted like the finest wine she'd ever drunk.

Her kiss of welcome went on an embarrassingly long time. And then she said, idiotically, "You're home."

"Sweet Cheelum, it is so," he replied and stepped away to grasp Telm into a hug and pound him on the back. "I swear, you are growing like your pup," he said. "I believe you've shot up nearly a hand span in the two months I've been gone."

The comment must have been the right one, for Telm glowed.

With Anlin tucked under one arm and Telm under the other, Faulk made his slow way into the manor, exchanging greetings with all, grasping Callip by the arm and contriving to leave Telm with his mentor, nodding Hettle away with a whispered, "Tomorrow."

Inexorably Faulk press forward into the hall. "We have a number of extra people to accommodate. I assume someone on the staff can handle this?" Faulk's voice was loud, as if making a general announcement.

"I'll take care of it," Anlin said, reluctantly starting to move away.

Faulk's hold tightened rather than released her. "No, someone else can do that. I have need of your private advice in the solar."

He then hauled her up the stairs. She knew she certainly didn't walk. As soon as they'd entered the solar, he turned and locked the door.

"Is there something of import I should know?" she asked, suddenly afraid the extra visitors were the harbinger of bad news.

"Only that I have missed you like life itself," he said. "And if you'll help me shed all these clothes, I'll be glad to show you just how much that is." As he spoke, Faulk had already dropped his gloves to the floor and draped the expensive cape over one of the chairs. He started the struggle to remove his mail.

"Let me help with that." Anlin moved forward and pulled on the heavy shirt as Faulk leaned over to facilitate the process. It brought back memories of their trip to Rennic. How foolish she'd been to reject his advances for so long. Cheelum had smiled on her when Faulk had won the tournament—for he'd gone on to win her heart.

The mail slid off to fall clinking onto the floor. Anlin backed away, used to Faulk's habit of hanging his mail shirt on the T-shaped tree in the corner of the room. To her surprise, he left it lying at his feet and began untying the laces of his gambeson.

He smiled at her. "Woman, I'd feel better if you were more enthusiastic in divesting yourself of your own clothes instead of just watching me."

She grinned at her own foolishness. "Even with your head start, I'll beat you to the goal," she challenged.

And then it was all speed and laughter as they simultaneously helped and impeded each other. The result was a trail of clothing that spread from the solar into the bedroom and Faulk rising naked over her. And then she knew at long last her husband was home.

꿍•꿍

Faulk lay completely relaxed, a sensation he'd not enjoyed since his departure. The faint winter light had long ago disappeared from the cracks in the shutters placed over the windows for winter, and the fire had died to glowing coals, so the room was in darkness.

Anlin rested across his chest making the odd little poof sounds she did in sleep. He ran a hand over her lengthening hair and down her back. He smiled into the gloom. Anlin still foolishly fretted that she lacked a proper matron's braid. As if he cared. One of the men on the King's Council bragged his wife's hair came to her knees when it was unbound, and a sillier woman Faulk had yet to meet. The mind that lay beneath the hair was of greater importance.

Anlin stirred and would have pushed herself to a sitting position had Faulk not banded her with his arms. She strained against his hold. "Sweet Cheelum," she said. "I have no idea how long I slept, but it is full dark and the manor has guests and there is dinner to serve and—"

"—and all of this will take care of itself. Or not. Whichever occurs, the world will not end. I had thought to order some food and wine... and then stay here until morning."

"What? People will wonder what it is we're doing behind a closed door."

He dropped a kiss on her forehead. "You goose.

Everyone over the age of six *knows* what we're doing—and I suspect a good many of the men from White Ford who returned with me are doing the same thing." He chuckled. "Shortly after harvest next year, there is likely to be a surge in the fief's population."

She poked him in the ribs and pushed back against his arms. This time he let her go. "You are being such a… such a… *man*."

"I hope you noticed that fact earlier."

That earned him another poke, but as she started to rise, he caught her hand. "Stay. I do have something serious to discuss and would like to get it done before the rest of the world intrudes."

He felt her body stiffen. "You've not taken any hurt, have you?"

"Since you've just carefully examined every inch of my body, you know this is not the case."

"Waylon?" she asked. "I didn't see him. Please tell me he hasn't died. Hilmar will be inconsolable."

"No, Waylon is on the mend. But his fighting days are over. He will never earn his knight's spurs. He will, however, make an excellent seneschal. As the chief steward for one of the Lords of High Places, Waylon will have the same honor as a knight, and I think he will be good at the job."

"I assume you have already made the arrangements, and I am glad for him. But I'll so miss Hilmar. I know they planned to marry when he had something to offer a wife."

This brought them to the heart of what he had to tell her, and yet, he still found himself reluctant to address the topic. It was supposed to be good news. Nay, incredible news. But Faulk wondered if, like him, Anlin would be uncertain of what was loss and what was gain.

"Hilmar can stay with you as long it pleases you. Waylon will be *our* seneschal. Perhaps as penance for something evil I did in one of those past lives Callip believes in, I have been named one of the Lords of High Places. I have the Letters Patent in one of my trunks. I—" He stopped when Anlin leaped from the bed and began rummaging in her chest. She drew out a heavy robe and draped it over her.

"I'm telling the truth," he said, surprised at her actions. "There is no need for you to immediately check the paperwork."

"Now you are the one being a goose. I'm going to order the fires built up and to arrange for dinner to be brought to our chamber. And I think at least two flagons of wine. I am not going to discuss something this important naked and in the dark."

He had no choice but to follow suit. He wrapped himself in a quilted robe and went into the solar to find Anlin issuing orders and the trail of clothing gone. The large room seemed packed with servants, all dashing about on their own errands, but each of them wore a broad grin. No one was fooled. Anlin might as well have left the strewn clothing where it lay.

Finally, his wife had all she wanted and the last of the servers had departed. Faulk gratefully slid the bolt on the door and went to join Anlin at the small table stacked with food. As he seated himself, she poured him some wine and said, "Now, please explain how I went to bed with Sir Faulk of White Ford and woke up with Lord...?"

"Tarn," he muttered into his wine glass.

Her hands hit the table with enough force to rattle the dishes. "Sweet Cheelum!" Her eyes were turned upward, so perhaps it *was* a prayer.

"I wanted no lordship," he said, "least of all Tarn. During the whole battle before the Eyrie, I did nothing. Fiddian and I were simply the tree Callip climbed so he could turn the king's magic back upon itself and win us the day. Consequently, I had a fresh horse to chase Lord Tarn—I guess I should specify the late Edmund Tarn—up to the castle where he was attempting to kidnap King Fremmor's heir.

"The queen stood before her child with a fireplace poker, and I'm sure she would have fought to the death to protect him, but Edmund was forced to face me."

"You slew him in battle, or so you wrote."

"Close enough to the truth. I killed him... and became the King's Protector. The queen, whose strength of will is second only to yours, would have it no other way. And this, naturally, sent the entire King's Council into complete disarray. There has never been a King's Protector who is not a Lord, nor a Lord who is without

Talent. It was a conundrum. But there was one of the major holdings in all of Fallucia lying empty... suffice it to say compromises were made and after nearly a week of wrangling, I somehow outrank all the other Lords of High Places."

"Did they perhaps decide this because they knew the old Lord Tarn had fathered you?" she asked.

"May Cheelum weep. I would hope none of the Lords know anything about that. Edmund taunted me with the fact when we fought, but the Queen was gone by then, and I doubt he ever told anyone. I certainly haven't, and never will. I think it was just one of those jokes that Cheelum, or the Goddess, or Whoever pulls Fate's strings, likes to play on humans.

"But when my elevation became inevitable, I did fight for some important things. If you look at the Letters Patent, you will see I am styled as Faulk of White Ford, Lord Tarn. And I have made it very plain I am to be addressed as Lord Faulk. But you will have the choice of being called Lady Faulk or Lady Tarn or even Lady Anlin, as has always been your right. And I refused to ever fight under that damned banner of a hand holding a bloody sword. I convinced the other lords the Tarn crest was attainted, and so the Lord Harold is designing a new one."

"Which is?" But the smile on Anlin's face suggested she already knew.

"A flying nightpiper." He held up his hand to ward off any comment. "I know you'd be happier if I chose something you see as more heroic, but I promise you that little bug eater, as you originally called my symbol, will be here long after all the falcons in the world are gone."

"You'll get no argument from me, Lord Faulk," she said, squeezing his hand. "I've spent hours trying to learn how to embroider a nightpiper, and I would hate to see that as wasted time."

He laughed and took a sip of wine as he steeled himself to give the last bit of his bad news. But it was something she had to suspect was coming. "We will have to take up residence at Tarn's Mount. It is by far my principal holding and there's no way around it.

"But I'm not relinquishing White Ford. I had to pay your father three knights' fees for scutage, since it's now impossible for me to swear service to him, but I would not let it go. While the castle at Tarn's Mount is massive and the lands go on for further than the eye can see, White Ford was my dream, and I'm not willing to let a dream go. Sir Kevin will hold it in my name."

She nodded, her eyes misty. Perhaps White Ford, or someplace like it, had been her dream as well. "Are there any other life changing events you conveniently left out of your letters?" she asked.

"No, this is all. And I wasn't keeping any of this secret. It has just taken some time for me to get my mind around all that has happened."

"Good, because there were some essentials I, too, could not put into a letter, and I think you should know them."

≈•≈

Faulk picked up a slightly withered apple and took a bite. All the hot dishes had now cooled and looked unappetizing. How ridiculous that two people, who were now some of the wealthiest and most powerful people in the land, would act as if someone had died? And Anlin realized what she had to impart wouldn't do anything to lighten the mood. At least there was plenty of wine. She took a drink.

"My brother Roland's death may have been more complicated than I indicated when I wrote to you," she began.

"You said he had run mad, attacked you, knocked over a lamp, which set his clothes alight, and later died of his burns. Which part of that was inaccurate?"

"The part about the lamp. We were in the barn, so there was no lamp. There was only Telm, who was tied up and gagged. But he caused Roland to burst into flames. Callip has interrogated me about the event, and kept asking about Roland's clothing, which were burned from the inside out."

She reached out and touched his arm—wanting to make contact, needing to pull some of his strength into herself. Her worry had eaten at her since the event had happened.

"Faulk, my son caused a man to burn up from inside. Even Callip was disturbed. He said it was a piece of Great Magic that no one could do anymore. That no one *should* be able to do, particularly a young, untutored boy.

"Callip has been reading all of the ancient scrolls the librarian at the Eyrie will send him, trying to learn more about how this magic is performed and more importantly, how it can be controlled."

"Callip made me feel as if I were being burned alive when we first went to Rennic," Faulk said.

"Yes, he told me. But he could only make you *think* it was happening. He couldn't make it actually occur. He said Telm had learned to control fire enough to light a candle or even start a fire that had already been laid. This falls within the ability of most shamans. And given enough time to do so, Telm could have burned through his bindings... which he did, in no time at all. But the other, the immolation, should not have been possible. And so Callip worries and tries to prepare. Evidently, Telm will not begin to reach his full power until well after puberty." She shook her head, not sure what else to say.

Faulk gave her a ghost of a smile. "I think Callip is a man undergoing a crisis of faith, and this adds to his concern," Faulk said. "He has found that many of the tenets on which he has based his life are in error. Perhaps part of his apprehension is caused by this and the problem with Telm is not so dire as he presents."

She returned his faint smile. She knew he was trying to lessen her own concern. "There is some truth to what you say. Callip is also worried about the reaction of other shamans and seerin when he tells them what he has learned. He hopes to find proof of where the Rennish fell into error in the Archive at Ridgemere, so he also frets about what he will discover when he returns."

"I fear he will discover that everything didn't happen *eight hundred years ago*." Faulk pitched his voice so he sounded much like Callip, and they both laughed in that odd way some men do after battle when they discover they are not among the dead. "If it will make you feel better, I'll make sure Callip feels it will be safe for both of them to return to Rennic. He is well respected and has the greatest magical ability."

Faulk paused for a beat. "You do realize this proves that Telm *must* go back with Callip. There is no one in Fallucia who can even begin to teach your son. And Callip may say no one can do Great Magic now, but that is what he called what was done on Eyrie's plain."

"Judging from how destroyed he looked when he returned here weeks after the battle," she said, "the effort nearly killed him. He also said it took a dozen Fallucian magicians to cast the spell, all aided with amulets, and that he was only able to counter it because he was reversing a spell that had already been cast and he, too, had dozens of magic enhancing stones."

She clasped Faulk's hand tightly. She wanted him to feel as well as hear her sincerity. "I know Telm can't stay here. However, Callip has made Telm take a vow that if Callip should die before Telm is thirty, Telm is to move heaven and earth to get back to be with you. You. Not me." The hurt still showed in the last three words, but when Callip explained his reasoning, Anlin could understand it. "Callip said I would mother him and this is not what Telm needs. He believes that you would help Telm grow straight. Magic can warp a mind, and Callip has great confidence that you would not let this happen."

"And I wouldn't—at least to the best of my non-Talented self. But I sometimes think this is a strength both you and I possess. We don't have the crutch of magic. Everything we accomplish we do ourselves, standing only on our own two feet. In every decision we make, we must examine our weaknesses and determine how to strengthen our defenses in that area. Perhaps it is this Talent of self-reliance that is something we can teach."

He yawned. "And I now recognize my limitations. We will not solve this problem tonight, if ever, and this knowledge makes us melancholy. So, I think we should go to bed and hold one another until we wake in the morning with the sure knowledge that we will begin again and eventually get where we should be. For now, let us imagine the future. Have you ever seen Tarn's Mount?"

"No, have you?" If Faulk thought a break would refresh them both, Anlin was willing to try it.

"Once. It's a mammoth building. One of the early

Lord Tarns obviously wanted something even more impressive than the King's Eyrie. But instead of choosing blindingly white stone as the king did, the builder of Tarn's Mount went for size rather than quality, and the whole massive place is made from ugly, gray stone."

He suddenly stood and pulled her to her feet. "How would you feel about painting the whole place pink?"

"Pink? Faulk, every other Lord would be looking for your Letters Patent in the hope of spilling ink on the page and obliterating your proof of ownership."

"Oh, I don't know. We could carry out the theme by having the Lord of Heralds put a pink ribbon in the nightpiper's beak."

She leaned against him as they wandered into the bedroom, exhaustion suddenly catching up with her, too. "Faulk, sometimes you are the most absurd man."

"I know," he said, "and that might be another of my hidden Talents."

The world dripped— but more from a heavy mist than actual rain. Faulk noticed Anlin kept using the rain as an excuse to wipe moisture from her face. If she wished to pretend she was not crying, Faulk would go along with her self-deception.

"Are you sure the passes will be open?" she asked Callip for perhaps the hundredth time.

"Yes. Only Questor Pass should present any problem, and we can get over it even if we have to leave the packhorses for later retrieval." Since Callip said this as he checked the covering over his precious scrolls, also for the hundredth time, Faulk seriously doubted any packs would be left behind even if the shaman had to dig a path through the pass all by himself.

The sound of rapid steps and the jangle of tack, accompanied by a cacophony of frantic barking and baying from the barn, indicated Telm was on his way— and Dragon had been locked in a stall.

Faulk and Callip had both tried to come up with a method to get the dog to Rennic. He couldn't make it on his own three legs. Just playing with Telm for less than an hour left Dragon exhausted. He would then lie on the hearth with tongue lolling. It would be some time before he would be ready to again frolic. But he'd become too large to ride with Telm and the journey couldn't be constantly delayed for the dog to recuperate.

Telm had been stoic when he heard the decision. As he approached leading his bay mare, however, it became apparent he had the same problem with getting rain on his face as his mother did. Partings were always hard.

Callip, who had taken his formal leave while waiting for Telm to arrive, mounted and held out his hand to take the reins of Telm's horse. The boy left his mare in care of the shaman, straightened his shoulders, and approached Faulk.

He bowed with great formality. "My Lord. I thank you for your wise counsel and friendship. You have taught me much of what a man should be and have opened my eyes to alternate views of the world. I will hold you in my heart while we are parted."

Faulk wasn't sure if there had been all that much wise counsel, but he hoped there had been friendship. Over the winter, Telm had often accompanied him on his errands around his demesne—the two of them riding contentedly side-by-side, their breaths misting in front of them like tangible thoughts. The topics of conversation had ranged far and wide, some of which were not always comfortable as they challenged each other's preconceived ideas.

A few nights ago, as a parting gift, Faulk had given Telm a carving he'd made of a nightpiper when he, too, was a boy. The carving itself was primitive, but Faulk thought he'd caught the bird's inquisitiveness in the turn of its head. "It's probably not a very accurate rendering," Faulk said, "but it's supposed to be a nightpiper. Do you have those in Rennic?"

Telm had frowned at the carving in concentration. "I'm not sure from the carving," the boy honestly said. "I know it is your emblem, and mother has been emphatic that it is not a falcon, but if you tell me what the actual bird is like, I might be able to identify it."

"When I first met your mother, I think she very much wanted it to be a falcon," Faulk said with a laugh, although he was gratified at how easily the word "mother" now rolled off Telm's tongue. "She was deciding if she should marry me, and I suspect she was looking for someone more heroic."

Telm looked at him as if to say he thought Faulk was very heroic. He'd been quite impressed with the title King's Protector and had believed every word of the embellished version of how Faulk had come by the title that Waylon told. Faulk decided it was a nice way to be viewed, and so he didn't disabuse Telm with the facts.

"The nightpiper is a medium-sized bird that flies at night on silent wings. He is seldom seen, but often heard. As the name would suggest, he has a chirring call that reminds the listener of a piper on a faraway hill. During the day, he disappears into the tall grass and makes not a sound. Does this sound like a bird you're familiar with in Rennic?"

"Yes!" Telm seemed as excited as if he'd won a tournament. "You're talking about the sky ghost. I love to listen to their call when I lie in bed at night."

"As did I," Faulk said. "My life when I was around your age was very harsh, and so I imagined in some way I could be like that bird. That I could disappear, but still be here, if that makes sense. And as an adult, I've tried to make my accomplishment my song, something I'm proud for others to notice. But the real Faulk—the essential man—I hope he remains hidden.

"I suspect when you're an adult, hiding yourself will be more difficult, but regardless of how public your life becomes, try to keep a part of it that is only yours."

Faulk wasn't sure if he could consider that wise counsel, but Anlin told him when Telm packed the carved nightpiper, he wrapped it as if the piece of wood was the most precious of Tremellian glass.

He would miss the boy. In good-bye, he reached out and squeezed Telm's shoulder. It was still bony, but further from the ground than it had been when he'd arrived all those months ago. "Travel within Cheelum's smile," Faulk said, feeling tightness in his own throat. Partings were damned difficult.

Telm went to stand in front of Anlin, who was openly weeping. He went down on one knee before her.

"I honor you as my mother," he began, but stopped, his face suddenly becoming blank. He reached his right hand out and placed it on Anlin's abdomen.

"So strong," he said, his voice awed. "I have never seen such a blinding light from such a tiny spark."

His eyes regained focus and he looked up at his mother. "Two," he said. "There are two. One who shines like the sun at noon and the other who reflects this light like the moon and makes its own beauty."

The boy closed his eyes and leaned forward until his forehead touched Anlin's abdomen. "I greet you, son and daughter of my mother. You will grow tall and strong, and each of you will walk your own path. One will be feared and one loved. People will call one Lord of Giffard's Crest and the other Lord of Tarn's Mount—and I will call you both, friend."

Faulk felt frozen with this pronouncement. Anlin must have felt the same, for she didn't move as Telm quickly stood and awkwardly hugged her. Judging from the flush of embarrassment that branded his face and the speed with which he dashed to his horse and mounted, Telm had not planned that display of affection.

Anlin raised her hand toward her son, but he had already gone beyond her grasp. "Travel within Cheelum's smile," she whispered.

Faulk took the two steps that separated them and slipped his arm around her shoulder. She nestled into him. He felt the faint tremors that shook her body. He thought either Callip or Telm might turn back to them or even raise a hand. But neither did, as if by the act of leaving, they had turned all those they left behind into nightpipers—no longer seen but a memory to be called to mind in the still of the night.

The two riders continued on their way until they were specks that disappeared behind a forested hill. Faulk and Anlin stood wrapped in each other's embrace and watched them go.

"I love him," Anlin said, "and so, as we agreed, I let him go."

"It was what was right for him. He didn't fit here. He might not fully fit in Rennic either. But there he is honored—just as I suspect he will eventually be honored here. It will simply take time to change attitudes on both sides of the border. Just remember he'll be back in two years. Callip would not lie."

"And then he'll be even less the boy I remember than he is now."

"True, but sometimes love needs to let go—and sometimes love holds on tight. I'm the one who holds tight." Faulk pulled her snuggly against him and kissed her forehead where the white blaze he so loved started. "Do you think he was right about there being twins coming?

"I'd like him to be." she said. "But what he said was so fantastic... I've seen Telm do amazing things, but I think in this he is in error."

"We could help make his prophecy come true?

Anlin looked at him in confusion "Help Telm? Young as he is, I doubt he needs our help."

"Well, we could help make his prediction come true. If there's not yet a child, or children, we could perhaps start one this morning. Remember I'm the love you hold on to."

"I've discovered I like you to hold me," she said with a watery smile. "And this morning is a good time. Some of the villeins will be here this afternoon to take down the bed in preparation for our move to Tarn's Mount."

"Then I will definitely have to spend the afternoon with Dragon in the barn," Faulk said. "He's barking himself hoarse—and I hate the idea of packing."

She chuckled and poked him in the ribs. He kissed her, tasting her tears but knowing all was as it should be. He had no doubt Telm spoke the truth, and Faulk was pleased Anlin's three magical children would be friends. And at least two of these Talented children would be his and Anlin's together. He smiled. People were wrong when they thought he and Anlin were without Talent.

"Let us go make magic," he said.

Author's Notes

A number of years ago, I wrote fantasy and science fiction short stories under another name. Anlin and Faulk arrived in my head at that time, but their story was too much a love story to fit into what I was then writing and the plot was too complex to be contained in the space requirements for short fiction. So I tucked notes and snippets of conversation into a file on my computer and went on to other things.

Recently, the couple again started yammering in my mind, "Write our story." They became quite insistent—I admit I don't think conversations with characters are in the least weird—and so I succumbed and here is their story. To write it, I had to abandon the strictly historical background I enjoy and build my own world.

The structure of Fallucian society is obviously based on the medieval feudal system. I have used some of the terms and attitudes from that period to reinforce this similarity. Rennish society, however, is completely imaginary. In it, I have tried to show how people with the best of intentions can create something horrible when they are convinced of the rightness of their vision and feel under attack.

Anlin and Faulk are products of this environment.

Anlin was horribly emotionally damaged by her years of servitude in Rennic, but she continues to have a solid and unshakeable core. Faulk is a seasoned warrior who will do what is expedient. He, nonetheless, still clings to the modest—but to him, impossible—dreams of having his own land and finding someone to love who will love him in return.

Since both Anlin and Faulk are without magic, they are considered "lesser." Neither would have imagined they would become part of the events that would shape their world.

Thank you for purchasing *Song of the Nightpiper*. I hope you enjoyed the tale. Please consider leaving a review on your favorite site to help guide others in their choice. I also love hearing from readers, and you can reach me through www.hannahmeredith.com. On the next page I have a list of other books that are available. None of them contains magic, but I hope the stories are still in some way magical.

Thanks for reading –

Hannah

Other Books by Hannah Meredith

Kestrel
Kaleidoscope
Indentured Hearts
A Dangerous Indiscretion

And a contributor to the Christmas anthologies

Christmas Revels
Christmas Revels II
Christmas Revels III
Christmas Revels IV